PRAISE FOR S

"I will read anything Susan Stoker . . . . because I know it's going to be amazing!"

—Riley Edwards, *USA Today* bestselling author

"Susan Stoker never fails to pull me out of a reading slump. With heat, action, and suspense, she weaves an incredible tale that sucks me in and doesn't let go."

—Jessica Prince, *USA Today* bestselling author

"One thing I love about Susan Stoker's books is that she knows how to deliver a perfect HEA while still making sure the villain gets what he/she deserves!"

—T.M. Frazier, *New York Times* bestselling author

"Susan Stoker's characters come alive on the page!"

—Elle James, *New York Times* bestselling author

"When you pick up a Susan Stoker book, you know exactly what you're going to get . . . a hot alpha hero and a smart, sassy heroine. I can't get enough!"

—Jessica Hawkins, *USA Today* bestselling author

"Suspenseful storytelling with characters you want as friends!"

—Meli Raine, *USA Today* bestselling author

"Susan Stoker knows what women want. A hot hero who needs to save a damsel in distress . . . even if she can save herself."

—CD Reiss, *New York Times* bestselling author

THE
Hero

The Refuge

Deserving Alaska
Deserving Henley
Deserving Reese
Deserving Cora
Deserving Lara
Deserving Maisy (October 2024)
Deserving Ryleigh (January 2025)

SEAL of Protection: Alliance Series

Protecting Remi (July 2024)
Protecting Wren (November 2024)
Protecting Josie (TBA)
Protecting Maggie (TBA)
Protecting Addison (TBA)
Protecting Kelli (TBA)
Protecting Bree (TBA)

SEAL Team Hawaii Series

Finding Elodie
Finding Lexie
Finding Kenna
Finding Monica
Finding Carly
Finding Ashlyn
Finding Jodelle

Eagle Point Search & Rescue

Searching for Lilly
Searching for Elsie

Badge of Honor: Texas Heroes Series

SEAL of Protection Series

THE Hero

Game of Chance, Book Three

SUSAN STOKER

Montlake

Text copyright © 2024 by Susan Stoker
All rights reserved.

No part of this book may be reproduced, or stored in a retrieval system, or transmitted in any form or by any means, electronic, mechanical, photocopying, recording, or otherwise, without express written permission of the publisher.

Published by Montlake, Seattle

www.apub.com

Amazon, the Amazon logo, and Montlake are trademarks of Amazon.com, Inc., or its affiliates.

ISBN-13: 9781662509698 (paperback)
ISBN-13: 9781662509681 (digital)

Cover design by Hang Le
Cover photography by Wander Aguiar Photography
Cover image: © Route 117 / Shutterstock

Printed in the United States of America

THE
Hero

Chapter One

Marlowe Kennedy jerked in surprise when one of the trustees yelled her name loud enough to be heard over the noise of the hundreds of sewing machines in the room.

Turning, she saw Yanisa scowling at her from just inside the door. She didn't immediately move because the last thing Marlowe wanted was to get into trouble. Trustees were prisoners who'd been given a bit of power over their fellow inmates. One word from a trustee to the guards and a prisoner could find herself in solitary. Most of the women here were scared of the trustees, and Marlowe couldn't blame them.

The ratio of guards to prisoners in this awful penitentiary in Thailand was something like twenty to one thousand. It was fear, or simply a lack of will, on the prisoners' parts that kept them from uprising. Most of the women had been sentenced to life, Marlowe included.

It was unbelievable that barely a month ago, Marlowe had been an esteemed archaeologist working on a dig not too far from Bangkok. She'd been respected and considered an expert in her field. But now look at her. She was a convicted drug dealer, according to the Thai government, thrown away as if she was a piece of trash.

Her days were spent hunched over a sewing machine, stitching cheap blouses, and her nights sleeping in a room crammed with at least a hundred other women, lying shoulder to shoulder on a thin mattress that didn't do a damn thing to cushion her from the hard concrete floor.

"Marlowe!" Yanisa yelled again, more impatiently this time. She gestured with her hand for her to come.

Standing, Marlowe made her way through the other women, who seemed not curious in the least why she'd been called out by the trustee. Or maybe they just knew better than to draw any attention to themselves by stopping what they were doing.

When Marlowe got close to Yanisa, the woman reached out and grabbed the front of her light-blue prisoner's shirt and shook her. Marlowe's first instinct was to smack the woman's hand off her, to shove her backward, but if she did that, she'd go right back to solitary. It was forbidden for any of the other prisoners to touch a trustee. But of course that didn't go both ways. The trustees could do whatever they wanted to the women in their charge. They frequently kicked, punched, and sometimes sexually assaulted others in the dark of night.

Such was life in this overcrowded and underfunded prison.

Yanisa turned, with a fistful of Marlowe's shirt still in her hand, and started walking toward the administrative building.

Dread rolled through Marlowe. She didn't like anything about the main building on the prison grounds. It was where the guards hung out. And where interrogations took place. Marlowe had spent more than enough time in one of the small rooms in the large brick building.

When she'd first been brought to the women's prison from the archaeological dig site, she thought she'd be able to explain that the yaba pills found in her belongings weren't hers. She thought she'd get a chance to explain her side, how she suspected her coworker, Ian West, of being the one to plant them.

But that hadn't happened. Secured in a room in that admin building, she'd been yelled at for hours in Thai. She didn't understand a word of what they were saying. She begged for an interpreter. For something to eat and drink. To use the bathroom. But no one seemed to care what she wanted.

She had no idea how long she'd been in the room, but finally a woman came in who spoke English. Marlowe had never been so relieved in her life to see someone she could understand, and who could understand her.

The woman explained that she was being charged with drug trafficking, and that she needed to sign an affidavit of some sort. Of course it was in Thai, and Marlowe couldn't read it. She'd refused at first, and the woman insisted that if she didn't sign it, she'd be found guilty on the spot and sentenced to death.

It had been a nightmare Marlowe had no idea how to get out of. She knew it wasn't smart to sign anything without reading it first, but the woman had been so calm and reassuring. And by that point, Marlowe was hungry, exhausted, and terrified. She'd seen the way the male guards had looked at her during the long interrogation. She'd heard the horror stories of women being assaulted.

In the end, she'd signed the papers.

Then she'd been brought into a room, her clothes were taken away, and she'd been forced to change into the light-blue shirt and dark-blue skirt all the prisoners wore, and taken to solitary confinement.

So yeah, needless to say, she didn't have good memories of the administrative building Yanisa was currently dragging her toward. At five feet, four inches, Marlowe wasn't a large woman, and with the amount of weight she'd lost while she'd been incarcerated, she was even more slight. Generally, Thai women weren't all that much taller than her, but Yanisa was an exception, which was probably part of the reason she was a trustee. She easily yanked Marlowe behind her as she walked, and it was all Marlowe could do to stay on her feet.

To Marlowe's surprise, instead of taking her to one of the small interrogation rooms, Yanisa dragged her toward the visitors' area.

For a brief moment, hope bloomed in Marlowe's chest. Was Tony here? Had her brother finally been able to get through all the red tape to come see her?

She felt almost dizzy with relief. Tony would get her out of this. Her big brother had always been her protector. He had connections thanks to his work for a US senator. If anyone could figure this mess out, it was him.

Yanisa jerked to a stop and practically threw Marlowe into a chair placed in front of a chain-link fence. The setup for the prisoners to talk to visitors wasn't ideal. She sat in front of the fence, and there was a second fence about eight feet away, behind which sat the visitors. There was absolutely no chance of them being able to touch, and in a room so large, with a dozen other women talking to those who'd come to see them, it was almost impossible to hear what anyone was saying.

"Five minutes," Yanisa told her gruffly, then turned and stomped away.

No one was sitting in the opposite chair on the other side of the large gap, and Marlowe frowned in confusion. She looked eagerly toward the door at the side of the room when it opened, expecting to see Tony.

But the man who entered wasn't anyone Marlowe had ever seen before. He stood out like a sore thumb from everyone else. He was tall. Had dark hair and a frightening scowl on his face, and was dressed impeccably in a white dress shirt, blue tie, and pair of khaki pants. He carried a briefcase, which he set on the ground as soon as he got to the space designated for her visitor.

He didn't lower himself to the chair, though. He frowned at her through the fence.

After a beat, his lips moved, but Marlowe couldn't hear what he was saying.

"I'm sorry, what?" she practically yelled.

His lips moved again, with what Marlowe thought might be a swear word, before he raised his voice. She could just hear him over the din. And English—American, unaccented English—never sounded so good.

"Marlowe Kennedy?"

She nodded.

"I'm your lawyer."

Marlowe blinked. This man didn't look like any lawyer she'd ever seen. Granted, she wasn't exactly an expert, but he seemed too . . . rough, despite the pristine clothing. She wasn't sure what gave her that impression. Maybe it was the anger in his eyes, or the muscles she could see bulging under his white shirt. But never in a million years would she have pegged this man as a lawyer.

"Did you hear me?" he yelled through the fence.

Marlowe nodded again.

"I'm going to get you out of here. Understand?"

She didn't. Not really. But she couldn't deny having someone on her side felt really good.

She nodded for a third time.

"You need to be ready," he told her, his dark eyes boring into hers. She had a feeling he was trying to tell her something, but she had no idea what. "In the meantime, keep your head down, don't bring attention to yourself. When the time is right, you'll know."

Marlowe tilted her head and studied the man across the gap. He hadn't introduced himself. Hadn't asked for her side of the story. Hadn't pulled out any paperwork. Hadn't done anything she suspected a lawyer would do when meeting a client for the first time. Of course, this wasn't exactly a normal circumstance. It wasn't as if they were meeting at a conference table where they could have a private and quiet conversation.

Suddenly, she needed to know this man's name. She wasn't convinced he could help her, didn't think anyone could at this point. The Thai government was in a war against drugs that they couldn't win, but they were more than willing to make examples out of anyone—foreigners especially—caught with anything, no matter how small the amount. It was why the prison was as overcrowded as it was.

But despite her lack of optimism, looking into this man's eyes, she felt a deep-seated need to trust him.

She stood slowly, not wanting to alarm Yanisa or any of the other trustees or guards in the room with a sudden movement. She gripped the metal fence in front of her so tightly, her fingers turned white. "What's your name?" she yelled.

The man stared at her for a beat before saying, "Kendric. Kendric Evans."

Kendric.

It fit him. Marlowe hadn't ever met anyone with that name before. His deep voice rumbled around in her brain as his name echoed within her. *Kendric. Kendric. Kendric.*

"How are you holding up?" he asked.

Marlowe shrugged. She knew better than to complain. She had no idea if Yanisa or anyone else could hear her over the noise in the room, but she wasn't going to take a chance that they would.

Kendric frowned. "I just need you to hold on a little longer. Can you do that for me?"

Marlowe wanted to say yes, but the truth was, she wasn't sure she could. This was the worst experience of her life, and after just weeks, she was already nearing her breaking point. The thought of spending the rest of her life here was terrifying to the point she'd do anything— *anything*—to get out. "Did Tony send you?" she shouted, instead of answering his question.

"Yes."

His answer was immediate, and the relief that swam through Marlowe's veins made her light headed. "Is he okay? Is he here?"

"He's fine. Worried about you. And no, he's not here. He sent me," Kendric said. His gaze moved slightly to her right, over her shoulder.

Marlowe turned her head to see what he was looking at, and saw Yanisa headed her way. She gripped the fence tighter. She didn't want to go back to the sewing room. She wanted to stay here, talking to Kendric. He was a link to her brother. To freedom. And she didn't want to lose it. She had the sudden suspicion that if she lost sight of Kendric, she'd fall right back into the pit of despair she'd been living in for what seemed like years instead of weeks.

As if he could read her mind, Kendric yelled, "Look at me, Marlowe."

She immediately turned her gaze back to him.

"I'm getting you out of here. You have to be ready. For anything. When the time comes, I'll be there. Understand? You just have to be brave enough to move."

Marlowe had no idea what he was talking about.

Yanisa grabbed her upper arm and said something in Thai.

Marlowe held on to the fence, not wanting to go. Not wanting to leave Kendric.

"Can you do that?" he asked.

There was an undercurrent to his question that Marlowe didn't understand.

"Marlowe!" he called again, as Yanisa pried her fingers off the fence. "When the time comes, be like Forrest Gump . . ."

He said something else, but the words were lost in the noise of everyone else yelling to be able to hear their visitors in the room.

Marlowe was so confused. Kendric couldn't have said *Forrest Gump*, could he?

But he had. She knew it.

Looking back before Yanisa pulled her out of the visitors' area, Marlowe saw Kendric standing right where he'd been before. He hadn't moved. He was holding on to the fence much as she'd been, staring at her as Yanisa manhandled her out of the room. The last glimpse she had of him, the man mouthed something.

The door slammed behind her, and Marlowe was once more being yanked along the grounds toward the sewing room. Yanisa was mumbling under her breath, and Marlowe was actually relieved she couldn't understand what she was saying. When they arrived back at the sweatshop, which was how Marlowe saw it, Yanisa shoved her toward the door.

Not expecting the violent movement, Marlowe flew forward and hit the door hard, barely avoiding smacking her face against the metal.

"Get work!" Yanisa growled.

Moving as fast as she could, Marlowe scrabbled for the knob and managed to get the door open. The air inside the room was stifling, and the familiar smell of body odor assaulted her senses.

It wasn't until she was once again seated at her sewing machine, fumbling with the material and trying to get the stitches straight, that Marlowe realized what Kendric had mouthed at her when she was being hauled away.

Run.

Was that the reference to Forrest Gump that he was trying to make? It made sense . . . but then again, it didn't. Run? To where? There wasn't anywhere to run *to*. And while there weren't a lot of guards at the prison, the walls were high and covered in barbed wire, and the bullets in the rifles of the men guarding the walls were as real as they could get.

She must've read what Kendric was trying to tell her wrong. She supposed it didn't really matter. Her brother was doing what he could to help her, and she had to have faith that eventually she'd be released. Someone would figure out that the yaba pills in her belongings at the dig site weren't hers.

She frowned. Shoot, she didn't get a chance to tell Kendric to look into Ian West. He was the reason she was in prison. She was sure of it. But if the man was smart at all, he'd be long gone from Thailand by now.

A sharp pain in her side made Marlowe grunt. Turning, she saw another of the trustees standing next to her, yelling and pointing at the sewing machine. The woman had kicked her because she was staring into space instead of working.

Lowering her head, Marlowe did her best to concentrate. She remembered what Kendric said. Not to bring any attention to herself. She had no idea what he was doing to free her, but she wasn't going to do anything to mess that up. Not when her freedom was at stake.

She could survive for a little while longer. She just hoped it wouldn't be months before Kendric and Tony could work through the red tape and get her the hell out of here.

Chapter Two

Kendric "Bob" Evans sat in his room two blocks from the women's prison and stared out the window with a frown on his face. He could just see the barbed wire on top of the walls, and he'd long since memorized the routes taken by the guards who walked the perimeter.

He'd seen some horrific things in his life, both as a Delta Force operative in the US Army and in the years he'd been working for Gregory Willis to rescue Americans overseas.

But today had taken the cake.

Willis, the FBI agent who was his contact when it came to rescue missions, had sent him a file on Marlowe Kennedy. It contained pictures and a fairly detailed account of her life history, including intel on her brother, Tony, the man she'd asked about during Bob's visit.

The truth was, Anthony Kennedy was moving heaven and earth to free his sister, with no luck. The issue was that the Thai government wanted to make examples of foreigners who dared try to sell drugs in their country. The problem had reached epidemic proportions, and so far, the government's crackdown and decision to imprison anyone caught with even one pill hadn't done much to stem the tide.

Desperate, Tony had finally reached out to Willis in an attempt to free his sister.

When finally given permission to talk to Marlowe, Bob, as he was known to his friends—a nod to the popular American diner Bob Evans—was shocked by her physical appearance. She'd only been incarcerated for a little over a month, but she looked as if it had been years.

In her pictures, she looked healthy, vibrant. He knew her height, so Bob suspected she was petite, but now she looked as if a strong wind would blow her over. Her cheekbones were sharper, her collarbones visible thanks to the gaping neckline of her shirt. Bob guessed she'd lost at least twenty pounds. Her hair was dull and lank, she had no color in her cheeks, the clothes she wore swam on her body. She looked . . . fragile.

Which wasn't good.

The plan that Willis had put into motion was risky at best, doomed to fail at worst, and Bob hated that he hadn't been able to talk to Marlowe today. Not *really* talk. He shook his head at his lame attempt at warning her with that stupid Forrest Gump reference. There was no way she'd understood. But he couldn't exactly come right out and say that when the shit hit the fan, she needed to run. Far and fast.

The plan had a few things going for it. The small number of guards, the age of the prison, the overcrowding. But the trustees might be a problem.

For the first time since he'd started doing these rescue missions, Bob wished his team was there to have his back. But Chappy, Cal, and JJ had no idea he was here, or even out of the US. They thought he was in Washington State visiting his sick aunt. A sick aunt who didn't exist.

He hated lying to them, but all three had settled into life in Maine without any issues. They were content to run their tree business and live a calm, quiet life.

Most of the time, Bob enjoyed it too. But he occasionally got restless. Needed the adrenaline rush that came with helping others get out of dangerous situations. Which was how and why he'd agreed to work for Gregory Willis.

Bob had completed a dozen or so missions in the last few years. He'd had no issues working alone before, in more dangerous situations than this one. So what was different now?

Deep down, Bob knew what it was.

Marlowe.

The look in her eyes had unsettled him. Desperation. Fear. Barely a hint of hope.

From what he'd read in the report detailing her brother's attempts to get the US government involved in the case, there was little chance the yaba pills found in her belongings were actually hers. An anonymous tip was called in, and it had resulted in Marlowe being hauled off her dig site and flung into a cell, with the key basically thrown away.

Determination rose within Bob. He wasn't leaving Thailand without her. It wouldn't be easy, even with the underground network of people Willis had arranged to shuttle them from hiding spot to hiding spot. Bangkok wasn't too far from the Cambodian border. If they could make it, they had a good chance of getting back to the States.

But getting to the border would be . . . a challenge.

Before he could even think that far, he first needed to get her out from behind the prison walls. There was a real risk she'd be hurt in the process, or he'd be caught and thrown into the Bangkok Hilton, as the Bang Kwang Central men's prison was often called. A prison break of this size and scope had never been attempted, and as crazy as the plan sounded when Bob had first heard it, after being inside today, he realized it actually had a mild chance of succeeding.

Still, all the things that could go wrong swam in his head, and Bob ruthlessly pushed them back. He needed to stay positive. As soon as the walls were breached, chaos would erupt, and all he had to do was find Marlowe and slip away undetected.

He snorted. Yeah, right. *All* he had to do. The prison had thousands of inmates. All of them wore the same clothes, and Marlowe had the same black hair and short height as most of them. Yes, she was American, which would help him find her once the plan was put into motion, but it was still going to be a difficult mission.

Despite that, he had every intention of succeeding. Hell, a few years ago, he wasn't sure he and his friends would be rescued when they'd been held as POWs. The chances were even lower then, and they'd made it out. He had to believe he'd be successful now.

"Hang in there, Marlowe," Bob whispered as he stared at the top of the prison walls. "Just a little longer."

∼

Marlowe lay in the stuffy room and stared up at the ceiling. The lights in the sleeping room were never shut off. It was as bright in there now as it was during the day, when sunlight streamed in from the dirty windows high above their heads.

The sounds of sleeping women were all around her. Some snored, others cried out when they had bad dreams, and others still mumbled under their breaths. Marlowe hadn't slept well since the day she'd arrived. It was impossible. The "bed" was uncomfortable, she was always hot and sweaty, and she didn't like being so crowded. She almost preferred the darkness of solitary. Almost.

The thought of spending the rest of her life here was . . . unimaginable. Tears threatened, but she squeezed her eyes shut and refused to let them fall. Crying wouldn't do a damn thing except make her even more miserable than she was right this moment. And she was already miserable enough to—

An extremely loud noise echoed through the room, interrupting her thoughts.

Marlowe sat up, as did most of the women around her. A low murmur began as everyone tried to figure out what the noise could have been, where it was coming from. One of the trustees lying near the door stood up and opened it, peering outside.

She gasped and said something in Thai under her breath.

Everyone was frozen in place for a moment, clearly surprised by whatever the trustee had uttered—until one of the prisoners near the door shouted something.

Marlowe had no idea what, but suddenly everyone was jumping to their feet and rushing toward the doors.

The three trustees were angrily trying to get the women to step back, to stay away from the doors, but with one hundred prisoners to their three, it was pointless. Marlowe was swept along with the crowd as everyone around her rushed to get out of the small building.

The second she was outside, she understood why everyone was in such a damn hurry.

A large truck had driven straight through the nearby east wall of the prison, leaving a massive hole in the brick.

Debris was scattered all over the yard—bricks, barbed wire, parts of the truck itself.

Even as the situation sank in, Marlowe noticed the women all around her rushing for the hole—toward escape, toward freedom— were eerily quiet. No one was screaming for joy, no one was hollering in fear. No one was trampling anyone else either. They were quickly and efficiently climbing over and around the truck still partially blocking the hole.

It was an orderly prison break . . . if there was such a thing.

Suddenly, Kendric's words from earlier came back.

I'm getting you out of here. You have to be ready. For anything. When the time comes, I'll be there. Understand? You just have to be brave enough to move.

Could this have been *his* doing?

Marlowe shook her head. It didn't seem possible. No lawyer would risk his license by orchestrating something like this. But she couldn't shake that one word he'd mouthed at her.

Run.

He'd told her to be like Forrest Gump. The old movie played in her head as she stood indecisively in the prison yard, frozen, staring at the other prisoners flowing through the hole in the wall. She heard the little girl from the movie yelling *Run, Forrest, run!*

Adrenaline shot through Marlowe's veins. She was terrified. If there was a chance Tony could grease some wheels and get her out of here through negotiations and lawyers, it would be smarter to stay put. To not give the Thai authorities any other reason to keep her locked up.

But what if she was well and truly stuck here? What if she had to spend the rest of her life in prison because her brother failed?

She wouldn't make it long. Marlowe knew that as well as she knew her name.

Her legs were moving before her brain had made the decision.

The only sounds in the night were the trustees and guards shouting. Marlowe assumed they were trying to corral the hundreds of prisoners still streaming out of various sleeping quarters. But no one was listening, countless women still silently but swiftly rushing toward the wall.

Freedom was at hand, and they were taking advantage.

Just as Marlowe reached the truck where it sat haphazardly in the wreckage of the brick wall, a shot rang out.

She ducked, as did the women around her, but no one stopped. They kept moving forward.

As soon as she was outside the prison walls, Marlowe wanted to stop and take a deep breath. For some reason, the air seemed cleaner out here, which was ridiculous, but seemingly true nonetheless. Another gunshot in the darkness kept her moving.

She tripped over something in the street and barely caught herself before she fell flat on her face. Looking down, Marlowe marveled at what she was seeing.

Hundreds of prison-issue shoes littered the street. As if the women who'd gone before her literally ran right out of them.

Which probably wasn't far from the truth. They were all given what Marlowe would call shower shoes. Cheap slip-on sandals that didn't have any kind of support. She considered kicking her own pair off her feet, knowing she could run faster without them, but at the last minute, she quickly slipped them off and held them tightly in her hand. She couldn't escape without shoes, even if they were crappy prison shower sandals.

Then she took a deep breath—and ran.

Marlowe had no idea where she was going, but the second she'd set foot outside that smashed prison wall, she knew there was no going back. She was a fugitive, and if the authorities caught her, she was in deep shit.

For a block or two, she ran in the same direction many of the other women were going, before her brain kicked in and she abruptly turned down an alley, away from the crowd. It only made sense that the authorities would follow the largest group of women, hoping to catch as many as possible at one time.

It was smarter to go it alone. Hide. Not that it would be easy. She was an American in a foreign land. Her feet slapped on the pavement as she ran blindly, doing her best to put as much distance between herself and the prison.

She was breathing hard already and trying not to panic. Marlowe had no plan. No idea where she was, where she was going, or how the hell she could get out of the country. Not only that, but she was tiring fast. She'd done her best to keep in shape while incarcerated, but that was tough to do when she was forced to sit in front of a damn sewing machine for ten hours a day.

Her steps slowed as Marlowe attempted to control her breathing. She could still hear the occasional gunshot echoing through the city streets, and each time she heard one, she flinched, expecting to feel a bullet tear through her flesh at any moment.

She'd just turned a corner to head down another alley when a hand reached out and grabbed her upper arm.

Instinctively, Marlowe used some of the self-defense techniques Tony had taught her years ago.

Instead of pulling away, she threw herself back into the person who'd grabbed her, pitching them both off balance. She brought her knee up as hard as she could and was rewarded with a grunt from her captor when she made contact.

She twisted her body, hoping to dislodge the man's grip, but he moved faster, pulling her close, her back against his chest. He threw his arm around her, anchoring her to his body.

He was taller than her by quite a bit. She could feel his hard muscles shifting as she squirmed frantically, doing her best to get out of his tight hold.

"Stop it, Marlowe! We don't have time for this."

She froze at hearing her name on his lips. And at hearing *English*. Doing her best to turn around, to see who he was, she growled in frustration when he held her so securely she couldn't move an inch.

As if he could sense her need—and knew that some of the fight had drained out of her—he turned her in his grasp, still keeping a firm hold.

There was hardly any light to see, but Marlowe recognized him immediately.

"Kendric," she breathed, shocked to her core.

His lips twitched as if she'd said something funny. "Yup," he agreed.

The man standing in front of her looked nothing like the staid and buttoned-up lawyer who'd come to the prison. Instead of the crisp white shirt, tie, and pressed khaki pants, he was wearing black from head to toe. A black T-shirt, cargo pants, boots. But the determination in his eyes was the same as she'd seen before.

"You good?" he asked.

Marlowe could only nod. Was she good? Not really. But then again, for the moment, she wasn't locked up for something she didn't do. There was a better-than-average chance she'd be caught and be sent right back to the hell she'd miraculously escaped, but for now, she supposed she was okay.

"Right." Kendric let go of her, but she could've sworn his thumbs swiped the skin of her upper arms in a reassuring caress before he turned and bent toward the ground. When he stood, he held her shoes out to her. "You should put these on. Smart making sure you didn't lose them."

Even that small compliment made Marlowe want to cry. It had been a very long time since anyone had said something nice to her. But she swallowed down the emotion. She wasn't safe, not by a long shot, and she needed to keep running. Get as far away from the prison as she could.

"You should go," she said urgently.

"What?" Kendric asked, his brows coming down in a scowl.

"You should go," she repeated. "The last thing you want is to be caught helping me."

To her surprise, Kendric actually laughed. "Who do you think orchestrated your escape . . . and the escape of all the other women? If we get caught, I'm definitely going to prison. But I have no intention of being captured. So put your shoes on, Mar, and let's get the hell out of here."

She stared at the slippers he was holding out to her and blurted the first thing that came to mind. "I can't run with them on. It's why I was carrying them."

He pressed his lips together, but simply nodded. "It's not ideal, but we don't have far to go."

"We don't?" Marlowe asked stupidly.

"Nope. Come on, let's get moving."

Marlowe stared at the hand Kendric held out to her for a beat. Then she took it with her own. He squeezed her fingers before turning and heading down the alley.

She felt as if she'd entered the twilight zone. Who *was* this man? Had he really run that truck into the prison wall, or perhaps arranged for someone else to do it? She couldn't wrap her mind around the risks he was taking—for *her*. She'd never met the man before he'd visited the prison.

"Stop thinking so hard, Marlowe. I'll answer all your questions once we're safe. For now, just know that I'm going to get you home."

Home. A longing so intense swept through her. Even if her job wasn't her passion, she definitely used to love traveling the world for various digs. Loved meeting new people, experiencing new cultures. But now, all she wanted was to get back to the States and never leave again.

Her mind still on overload, Marlowe followed Kendric without complaint, relieved to put her life in his hands, even temporarily. The adrenaline rush was ebbing, and she was suddenly exhausted. The lack of sleep, the crappy nutrition, the worry, the fear. All of it was catching up with her, and she knew without a doubt that if she hadn't run into this man . . . she'd be in big trouble.

~

Bob tightened his fingers around Marlowe's as he led them farther and farther away from the women's prison. They weren't out of danger, not by any stretch, but with every step they took, they were a little closer to getting her home.

He'd watched anxiously as one of the many people working with Willis and his underground network—a *very* well-paid underground network—ran the truck into the brick wall surrounding the prison. He'd chosen the perfect place for the ambush, the only spot in the prison that didn't have a building right up next to the outside wall.

As planned, the wall crumbled under the onslaught of the truck and the driver quickly fled the scene. It didn't take long for women inside to take advantage of the crash. They began pouring out of the prison, and Bob had held his breath, praying that Marlowe would be brave enough to make her escape.

He'd tried to warn her when he'd visited previously, but the setup for visitors wasn't ideal. Wasn't private in the least. He'd wanted so badly to tell her what was going to happen, but he couldn't risk anyone overhearing.

His sources had said that the women weren't actually locked inside their sleeping quarters at night. They were crowded into the buildings and only watched over by trustees. He'd had to hope that when the truck crashed into the wall and the alarms sounded, people would be curious enough to investigate. Thankfully, the crazy strategy had worked.

Freedom was a powerful motivator.

Bob didn't even feel bad that the plan to rescue Marlowe meant hundreds of other women would also escape. Many of them were no doubt also there under bogus charges, or the amount of drugs they'd been caught with didn't warrant their punishment. America's justice system wasn't perfect by any stretch of the imagination, but it was nothing like it was here.

He'd waited outside the prison in the shadows, close to the area where he knew Marlowe's sleeping quarters were located, watching as women ran for their lives. Holding his breath as he strained to catch a glimpse of his target. She was slight, had short black hair, and blended in fairly well with so many of the other prisoners.

Just when he'd thought she wasn't going to take the chance to escape, he'd spotted her.

At first, she'd run along with the other women, and he'd had to circle around a block to avoid detection before trying to catch up with her.

But when he'd intersected the path of the women, she was no longer with them.

She'd peeled off at some point, and for a brief moment, Bob had panicked. He couldn't lose her now.

By some miracle, he'd caught a glimpse of her as she was about to run around a corner, farther down the street. She'd looked back, as if to see if she was being followed, and the look on her face had etched itself onto his brain.

She was completely terrified.

He sprinted after her, and it still took a bit to catch up. He hadn't wanted to add to her terror, but when he'd grabbed her, he'd done just that. To his surprise—and satisfaction—she didn't simply give up. She fought against his hold. Hard. She'd managed to knee him viciously in the thigh. Thank goodness she wasn't taller than she was, otherwise she could've nailed him in the nuts. It wasn't until he'd trapped her tightly in his embrace that he'd been able to speak and calm her down.

The relief, disbelief, and confusion was easy to read on her face, but he didn't have time to reassure her much. To tell her the plan to get them out of there. They had to get to the next phase of the escape plan before dawn, which was little more than an hour away.

He hated that she wasn't wearing shoes, but he couldn't do anything about that right this second. She was quiet behind him, and Bob was glad. She had to have a million questions, but the fact that she was holding her tongue meant she trusted him at least a little bit.

And trust was essential during rescue missions like this one.

Bob squeezed her hand without thought, wanting to reassure her wordlessly that everything would be okay. Of course, he had no idea if that was true, but he'd do his part to get her back to her brother, or die trying.

They walked fast for ten more minutes until they reached their destination. Bob let out a sigh of relief as he walked around the dilapidated hut in one of the worst parts of the city. He slipped through a hole in a fence, then into a small shed behind the home. He didn't know who lived there, and he didn't need to.

He smiled as he saw what he'd hoped would be waiting for him behind the wooden door of the shed. A scooter. This was their ticket out of the city, and to the next step in their journey for the Cambodian border. A small bag sat next to the bike.

Bob let go of Marlowe's hand—and was surprised at the pang of discontent that flashed through him when he was no longer touching her. She was a job. Nothing more, nothing less.

But even as he thought the words, Bob knew they were a lie.

Marlowe Kennedy wasn't just another job. Seeing the complex emotions behind her eyes, the fear that couldn't disguise her determination to get away . . . he was drawn to this woman in a way that was unfamiliar.

Leaning over, he picked up the bag and peered inside, determined to keep things between them professional. Satisfied, he pulled out two of the items and turned to Marlowe.

"Shirt and leggings. Put them on. The authorities will be looking for women wearing that prison uniform."

She nodded and reached for the clothes. Turning his attention back to the bag, Bob pulled out the last item. He looked up—and blinked in surprise.

Marlowe was standing next to him wearing nothing but a cheap, grungy-looking bra. She'd stripped off the prison top without a second thought. She frowned as she attempted to figure out where the armholes were in the shirt.

Bob tried to look away, he really did, but he couldn't take his gaze from the sight before him. Marlowe's ribs were clearly visible. She was so skinny, it almost hurt to look at her. He was right; she'd lost quite a bit of weight in the weeks that she'd been incarcerated. Too much.

She also had a dark bruise on her side, indicating she'd either bumped into something . . . or someone abused her.

Before he could become too outraged at the thought, she got the material straightened out and pulled the dark-gray long-sleeve shirt over her head, hiding her body from him. Then, as if she didn't have a drop of modesty, she shoved the dark-blue skirt over her hips and reached for the black leggings.

Bob swallowed hard. Despite needing to put on some weight, Marlowe was gorgeous. The woman was only five-four, yet her legs seemed to go on forever.

Shaking his head, he internally reprimanded himself. This wasn't the time or place for him to have such inappropriate thoughts. The past month had been hell for the poor woman, and he was there to get her home in one piece. That was it.

But somehow, her stoicism piqued his interest all the more. He was used to the people he rescued being overwhelmed. Nervous. Angry. Helpless. Marlowe was . . . practical. She hadn't asked a hundred questions. Hadn't slowed him down. Hadn't hesitated to put on the clothes. She'd simply done whatever he'd asked.

Irrationally, that acquiescence itself frustrated him. He could have led her to this dangerous area to violate her. Kill her. He could've led her straight back to the Thai authorities. He'd never do any of those things, but she didn't know that.

"You're too trusting," he said quietly.

She looked up at him in surprise. "What?"

"You don't know me. Yet you just took your clothes off in front of me."

Bob saw her cheeks darken. Jesus, he was being a complete ass. But before he could apologize, Marlowe lifted her chin to look him dead in the eye. "I was pretty self-conscious before I was arrested, but after being strip-searched and having zero privacy for the last month—including in the bathrooms—I guess I just didn't think about it. The prison clothes *would* be a huge giveaway, so I further assumed I needed to change immediately. Also, if you wanted to hurt me, you could've done it already. So for now, I'm trusting you. I literally have no other options."

The last bit was said defensively and with force. As if daring him to contradict her.

Yup. He was a total dick. And she was right. They didn't have any time to spare. He held up the last item from the bag.

"This should help keep people from realizing who you are."

She stared at it for a moment. Bob saw a look of distaste cross her face before she masked it. "Smart." That was all she said as she held out her hand.

For some reason, Bob didn't like that she was hiding her true feelings from him. He preferred her to say what was on her mind. "You don't like wigs?"

Marlowe shrugged. "Under normal circumstances, when I haven't gone a week since washing my hair? When we aren't in a tropical environment? When I'm not wearing one to hide the fact that I'm a fugitive on the run? I wouldn't care."

Bob couldn't help but smile a bit at that. Instead of handing her the long blonde wig, he asked, "May I?"

She stared at him for a long moment before saying, "Yes."

There was something intimate about easing the wig over her head and arranging it so it looked natural, carefully ensuring that none of her short black hair was showing around her nape.

"Won't this make me stand out more?" she asked after a moment. "I mean, long blonde hair doesn't exactly blend in around here."

"True. But if the authorities are looking for an American with short black hair, maybe they won't bother to stop and interrogate us."

Marlowe reached for him and put her hand on his forearm. The hair on the back of Bob's neck stood up at her touch. Electricity seemed to arc between them for a moment before she said, "I don't want you to get in trouble for helping me. If we get caught, you run."

Anger swept through him, an emotion that felt more comfortable than what he'd been feeling a moment ago. "Not happening."

"But—"

"No," he said firmly. "We aren't going to get caught. We're both getting back to the States. Now, come on. Let's put some miles between us and that prison, shall we?"

He turned to the bike and threw his leg over the seat. He'd prefer Marlowe not be exposed behind him, but there wasn't anything he could do about that. It was still dark outside. Hopefully he'd be able to avoid any roadblocks and get them outside the city limits and to their next stop before the sun came up.

He turned and looked at Marlowe a little impatiently. "Get on behind me."

She frowned slightly at the scooter. Bob couldn't help being pleased with how different she looked. The blonde wig changed her appearance drastically, but he actually preferred her short black hair. Shaking his head a little, he held out a hand.

"It won't bite, Mar, get on."

"I've never ridden a motorcycle," she said uneasily.

Susan Stoker

He chuckled quietly. "This isn't even close to being a motorcycle, Punky. Just sit down and hold on to me."

She finally nodded and swung a leg over the seat behind him. Her hands gripped his T-shirt gingerly at his sides, and he could feel her body stiffen.

Bob pulled her hands off his shirt and wrapped her arms around his waist. The move drew her closer, and he felt her heat along his back. He patted one of her arms. "Tighter. You're gonna have to pretend you like me, Punky. We're just two American lovebirds on a little nighttime joyride."

She jerked slightly at his words, but he felt her nod, then tighten her hold.

Not wasting any more time, Bob walked the scooter toward the door. He nudged the surface with the front tire and, once outside, headed toward the fence. As soon as they were on the street, he started the scooter, gave it some gas, and headed toward the road that would lead them away from the center of town.

Several minutes went by before he felt Marlowe relax. She'd clearly gotten used to the scooter. Long strands from the wig blew around them as he drove as fast as he dared away from the neighborhood.

"Punky?" she asked after a while.

Bob smiled. "Yeah."

He heard her huff out a breath. "What does that mean?"

"Punky Brewster," he told her.

"The kid from that eighties show?" she asked, a hint of incredulity in her tone. "You've seen it?"

"I don't sleep much," he admitted. Something his friends didn't even know. "I watch a lot of reruns on TV when I can't sleep. You remind me of her. Scrappy. Determined. Optimistic, even when things aren't going your way."

"I'm not *any* of those things," she protested.

"You are."

"Not."

24

Bob smiled again. "Are we really arguing about this?"

"You started it."

A chuckle escaped that time. "Well, I'm gonna call you what I want, so there."

"You're weird," she told him after a beat.

It was hard to believe he was in the middle of a dangerous op and actually having a little fun. "Yup."

She was leaning against him, speaking into his ear. It was an intimate position, and Bob regretted that he couldn't see her. Couldn't pay as close attention to her as he'd like. He had to concentrate on the road, on not hitting any of the numerous potholes in the street. Be on alert for any kind of police activity.

"Did Tony really send you?" she asked, warm air from her words brushing over his ear and throat.

"In a roundabout way," he told her honestly. "I've never spoken to your brother, but he knows the man who I work for, and he started the ball rolling."

Another annoyed huff left her, and Bob smiled again. "That tells me nothing," she complained. "Who are you? Is your name really Kendric?"

"It is," Bob told her. "Kendric Evans. My friends call me Bob."

It took a few seconds for her to respond, and when she did, Bob wasn't really surprised by her reply. "Are you kidding me? Bob? Like Bob Evans, the restaurant?"

"One and the same."

"That's ridiculous."

"It is," he agreed.

"Why do you answer to it then?" she asked.

Bob opened his mouth to explain—until he caught sight of the one thing he hoped he wouldn't, several blocks ahead. "Roadblock," he told her. "Stay calm." Adrenaline spiked in his own bloodstream, but he did his best to control it.

"Kendric," she whimpered.

"Follow my lead," he told her as calmly as he could.

"Why aren't you turning off? Going down a different road?" she asked, and Bob could hear the panic in her voice.

"Because they've already seen us. If I turned, they'd get suspicious. I've got this," he reassured her. "Like I said, follow my lead."

"My shoes," she said. "They're going to recognize them."

"They won't look at your feet. Promise. Just go with whatever I do. Okay? We're two Americans, madly in love, on the trip of a lifetime."

"I can't deal with the guilt if you get arrested," she told him.

Bob didn't have any more time to reassure her. They were approaching the two police cars parked across the road.

Taking a deep breath, he centered himself. He'd gotten out of worse situations than this. He had faith in Marlowe that she could play her part. And if worse came to worst, he'd gun it and do his best to outrun the cops. That would be difficult on a scooter . . . but he'd faced more than his fair share of difficulties in his lifetime.

Chapter Three

Marlowe felt like she was going to throw up. She couldn't go back to that prison. She just couldn't. She held on to Kendric with a grip she knew was too tight, but she was unable to relax her arms. The man had told her to trust him, and she was trying her best, but it was hard when merely the sight of the officers brought back horrible memories of her interrogation.

One of the police officers held up his hand, gesturing for them to stop, and said something in Thai.

"Sorry, I'm from the US, and I don't know a lick of Thai," Kendric said almost cheerfully. "My fiancée and I are on holiday. Driving through Thailand, seeing the sights."

Marlowe held her breath.

"Where are your bags?"

Crap. She hadn't even thought about that. But Kendric didn't miss a beat.

"Back at our hostel. I thought I'd take my muffin cake out to see the sunrise. One of the people we met said there's a particular place about ten miles outside the city that has the most amazing view."

The officer's gaze flicked to her, and Marlowe did her best to look relaxed, even though she was anything but. As subtly as possible, she reached for the hem of her shirt and pulled it down, trying to flash some cleavage at the man. Not that she had much. Her boobs were a size B on a good day, and the weight she'd lost hadn't done her any favors, but she hoped maybe, just maybe, flashing some skin might be helpful.

"IDs?" the second officer asked.

Once again, Marlowe felt her gut squeezing with panic, but Kendric merely nodded and leaned to the side, reaching into his back pocket. His fingers brushed against her inner thigh, and he turned to smile at her. "Sorry, babe."

She did her best to get into the act. She ran her hand down his arm as he fumbled for his wallet. "It's okay. You know I like when you touch me."

Kendric winked at her and pulled out his wallet. To her surprise, he pulled out two drivers' licenses and handed them to the officer. Then he put his hand on her knee and ran it up and down her lower leg.

Marlowe noticed the second officer's gaze was glued to Kendric's hand. It seemed to take the other man forever to examine their licenses. And Marlowe was beginning to get nervous.

To her surprise, Kendric twisted on the seat in front of her and cupped her cheek. Then he wrapped those fingers around her nape and kissed her. And it wasn't a small peck either. His lips covered hers, and his tongue immediately demanded entrance to her mouth.

On a quiet gasp, Marlowe opened for him.

The second his tongue touched hers, she was lost. Literally forgot she was a fugitive. That at any moment, the police officers could haul her off the scooter and lock her up again. That she didn't know Kendric. That she hadn't properly brushed her teeth in ages.

All she could do was hang on to Kendric as he rocked her world.

She'd been kissed before, but had never felt the earth move. Never felt electricity shoot from her head to her toes. Never gotten wet from a simple kiss. But kissing Kendric was everything the sappy romantic movies she liked to watch made it out to be. She felt like Sleeping Beauty, awakened for the first time by true love's kiss.

When he pulled back, their eyes met, and Marlowe could only stare at him in wonder.

Kendric groaned low in his throat and leaned toward her again.

Eager to experience more of the amazing feelings he brought out in her, Marlowe grabbed his thigh and dug her fingers in as she lifted her chin.

"You should be careful," the officer said, breaking the moment between her and Kendric.

Marlowe wanted to cry. She needed more of this man. Wanted to inhale him. Wanted to become one with him.

Her only consolation was that it took Kendric a long moment to compose himself. His eyes remained locked onto hers, as if telling her they'd continue this later. Then he twisted back to face the officers, as if he hadn't been turned inside out by their kiss, and said, "Oh? Why?"

"There was a prison break. Many escaped."

"Oh, that's why y'all have this roadblock, huh? Makes sense."

"Dangerous criminals," the officer said with a nod.

"Well, I hope you catch them all," Kendric said as he put the licenses into his wallet and leaned forward to put it back into his pocket.

"If you see anything suspicious, anyone suspicious, you must report to authorities," the officer warned.

"Oh, yes, of course I will. I have to keep my cookie safe," Kendric said, patting Marlowe's knee. As if on cue, both men's eyes went back to Marlowe's legs.

Lights flickered behind them as another car approached.

"You may pass," said the officer who'd scrutinized their licenses, motioning for them to go around the front of one of the cars to get back onto the road on the other side.

"Thank you. Be safe. I hope you catch all the prisoners," Kendric said.

"We will."

Marlowe shivered at the determination in the man's tone. But she managed a smile. Kendric waved at the officers and drove around their cars, and soon they were back on the road.

She rested her forehead against Kendric's shoulder and released a long breath.

"Easy, Punky. You did it. You did so good," he said, patting her hands, which were in a death grip around his waist once more.

"You had IDs for us?" she mumbled into his shoulder.

"Yup. All part of the plan."

"The plan," she huffed. "What plan?"

"The plan to get you home," he said easily.

They drove for a few minutes, and Marlowe thought back to their kiss. He hadn't hesitated. Hadn't seemed even the least bit shy about what he'd done, as if he went around kissing strangers all the time. And Marlowe supposed maybe he did, if he rescued women often. She didn't know him. Didn't know anything about him.

"I'm sorry about that back there," he said, breaking into her thoughts. "That one guy was getting a little too interested in checking you out, and I figured we needed to give him something else to think about . . . namely, his dick."

Marlowe felt herself blushing. "It's okay," she told him.

"For the record?" Kendric said.

She waited, but when he didn't continue, she asked, "Yeah?"

"I can't remember a kiss I enjoyed more." He was looking straight ahead as he confidently drove the scooter through the light early-morning traffic. "It wasn't appropriate, and I feel as if I took advantage of you . . . but I don't regret it."

"Me either," Marlowe admitted. "You can kiss, Bob."

"I'm thinking I like you calling me Kendric better. Ken works too."

"Good. Because you aren't a Bob. Not even close."

"Carlise, June, and April would love you."

Marlowe frowned. "Who?"

"My friends' wives. And April is the admin assistant for the business my friends and I run together. She and JJ have a thing, but neither wants to admit it."

A few minutes of silence went by before Kendric said her name. "Marlowe?"

"Yeah?"

"Do you forgive me for doing that back there?"

She snorted. "For doing what? Having an ID for me? Distracting the cops so they wouldn't look at my prison-issue shoes? Giving me a kiss that curled my toes and made me forget for just a moment that my life has gone to shit? Yeah, Kendric. I forgive you."

"Curled your toes?" he asked, turning his head slightly so she could see his grin.

Marlowe realized she was also smiling like a loon. "Yeah."

"Me too," he admitted.

She closed her eyes for a moment. The admission that he'd been just as affected by the spontaneous kiss seeped into her bones. Made her feel as if maybe she'd get back to the woman she'd been before getting thrown in jail.

Suddenly overwhelmed with gratitude, she hugged Kendric hard.

He squeezed her hand and said, "We're going to be at our stopping point in just a few minutes. The Cambodian border isn't too far, just the equivalent of about three hundred miles. But the roads aren't great outside the city. We can't go as fast as I'd like on this scooter, and I don't want to look suspicious to any authorities we might run into along the way, so we'll take our time. Act like tourists. My plan is to lay low during the day and set out again after dark. That okay?"

"This is your rescue. I'll do whatever you say, when you say it, as soon as you say it."

He twisted his neck and caught her gaze for a second before returning his attention to the road. "Yeah?"

Remarkably, she giggled. "Well, maybe I should clarify that."

"You're safe with me," Kendric fired back, no humor in his tone at all.

"I know," Marlowe told him. And she did. She felt safer with this man than she had in a very long time. Maybe ever. There was just something about him that screamed safety. She didn't know much about him, but one thing was clear—he'd do whatever it took to get her back to her brother, even if that meant getting hurt himself.

And the more time she spent with him, the more abhorrent that idea was. She didn't want him getting injured on her behalf. Or killed. She shivered at the thought.

"Cold?"

That. Right there. He was so in tune with her, it was almost scary. "No, just an unpleasant thought."

"Soon this will all be a bad dream," he reassured her.

"Will they come to the States to get me?" she couldn't help but ask.

"No."

His answer was short and to the point. "How can you be sure?"

"I just am. Trust me, Punky."

Not wanting to think about being hauled out of her bed in the middle of the night by immigration or the FBI or someone hell bent on sending her back to Thailand, Marlowe nodded against him.

About ten minutes later, Kendric slowed and once again steered the scooter between the slates of a fence, into a wooden building that looked as if it was one strong storm from being blown over. He turned off the engine and hopped off the seat. Then he took her arm in his and said, "Slowly."

Wondering why he was so concerned, Marlowe swung her leg over the seat and stood—and immediately swayed on her feet. Her legs didn't seem to want to work. "Oh!" she exclaimed.

"Give it a moment for the blood to start flowing again," he told her, still holding her steady.

"You just leaped off as if you weren't on there the same amount of time I was," she complained.

Kendric's lips twitched. "I'm used to it. Come on, lean on me and we'll head inside."

"Wait. Kendric?"

"Yeah?"

"Will being around me put anyone else in danger?"

She couldn't read the expression on his face. Perhaps a mixture of anger and tenderness. "No."

"Are you sure?"

"Yes."

She didn't know if he was lying or not. "I can't deal with anyone getting in trouble because of me."

Kendric wrapped an arm around her waist and pulled her close. Marlowe braced her hands on his chest as she looked at him in surprise.

"Everyone we'll meet along our journey knows the risks they're taking. And trust me, they're being well compensated for their assistance. Besides, they know how corrupt the officials here can be. Many have had loved ones incarcerated just like you were. With no chance of fighting the charges. They're glad to help. Eager, in fact. You'll see. I know this is going to sound impossible, but relax, Punky. I've got you."

Marlowe closed her eyes and rested her forehead against his chest. "I'm scared," she admitted. "I have been ever since the police officers came to the dig and accused me of being a drug dealer. I just . . . I want to go home." The last few words were almost a sob, and Marlowe hated the weakness they exposed.

"You will. You *are*," Kendric said. Marlowe could feel him running a careful hand over the wig on her head. Even though the touch was light because of the material between his hand and her scalp, she still felt it down to her toes.

Taking a big breath, she opened her eyes and looked up at him. "I'm okay. It's just . . . it's a lot. But I'm all right now."

Kendric stared at her for a beat. "You're pretty amazing."

She huffed out a disbelieving breath. "I'm not."

"You are," he insisted. "You have no idea. I've done this many times before, and trust me when I tell you that you're holding up way better than most people."

Marlowe didn't like to think of Kendric putting himself in danger like this as part of his job. Then she frowned. Hadn't he said he owned a business with some friends? Was *that* his job, or did they all do this? Rescue people?

"You're tired. We need to eat, get clean, and then sleep."

A low moan escaped her throat at the thought of any one of those things.

Kendric smiled. "Come on. We'll go meet our host and get you sorted."

Nodding, Marlowe allowed herself to be turned, loving that Kendric kept an arm around her shoulders and walked by her side toward the run-down-looking dwelling nearby.

~

Bob couldn't take his eyes off Marlowe for more than a few seconds. The memory of the kiss they'd shared looped through his brain like a broken record. He hadn't meant to kiss her like that, but when he'd seen the second officer looking suspicious about their story, he'd simply acted.

And that kiss had rocked him to the core. It was a good thing they were sitting, otherwise his knees would've gone out from under him. Because in that second, he knew.

This woman was his.

His.

He'd been looking for his perfect match for years. And as luck would have it, he'd found her on the other side of the world.

She was his responsibility. She was relying on him to get her out of the country safely. One screwup on his part and she'd go right back to prison and likely spend the rest of her life there.

That wasn't an option. No way in hell.

Most people would tell him he was being ridiculous. That there was no way he could know she was his after a single kiss. They'd insist he was just horny because he hadn't had sex in too long to remember, and *that's* why he was so drawn to her. But those people would be wrong.

Bob felt their connection down to his bones. He hadn't recognized the pull toward her when he'd visited her in the women's prison, but as soon as he'd touched her, it sprang to life.

Then that kiss . . .

His friends would understand. Chappy and Cal had fallen just as hard and fast, and now they were both married and living happily ever after. If anyone deserved to be happy, it was his friends.

Even JJ, despite currently resisting their admin assistant himself, would tell Bob not to let anyone talk him out of going after what he wanted. What he wanted was Marlowe Kennedy.

And yet, despite his convictions, he had no illusions about the more likely scenario once they were back in the States. She'd go live with her brother for a while, until she was back on her feet. He'd go back to Maine, and their time together would come to an end.

If that happened, she'd be his biggest regret . . . and his proudest accomplishment. She might never be his, not the way he wanted her to be, but he'd have to worry about that later. For now, his only goal was to get her out of Thailand and back to the States safely. After that . . . who knew.

The last thing he wanted was anyone being with him out of a sense of obligation or gratitude. He wanted, *needed*, more.

Needed her to feel their connection as intensely as he did. Needed her to want to get to know him as someone other than her rescuer. At the moment, he wasn't sure if that was possible.

Putting thoughts of the future aside, Bob concentrated on the here and now. They'd been welcomed into the small, poor hut of another member of Willis's network and shown into a back room. The man who'd let them in didn't speak English, but through hand gestures made them understand that he'd be back with food and drink.

The room was small and sparsely furnished. It was likely where the man slept with his wife. A pallet lay on the floor, and a small, rickety dresser sat against one wall. The floor was old wooden planks that were probably full of splinters. There was no window in the room, and it was already heating up as the sun made its appearance in the sky. It would only continue to get warmer as the day went on . . . but for Bob, it was perfect.

They were safe. He had to believe that. Willis was very good at what he did, and his contacts thus far had operated flawlessly.

"There's no way out," Marlowe said uneasily as she looked around. "No windows. What if the cops come?"

"They won't. And trust me, if we need to get out of here, I'm thinking one strong kick to the wall will give us an egress point. You're safe, Marlowe. I promise, you aren't going back."

She sighed. "I'm trying to believe it, but . . . it was awful, Kendric. You just don't know."

"You might be surprised. But I'm thinking things will look better after you eat something and get some rest."

"What about you?" she asked.

"What *about* me?"

"Will you get some sleep too?"

"Of course," Bob answered immediately, but the truth was, it was unlikely. He didn't sleep well under the best circumstances. And this was far from ideal.

"Good. Can't have you falling asleep at the wheel . . . or handlebars," she said with a small smile.

This was another thing Bob admired about this woman. She was able to make jokes, even when she was unsure and scared.

"Come here," he said, holding out a hand to her. He hadn't given her a choice with the kiss back at the checkpoint, and he was still kicking himself about that. He wouldn't force her to do anything again if he could help it.

She immediately stepped toward him and instead of taking his hand, kept coming until she was hugging him. She fit against him perfectly. She was a small thing, and she felt fragile in his arms. But Bob suspected under normal circumstances, this woman was tough as nails, and he couldn't be prouder of how she'd managed so far.

Way before he was ready to let go, their host opened the door. He had a tray in his hands that had two bowls and a plate piled high with various bite-size pieces of food. Bob had no idea what any of it was, but his stomach growled impatiently.

Marlowe grinned and stepped back as the man lowered the tray to the floor. He didn't say anything, didn't even meet their gazes, as he backed out of the room and shut the door behind him.

"Was it something I said?" Marlowe quipped.

Bob chuckled. "Come on, let's see what we've got so you can eat and get some shut-eye."

Marlowe didn't eat nearly as much as Bob would've liked. She picked at the food on the plate, but drank most of the broth that was in the bowl.

"You don't like the food," Bob said. It wasn't a question.

Marlowe shrugged. "Not really. I've tried. I mean, I know I need the calories, but I've never been much of a seafood fan, and everything here is just so different from what I'm used to."

"What are you used to?" Bob asked.

Marlowe gave him a small, sheepish smile. "Chicken nuggets, hot dogs, Doritos, potato chips, candy, ramen, SpaghettiOs."

He stared at her in disbelief. "Good lord, woman. All that's crap."

"I know," she said with a shrug. "I eat like a ten-year-old. What can I say? I'm single and can't cook. So I make do."

"I love to cook. Although it sucks cooking for one," he admitted.

"We'd make a good pair. You love to cook and I hate it," Marlowe said. Then she blushed and bit her lip. "I mean, you know, if we were together. Which we aren't! I mean . . . shoot."

"I know what you meant," Bob said gently, letting her off the hook. But he was thinking the same thing. If she was his, it would be his pleasure to cook for her every night. To make sure she got the nutrition her body needed.

"I usually bring MREs with me on a dig. To help supplement the local food. Along with a bag or two of candy, although that's usually gone way too fast," she admitted with a shrug.

"What's your favorite?"

"What, candy?"

"Yeah."

"Anything with sugar in it," she said with a small laugh. "I mean, you know, not chocolate. Smarties, Spree, SweeTarts, Runts, that kind of thing."

Bob couldn't help but smile. "Sweet tooth," he muttered.

"Yup," she said without a shred of embarrassment.

Bob made a mental note to find her a bag of candy as soon as he could manage it. He opened his mouth to tell her as much, but she yawned then, quickly covering her mouth.

"Sleep," he ordered, pointing to the pallet on the floor.

"I can't sleep there," she said, shaking her head. "I mean, that's their *bed*. First of all, that's rude. Secondly, and this is going to sound ridiculous, considering where I just spent the last month, but . . . I can't help thinking about what they might've done on those covers."

Bob snorted. "Right. How about this?" He walked over to the dresser and opened one of the drawers. He pulled out a man's shirt, then went over to the wall and spread it out on the floor. He sat next to it and patted his leg. It wasn't ideal, but now that Marlowe had brought it up, the thought of lying down on the pallet where the man may or may not have made love to his wife hours ago wasn't exactly high on his list of things to do either.

"It's probably not all that comfortable, but . . ."

"It's perfect," Marlowe said with a small smile as she approached. She lay down on her side, resting her head on his thigh. "Are you sure this is okay?"

"It's more than okay," Bob assured her. And once more, she'd impressed him. She could've pitched a fit about having to sleep on the floor, but she didn't. She was grateful for what she had. He supposed being in prison had a lot to do with her easy acceptance of her situation, but he also had a feeling it was just who she was naturally. "Sleep, Punky," he told her.

"Has anyone told you that you're bossy?" she asked sleepily.

"Yes."

"Well, they weren't lying," she said.

Bob chuckled again, and he couldn't stop himself from reaching out and stroking his hand down her hair. It was then that he realized she was still wearing the wig. "Lift up," he told her.

"What?" she asked, lifting her head from his thigh in confusion.

He quickly pulled the wig off her head, and she sighed in contentment.

"Oh, that feels so good."

Bob ran his hand over her hair, feeling the sweaty strands at the back of her neck.

"Kendric?" she asked.

"Yeah?"

"Thank you," she whispered. "Thank you for coming for me. For keeping me safe."

"You're welcome," he told her, but he wasn't sure she heard him, as she was already snoring. She was out so fast, it was as if she hadn't slept for days or weeks. He had a feeling he wasn't too far off. When he'd been a POW, he hadn't slept much at all. Always aware of every little sound, waiting and wondering when it would be his turn to be tortured again.

Turning his attention to the woman next to him, Bob refused to think about that time in his life. He and his friends had been rescued, and now he was paying back the debt he owed to the men and women who'd restored his freedom by returning the favor. Helping others in need.

But being here for Marlowe didn't feel like a favor. It felt like fate.

Bob shook his head and rested it against the wall behind him. He really needed to stop thinking like that. Marlowe would go her own way once they were back home.

She couldn't be his. This wasn't fate. She wasn't his soulmate.

But no matter how many times he told himself those things, the feeling that he was destined to be right where he was, right this second, wouldn't rest.

Not able to look away from Marlowe for long, Bob lowered his head and stroked her hair. The strands were filthy, she was covered in dirt . . . but he'd never seen a more beautiful woman in his life.

He was in big trouble. This woman had him wrapped around her little finger after a total of a few hours . . . and she had no clue.

When he got home, he'd call his friend Tex and have him keep tabs on her. Scrub her fugitive status, if possible. Make sure she was safe when she went on future archaeological digs. Maybe he'd even see if the former SEAL could covertly put a tracker on her.

Shaking his head, Bob snorted. He wouldn't do that to Marlowe. What was he thinking? Track her without her knowledge? No, only psychos did that kind of crap. Besides, if Tex let anything slip, and Chappy, Cal, or JJ found out about his little extracurricular rescue trips, he'd have his hands full trying to explain and earning back their trust.

He'd have to let Marlowe go. Had a feeling it would be the hardest thing he'd done in his life so far . . . even more difficult than surviving his time as a POW. But he'd do it, because Marlowe deserved her freedom too.

Chapter Four

The next two nights went by much the same as their first. And Kendric hadn't lied: they were traveling extremely slowly. A big part of Marlowe wanted to race as fast as they could on a straight path to the border, to get out of this country. But she understood the need to stay under the radar, to try to avoid coming into contact with anyone who might identify them.

So they traveled a somewhat meandering path by night, sticking to back roads and trails, and stopped at safe houses before dawn. They hadn't come across any more roadblocks, and the farther they got from Bangkok, the more Marlowe's hopes rose.

She was beginning to think she might just make it to the border without being caught. But there was still the issue of getting into Cambodia. It wasn't as if they could just go through one of the official crossings. She wasn't sure what Kendric's plan was, but she was confident he had one.

Ever since he'd found her, he'd taken care of everything. It was a relief to put her trust in someone. She didn't have to think about anything other than holding on to him while he drove them farther and farther away from the hell she'd experienced.

It should've scared her how fast she'd given up control to Kendric, but it didn't, simply because he made her feel protected. While Marlowe liked her job, she didn't enjoy going into some of the more dangerous countries she'd visited. Feeling safe was sometimes a rarity.

It was rather funny that she was an archaeologist at all. She'd kind of fallen into it when she'd been in college. Her roommate her freshman year had been interested in the field, and since Marlowe hadn't known what she wanted to do, she'd basically latched on to her friend, taking a lot of the same courses. The friendship eventually ended after a couple of years, but by then, Marlowe found she enjoyed her studies.

Archaeology wasn't really her passion, but it had allowed her to see the world. In fact, she hadn't stayed in one place for years. Ironic, considering what she *really* wanted to do. Something that wasn't always respected by society any longer, especially since she was a single woman.

She wanted to be a mom.

Because she had neither a boyfriend nor a husband, she wanted to adopt children in the state's system. Those who didn't have a parent to love them. She knew it would be an extremely difficult road to adopt a child as a single woman, but it was what she longed for.

Of course, she couldn't exactly be a single parent without a job, and that's what had kept her doing what she was good at, even if she didn't love it like she should.

But after this experience, Marlowe was more determined than ever to do what *she* wanted to do. She didn't know how she'd afford it, but she had no doubt Tony would help her figure it out.

For now, her attention returned to the man sitting in front of her. The farther they got from Bangkok, the more Marlowe worried about Kendric. He'd admitted that first day that he didn't sleep well, but she wasn't sure he was sleeping at all. At least nothing more than catnaps. When he got her settled after they ate, most of the time using him as a pillow, he was always in the same position when she woke up hours later. She wanted to insist that he lie down, but every time she brought it up, he'd brush off her concerns, insisting he was fine, that he slept while she did.

She was determined to get him to lie down today, as they slowed near a surprisingly nice-looking house, a two-story cinder block structure with a well-maintained yard. The other places they'd stopped at were run down and looked like they were on the verge of collapsing, but this house was in a city that was fairly well populated. They'd seen more people on the way to this safe house than in the last two days combined, which made Marlowe very nervous. She could feel Kendric tense up every time they spotted a member of the Royal Thai Police.

"Are you sure this is where we're supposed to stop?" she asked as he drove the scooter around to the back of the house.

"I'm sure," he said confidently. "We're getting close to the border, and Willis figured we needed a more comfortable place to regroup before the stress of crossing."

Kendric had told Marlowe only a little about the mysterious contact responsible for setting up the network of people helping them get across Thailand, though he'd called him more than once during their journey.

She swung her leg over the seat, pleased at how she was holding up, now that she was more used to straddling the bike. She took off the backpack they'd received at the second house. Kendric insisted on taking it from her the second they stopped anywhere. He couldn't exactly wear it while driving, with her plastered to his back, and Marlowe actually liked that she had some kind of responsibility on their journey.

"Come on, I have it on good authority that the owner of this place has a shower we can use."

"A shower?" Marlowe asked excitedly. They'd been making do with bowls filled with warm water, cleansing a bit before setting out again each night. She couldn't wait to take the hated wig off and scrub her hair. Not to mention the rest of her as well.

"Yes. A shower," he said with a grin.

He reached for her hand as naturally as if they'd been holding hands for years, rather than a couple of days. It was hard to believe she'd just met this man. Maybe it was because of the circumstances, but already, Marlowe couldn't imagine not having him in her life.

She refused to think about what would happen when they got back to the States. How she'd have to watch him walk away. She was just a job to him, nothing more. She had no claim on the man. But every time she held him as he drove them through the night, he sure *felt* as if he belonged to her, just as she belonged to him.

They hadn't kissed again, and with each day that went by, Marlowe longed more and more to feel his lips on hers. She was beginning to think she'd imagined the feelings that had coursed through her the first time.

Kendric knocked on the back door, and it opened almost immediately. The woman at the door had a smile on her face—but as soon as she saw them, it faded. Her gaze flicked past Marlowe's shoulder, as if looking for someone else, before returning to them.

"Marlowe and Bob?" she asked in accented English.

"That's us," Kendric said.

"You are male and female," the woman said, still frowning.

"Yes," he agreed.

The three of them stood there staring at each other for a heart-stopping moment before the woman gestured for them to enter. They walked into a kitchen, and once the door was shut, the woman wrung her hands together as she spoke again. "I believed you were two men. You married?"

"No. Does it matter?" Kendric asked.

"Yes. Hiding space, it is small. One bed. Man and woman cannot stay together unless married."

Marlowe tensed. Everything on their journey had gone pretty smoothly. She wasn't sure what would happen if they couldn't stay here.

Kendric looked down at her, then back at the woman. "Customs are different in America," he said. "It's not necessary. We are friends. We just want to rest. Eat. Get clean. That's it."

But the woman stubbornly shook her head. "No. Not allowed to sleep together if not married."

"I can sleep on the floor in a different room," Kendric tried.

But the woman continued to frown at them. Marlowe had a feeling she wouldn't relent.

And no way did she want to be separated from Kendric. He'd literally saved her life. She could already feel the panic welling inside her at the thought of not being near him while she was sleeping and vulnerable.

Kendric sighed. "All right. We'll go. Find somewhere else to stay until tonight."

Marlowe's heart sank. She'd so been looking forward to a shower. And her butt hurt from sitting on the scooter all night. And she didn't know what this change of plans would do for their schedule. How difficult it would be to find somewhere else to hide during the daytime.

Instead of looking relieved, their host actually seemed more distressed. "My sister, she in next village. She tell me police are looking for escaped prisoners. Searching houses, roads. Jungle. If you leave, they maybe find you."

Kendric frowned, and Marlowe's head spun with worry.

Their hosts at the previous safe house had told them that Thai authorities had widened their search for the women who'd escaped the prison, that very few had been recaptured so far. There was a long list of every name, along with each woman's picture, on the news and in the papers.

That was why she'd continued to wear the wig, even though they were now less than fifty miles from the border. Monetary rewards were being offered, enough to convince almost anyone to turn them in if they were spotted. They might not be in the city anymore, but they were still in danger.

"Marry now," the woman said suddenly.

Marlowe's eyes widened at her words. "What?"

"Marry now. Here. Then can stay in safe place under floor. Together. Even if police search, they will no find you. I can make arrangements. Now."

"Give us a minute?" Kendric asked the woman, already putting his hand on Marlowe's arm and pulling her to the side of the room. "This isn't necessary. I'll find us somewhere else to hunker down. You'll be safe. I promise."

"But she said the police are searching the area. And before we got here, you saw a police car and took that shortcut through the jungle so we wouldn't be spotted. Where else would we go?"

"I don't know. But I refuse to force you into something so drastic, not with everything you've already been through."

Marlowe blinked—then suppressed a hysterical giggle. "I can't believe you're comparing *marriage* to being falsely accused of selling drugs, being thrown into a foreign prison, breaking *out* of said prison, then driving through the night, through pitch-dark jungles and on roads that are more ruts in the ground than actual roads," Marlowe huffed.

Kendric's lips twitched. "Well, when you put it that way . . . ," he said sarcastically.

Marlowe lowered her voice and looked earnestly into Kendric's brown eyes. "I'll feel safest wherever *you* are, be it here or in some other safe house. But you're tired, Kendric. Please don't lie and tell me you're not. And it could take hours to find another safe location.

"Does it really matter if we get married? If it ends up being legal in the States, so be it. We can get a divorce once we're home. Or an annulment. If it makes our host happy, helps us evade the authorities, and means we don't have to be separated or sleep under some bush . . . why not? But if you truly hate the idea—and I won't blame you if you do—then we can go. I trust you."

He stared at her for a long moment with a look she couldn't interpret. Then, finally, he leaned down and kissed her forehead. "You're right. If it means we can stay together, stay safe, and you can have that shower I know you want so badly, we'll do it. But I'll be damned if I cheat you out of this . . ."

To Marlowe's surprise, Kendric dropped down to one knee. He took hold of her hand and kissed the back of it before looking up at her.

"Marlowe Kennedy . . . will you marry me?"

Surprisingly, her eyes filled with tears. This wasn't real, she knew that, but somehow it felt *very* real. And right. The look in Kendric's eyes was loving and patient and . . . determined.

"Yes."

He grinned at her, then stood and hugged her hard. His lips by her ear, he whispered, "I seem to have misplaced the ring, but I promise to get one on your finger as soon as I can."

Marlowe giggled. "Misplaced?" she asked when he pulled back a fraction.

"Yup."

She shook her head. "I don't need a ring."

"Try telling *her* that," Kendric said, motioning behind her to their host.

Turning, Marlowe saw the woman had a huge smile on her face and was practically vibrating with excitement. When she turned back to Kendric, the smile had left his face and he looked as serious as she'd ever seen him.

"This'll be fine, Punky. I promise."

"I know," she whispered.

He turned to the woman and said, "All right. If you can make the arrangements, we'll get married. Here. Now."

Their host beamed. "Yes! Good. Bathroom upstairs. You first." She pointed at Marlowe. "I will find you the dress."

"Go on," Kendric said softly. "Take your time in the shower. I'm sure our host needs some time to put this ceremony together."

"Okay. Kendric?"

"Yeah?"

"If you really don't want—"

"I do," he interrupted her.

"Okay. I just had to ask." She smiled. "Let's do this."

"Let's do this," Kendric echoed.

The woman behind them started talking a mile a minute in Thai as she walked over and grabbed Marlowe's hand.

"See you later?" she asked Kendric as the woman led her away.

"Later," he agreed.

The last thing Marlowe saw before turning a corner was his gaze glued to her own.

~

Bob had been wrong about their host needing time to put together a wedding ceremony. By the time he'd stepped out of the shower and put on the traditional gold pants and red button-up, long-sleeve shirt that had been procured for him, their host was waiting impatiently.

She led him down the stairs and into the kitchen, where he got his first look at Marlowe since she'd been led away less than an hour earlier. He was momentarily frozen by the sight.

Her skin was pink and glowing from the shower. She'd left off the blonde wig, and her hair was shiny and still a touch damp, with small tendrils curling in to frame her face. Their host had found a cream dress that fit Marlowe's slight curves as if it had been made for her. A long sash draped over one of her shoulders and touched the floor. She was barefoot, and the sight of her tiny toes made the entire situation seem even more intimate.

"Hey," she said uncertainly.

"Hey." Bob turned to their host. "Can we have a moment before we start?"

The woman nodded, still beaming, and backed away, giving them a bit of privacy.

Bob turned back to Marlowe. "You okay?" he asked quietly.

Marlowe nodded. "You?"

"We don't have to do this," he said, not answering her question. The truth? He was suddenly more than okay. This was a strange situation— but he wasn't upset in the least about having to marry this woman. If he'd been with anyone else, he would've found a way around what they were about to do. But now, he was silently praying Marlowe wouldn't take the final out he was giving her.

"She's really excited," Marlowe replied, her gaze going to their host hovering in the background, before returning to Bob's. "This is going to sound crazy . . . but after everything I've been through, after spending the last month in that prison, being yelled at, being shoved around, looked down at, spit on, slapped, kicked, and generally treated like crap . . . it feels almost cathartic to be participating in something good. I just . . ." Her voice faded as she struggled to find the right words to explain what she was feeling.

Bob reached out and put his hand on Marlowe's cheek. His thumb brushed against her jawline. "I understand." And he did. This woman deserved some goodness after what she'd experienced. He'd never believed she was the dangerous drug dealer the Thai authorities had tried to portray her as. And the longer he was around her, the more sure he became.

Their host asked them something from nearby, and Bob assumed she wanted to know if they were ready to start. But he wasn't going to be rushed.

"You're amazing, Marlowe," he said earnestly. Any other woman in her shoes would probably be freaking out. Demanding he do something so they could stay and not have to get married. But she was stoic and determined and unwilling to complain, even when she had every right in the world to do so. She'd held up extremely well so far, and he couldn't be prouder.

"I'm just me," she said with a shrug.

"Let's do this," he said firmly. "Then we'll eat something and get some sleep."

Marlowe grinned. "Reception and honeymoon, huh?" she teased.

Bob chuckled. "Yeah, I guess so." He reluctantly dropped his hand and reached for her own. She wrapped her fingers around his without hesitation.

They turned to their host. "We're ready," he told her.

The woman beamed and gestured for them to follow. They went into a small room off the kitchen—and Bob blinked in surprise. The woman had been busy while they'd been cleaning up and getting dressed. There was an altar set up at one end of the room, and a man dressed in ceremonial garb stood there smiling at them.

"Holy cow," Marlowe said under her breath. "How many weddings does this woman arrange, anyway?"

Bob wondered the same thing, but didn't hesitate to step toward the officiant. He held on to Marlowe's hand as the man immediately began speaking in Thai. Neither he nor Marlowe had any idea what was being said, but it didn't matter. The feeling in the intimate space was momentous.

Bob turned to look down at Marlowe. Their gazes met, and he smiled. She didn't look nervous in the least. She seemed calm and serene.

Marlowe squeezed his hand. This wasn't the wedding Bob envisioned for himself. Hell, he'd begun to suspect he'd never get married at all, no matter how much he wanted to. But standing here with Marlowe felt so right. As if it was meant to be. The two of them against the world.

"Do you, Kendric, take this woman to be your wife, to have and hold from now to forever, for better and worse, for rich and poor, when sick and healthy, to love and protect, cherish and honor, respect and nurture, in this life and the next?"

Bob jerked his gaze to the officiant. Honestly, he'd tuned the man out since he previously hadn't understood a word. But now he spoke in English, prompting him to agree to the sacred vows of marriage. They were a little different from the traditional vows back in the States, but just as meaningful. "I do," he blurted, not wanting Marlowe to think he was having second thoughts.

The officiant turned to Marlowe. "Do you, Marlowe, take this man to be your husband, to have and hold from now to forever, for better and worse, for rich and poor, when sick and healthy, to love and protect, cherish and honor, respect and nurture, in this life and the next?"

"I do," she said softly.

The officiant began speaking in Thai once more. Bob's gaze never left Marlowe's. He already felt different. Which was ridiculous. Fancy clothes and a Buddhist officiant didn't necessarily tie their lives together forever.

This wedding was for show. For convenience, so he didn't have to venture out and find somewhere else for them to rest for the day. To allow them to stay together. But deep down, Bob felt the connection he had with Marlowe solidify even more. His determination to get her safely out of Thailand and back home to her brother even stronger.

The officiant cleared his throat, and when Bob looked at him, he smiled, nodded, and said, "You may kiss."

Bob turned back to Marlowe. She was smiling. He lowered his head without a second thought. Their lips brushed together lightly, once, twice.

Then Bob wrapped an arm around her waist, pulling her against him and kissing Marlowe like he'd longed to do again, ever since that first night.

And just like then, the second their tongues touched, he was lost in her.

It took every ounce of strength he had to pull back. He stared down at her and realized they were both breathing hard. She'd grabbed hold of his shirt and fisted the material as they'd kissed. She looked as shell shocked as he felt.

Their host approached, speaking a mile a minute, and pulled them to the other side of the room, where there were two pillows on the floor with a basin of water in front of each. She gestured for them to kneel on the pillows. Then she demonstrated how they should each clasp their own hands together and hold them over the basins.

Mentally shrugging, Bob did as the woman requested.

Their host grabbed a small, elongated shell and dipped it into another bowl of water sitting on a nearby table. She spoke in a low, even tone as she slowly poured the bit of water over Bob's hands. Then she refilled the shell and did the same over Marlowe's hands. The officiant came over and did the same thing, pouring water first over Bob's clasped hands, and then Marlowe's.

Their host handed them small towels to dry their hands and tugged them to their feet, before pulling them toward the kitchen.

"I guess that was some sort of wedding ritual?" Marlowe asked softly as they followed the woman.

"I'm sure it was," Bob said with a nod. Even though they were on the run, could be discovered at any time, turned in by a neighbor or even the officiant himself, Bob relaxed as he sat at a small table in the kitchen. This was his wedding day, after all.

His lips turned up. Honestly, those were words he never expected to say or think.

Once they were seated, their host presented them with a large platter piled with different foods. He looked over at Marlowe in time to see her wrinkle her nose. His Punky really did eat like a ten-year-old.

This time, Bob didn't even think twice about the possessive pronoun. Marlowe really was his now. Ignoring their host standing nearby, waiting for them to dig in, Bob leaned over and whispered in Marlowe's ear, "I promise that as soon as I can, I'll get you some Oreos, Pop-Tarts, and maybe even a Twinkie to celebrate our marriage."

She giggled and looked at him almost shyly. "It's okay. I mean, she went to a lot of trouble to put all this together for us. I should be used to this kind of food by now."

"Used to it, but not liking it," Bob said dryly.

"It's good for me," she said with a shrug as she turned back toward the platter.

"Do you trust me?" he asked.

She looked at him again and without even one second of hesitation, said, "Yes."

"Let me serve you then," he told her as he reached for a fork.

Marlowe nodded.

Bob carefully picked through the platter, looking for items he thought she might enjoy more than others. He avoided the seafood, already knowing she didn't particularly like it. He speared a bite of what he thought was chicken and brought it up to his own lips. It was definitely chicken, but he suspected it was too spicy for Marlowe.

He found another piece that looked like chicken, tasted it, nodded, and brought a bite up to her mouth.

Marlowe didn't take her gaze from his as she took his wrist to hold the fork steady and leaned forward. She opened her mouth, and he fed her the piece of meat.

"Okay?" he asked.

She nodded after she swallowed. "It's good."

They continued like that for a while, with Bob tasting the bits of meat and vegetables on the platter to find something he thought she'd enjoy. It was an intimate experience for them both, and neither spoke much as they ate.

Their host approached and placed a bowl next to the platter. It sounded as if she was apologizing for something, maybe for delivering the new dish late, but it was the gasp of surprise and delight from Marlowe that had Bob smiling.

"Ramen!" she exclaimed. "Oh my God, it looks amazing! We had lots of rice at the prison, which was what I was basically living off of, but ramen is one of my favorite things to eat back home."

Bob frowned. "Surely that's not all you could afford?" he asked.

Marlowe laughed. "Oh no. I mean, it's cheap, but I actually like the taste," she said a little sheepishly.

Bob let out a sigh of relief. "Good. Here, the fork's all yours."

She took it and dug into the bowl of noodles with enthusiasm. They weren't ramen, not like she was probably used to. It was actually pad thai, a style of noodles popular in the country, but Bob was pleased Marlowe had something to eat that she truly enjoyed.

After a moment, she looked up and frowned. "I'm hogging them. Sorry. Here," she said, holding out the fork with a huge bite of noodles twined around the end. She had one hand under the fork to catch any noodles that might fall and smiled at him.

Bob couldn't resist. He reached out for her wrist, just as she'd done with him, and leaned forward slowly, holding eye contact with her the entire time. He slid the food off the fork, chewed, swallowed, then said, "Delicious."

"Right?" She beamed. "Best meal ever," she declared as she returned her attention to the bowl in front of her and twirled the fork to scoop up more.

Once again, her enthusiasm struck Bob hard. This woman had no reason to be so happy. She'd been incarcerated on bogus charges and abused, was now on the run with a stranger, and had been forced to *marry*, for God's sake. And yet, she still found pleasure in a bowl of noodles.

Bob was humbled. Just being around her made him want to be a better person.

When they'd eaten as much as they could, their host was right there to take the leftovers and dishes away. The sun had risen a few hours ago, and it was time for both of them to get some rest.

They followed their host to what looked like a home office and watched as she moved a rug to the side, gesturing toward what was literally a trapdoor in the floor. Bob lifted the square wooden door and studied the space with a frown.

He and Marlowe had slept in some tight spaces over the last few days . . . but he understood for the first time why the woman had insisted they had to be married.

The space beneath the floor was literally only big enough for a narrow pallet. It didn't even look to be twin size. Morbidly, he figured it was a foot or so wider than the average coffin. It wasn't really ideal for *one* person. For two? They literally would have to wrap around each other to fit.

The woman began speaking again and gestured to the clothes they'd been wearing when they arrived. They'd obviously been cleaned and were now folded neatly on a desk nearby. She pantomimed putting them on and leaving what they currently wore on a chair. Then she picked up the backpack with the few supplies they'd gathered along the way and dropped it in the hole, along with Marlowe's blonde wig. She smiled once more and left the room.

Throughout it all, Marlowe hadn't moved. She was staring down at the hole with a blank look in her eyes that Bob didn't like.

"Marlowe?"

"I can't," she whispered, sounding terrified. The woman who'd been so happy about ramen noodles was gone.

Alarmed, Bob took two strides until he was standing in front of her, blocking her view of the hole in the floor. Because that's all it was. It wasn't a room. Didn't have a real bed. It was literally just a small space under the floorboards. This might be the largest house along the network so far, but it was the smallest space they'd slept in yet.

"Look at me, Punky."

It took a few minutes, but he didn't rush her. Finally, she lifted her chin and met his gaze.

Bob wanted to tell her that they didn't have to stay. That he'd find them somewhere else to go. But it was already well into morning, too dangerous to take her anywhere. Not with her picture being broadcast across the country. Besides, they'd gotten married just so they could stay here. He didn't want her sacrifice to be for naught.

"What's wrong?" he asked.

"I can't," she repeated, shaking her head. "The hole . . . it's too small. I . . . when I was first brought to the prison, I was put in solitary. It was so small. And dark."

"You can do this," Bob insisted.

She shook her head violently.

"Marlowe, you won't be alone this time. I'll be there. And I'm not going anywhere. Understand? I'm not leaving you. You're safe. For better and worse, for rich and poor, when sick and healthy, to love and protect, cherish and honor, respect and nurture . . . that's what I promised, right?"

She blinked, and Bob saw her gaze focus. She lost that blank look that worried him so much. "You remember our vows word for word?"

"It's not every day a man gets married," he told her. "Of course I remember. I've got you, Punky. That hole isn't going to be terribly comfortable. It's going to be hot and cramped. I'm not all that thrilled about small spaces myself . . . but we can do this."

"Why?" she asked.

"Why what?"

"Why don't you like small spaces?"

Bob grimaced. He didn't like to talk about the time when he was a prisoner of war. Didn't like to think about what he'd been through, what his friends had suffered. He preferred to put it behind him and move forward. But he'd do whatever it took to help Marlowe through this.

"I'll tell you when we're settled," he bargained.

She stared at him for a beat, then took a deep breath and nodded. "Okay. We need to change."

Then she turned and reached for the shirt she'd been wearing for the last few days. She looked over her shoulder at him. "Will you undo the dress for me? I don't think I can reach."

Bob nodded, and when he reached for the delicate zipper on the back of the dress, he noticed his hands were literally shaking. All he could think about was peeling the material off his *wife*, draping her on a real bed, and showing her how much he admired her. How badly he wanted to explore every inch of her body. But this wasn't a real honeymoon, and honestly, she wasn't in the right mindset . . . and may *never* be where he was concerned.

It took every ounce of strength he had to lower that zipper and step away from her. The smooth skin of her back beckoned, and it was all he could do not to slip his hands around her body and cup her breasts as he pushed the dress off her shoulders.

He saw her reach for the ugly gray bra she'd been issued at the prison before he turned and reached for his own black clothes. He didn't turn around until Marlowe said softly, "I'm decent."

It was on the tip of his tongue to say that yes, she was more than decent. She was fumbling with the wig, about to put it on, when Bob said, "Leave it off."

She looked up at him. "I thought you said I should always wear it."

"I did. But it's going to be hot enough in that hole without it on. We'll get it sorted tonight when we get ready to leave."

The relief that crossed her face told Bob exactly how much she hated wearing the hot, itchy wig. But as usual, she hadn't complained even once about it. She nodded, then looked down at the hole. She took a deep breath, and with her typical can-do nature, stepped into the space. When she was standing inside, the floor barely reached her hips. It was going to be a tight fit for sure.

She stuffed the wig into the backpack, arranged it to act as a pillow, then stretched out on her back, hugging the wall and giving him as much room as she could.

Now that she was in, Bob didn't want to prolong things. He stepped inside as well, grabbed hold of the lid, and lowered it as he lay down. The hiding spot was well insulated, because as soon as he closed the door, it was pitch dark.

Bob heard Marlowe inhale sharply, but that was the only indication she gave that she was upset.

Figuring their host would come in and remove their wedding clothes and replace the rug over the trapdoor, Bob turned his attention toward making Marlowe as comfortable as he could. He reached for her and pulled her against him.

She immediately latched on to him, burying her face in the crook of his neck. Bob couldn't fully lie on his back with Marlowe beside him, so he maneuvered them both onto their sides. Marlowe curled up in front of him, holding on to his shirt with both hands. He wrapped his arms around her and could feel her heart thumping in her chest. She was breathing way too fast.

"Relax, Marlowe. I've got you. We're good. Safe."

It took a minute or two, but finally he felt her start to relax against him.

"I understand now why she wanted us married," she said with a small chuckle.

Bob huffed out a laugh. "Right? Although the fact that she thought it would be okay for two men to hide out here is confusing as hell."

Marlowe's giggle was music to Bob's ears. "Oh my God. I can't even imagine how that would work. I mean, I'm small. I can't imagine two men your size down here."

Bob couldn't either. But if it had been necessary, he would've done it and felt no shame or embarrassment. Survival was a powerful motivator.

After several minutes, Bob realized that Marlowe wasn't sleeping. She had to be tired after traveling for most of the night, but he supposed being in this hole wasn't allowing her brain to shut down.

They hadn't had much of an opportunity to talk while they were on the run. Between being on the scooter and sleeping during the day, they hadn't really gotten into any deep conversations. But now that they were man and wife, Bob figured it was as good a time as any.

He rarely opened up to people, and never to someone he was tasked with rescuing. But Marlowe was different. And not only because he'd married her. For once, he *wanted* to tell his story. He had a feeling that hearing what he'd been through could help her get through her own trauma.

He took a deep breath. Then said, "My friends and I were held captive and tortured when an Army mission went sideways."

Chapter Five

Marlowe opened her eyes, but all she saw was darkness. She hated that feeling. It reminded her too much of being in that solitary cell. And upon hearing the fear in Kendric's tone as he informed her that he'd also been held captive once, the odd feeling of relief that swept through her made Marlowe feel like a horrible person.

How could she be *glad* that he'd been through anything similar to what she had?

She adjusted in his arms, wrapping one hand around the side of his neck. She didn't interrupt his story, but hopefully her touch let him know she was listening.

"The mission was shit from the start, and we all had a feeling it was going to go sideways. It did. We fought back as long as we could, but eventually we ran out of ammo, and rather than die, we chose to surrender."

Marlowe gasped quietly. She could only imagine how horrible that must've been. To give up, knowing you could be killed or tortured.

"I think our captors thought they were being cruel when they put my friends and I all in the same cell. But it was the best thing they could've done. Yes, we all had to listen as they beat on one of us outside the cell, but together, we were four hundred percent stronger than if we'd been chained up by ourselves."

"Being alone is the worst," Marlowe agreed softly. "It feels as if you're the only person in the world. Like everyone has forgotten you. Like you're less than human."

Kendric's arms tightened around her, and she felt him nod before he went on. "Honestly, Chappy, JJ, and I didn't have it all that bad compared to Cal. Once our captors found out who he was, they concentrated most of their attention on him. That was harder to bear than being tortured ourselves."

When he paused and didn't say anything else, Marlowe asked, "Who was he? Why did they focus on him?"

"He's a member of the royal family of Liechtenstein. Those assholes were so thrilled to have royalty in their clutches, they did their best to break him. They wanted him pleading for his life on film."

"They filmed it?" Marlowe asked, horrified.

"Yeah. And sent that shit out on the web. There are still videos out there of Cal being sliced to ribbons. It's sick. And the worst was not being able to do anything to help him. But Cal being Cal, he didn't say one damn word. Didn't give our captors the satisfaction of even one grunt of pain. When they rechained him to the wall after a session, he'd bleed so badly, a river of blood would literally snake down to the drain in the middle of the room. And all we could do was beg him to hold on."

"I can't imagine," Marlowe said, feeling as if her words were woefully inadequate.

"Good. I wouldn't ever want you, or anyone, to experience that hell."

"When I was put in solitary, I was still in shock from everything that had happened," Marlowe admitted. "One minute I was on the dig site, minding my own business, and the next I was being handcuffed and thrown into a police car. I had no idea what was going on."

"What can you tell me about what happened?" Kendric asked.

Marlowe sighed. "Not much. I mean, I have my suspicions, but because I don't understand Thai, I have no idea what was said during my interrogation."

"Did they hurt you?" Kendric asked in a tight, very dark tone.

"No. But . . . I thought they were going to. They yelled a lot. Hit the desk. Even pressed me up against the wall. That's why I ultimately signed that paper. I figured they would do whatever it took to make me sign it. I'd read a lot of horror stories about foreigners in custody, women especially, and what happened to them."

Kendric's arms tightened around her almost to the point of pain. Marlowe rubbed her thumb back and forth on the skin of his neck, trying to calm him. "I'm okay," she soothed. "They didn't do anything."

It took a minute or two, but eventually Kendric asked, "What are your suspicions? How did those yaba pills get in your stuff?"

"You don't think I was selling them?" she asked, genuinely curious about his answer. She wouldn't blame him if he did. Everyone else thought the worst of her. Why wouldn't he?

"No."

That was it. Just no.

His belief made a previously unnoticed tension ease inside her.

"I worked with a guy, his name is Ian West. He's younger than me and was new to the dig site. He seemed okay enough. A little overenthusiastic. And he liked to drink on his time off. Which is fine. I mean, each to his own. Anyway, as you know, it's hot here. I mean, *really* hot. The temperature combined with the humidity makes it unbearable at times. One night, I couldn't sleep because of the heat. I was walking around the dig site, which wasn't uncommon for me. It was better than sweating in my bunk. And I saw Ian in one of the trenches we'd been working on earlier that day. We *do* dig at night, especially when grant funds are running low or a dig season is ending. But we use lots of floodlights, we stop at a certain time, and no one works by themselves. Ever.

"I watched him digging for a minute, about to approach to find out what the hell was going on, when he held up something to the light. He laughed quietly, stood, and put whatever he'd found in his pocket.

"I was shocked. That's not something you do on a dig. Take something you found. Anything we discover belongs to the country in which we're working. We're just the hands that unearth stuff, none of it is ours.

"He quickly walked away, never even saw me standing nearby. Probably because he was using a single lantern, and he took it with him. I always keep a small flashlight on me when walking the dig site at night. After he went back to his tent, I walked over to the trench. I don't know what I expected to find, maybe evidence of pottery shards or something. But I looked in . . .

"Coins. He was stealing *coins*. There were about two dozen still sitting in the dirt in the trench, waiting to be tagged and collected. There's no way the team would've left them there like that, so I'm guessing Ian must've found them earlier in the day and didn't tell anyone. I have no idea why he didn't take them all. Since no one knew they existed, no one would miss them. I may never know the answer to that question."

She sighed heavily. "I didn't want to believe he was a thief. I tried so hard to justify what I saw, but it was impossible. When we find something, there's a protocol to follow before an item's extracted. Pictures taken, data collected, et cetera. And it goes without saying we use gloves to handle artifacts. And he put the coins in his *pocket*! As if they were just quarters or something."

Marlowe took a deep breath, trying to get control over her emotions. Every time she thought about what happened next, how stupid she'd been, it enraged and embarrassed her.

"What did you do?" Kendric asked. She felt his hand slip under her shirt, his fingers lightly stroking her lower back, as if he was trying to soothe a wild animal. His touch felt wonderful. And surprisingly, she felt her anger waning.

"I was an idiot," she said with a sigh. "I went to his tent and confronted him. Told him I saw him take the coins. He sounded genuinely panicked. Said he was sorry, acted so contrite. Told me he just made a rash, stupid mistake. I insisted he go to the site leader and tell him what he'd done, show him the coins so official steps could be taken to record the find. He promised he'd do so in the morning, kept apologizing and begging my forgiveness.

"I was going to go straight to our project leader—and I should have. But it was the middle of the night after a long workday. I didn't want to disturb him, and like a moron, I trusted Ian when he said he'd make things right.

"I went back to my tent, finally fell asleep . . . and in the morning, the police were there. They found the drugs in my tent, and I was hauled away."

"You think Ian planted the pills in your stuff after you went to sleep?" Kendric said.

"Yeah. And despite the theft . . . I think I hate that part even more. I mean, there were only three Americans on the dig, and we all usually hung out together."

"No one spoke up on your behalf?" Kendric asked.

"Ian had gone to the project leader before I even woke up, as promised—and accused *me* of attempting to steal coins. They found one of those in my tent as well. And just one could fetch hundreds of thousands from the right buyer. They searched Ian's tent at my insistence, and of course, they found nothing. After that . . . everyone just kind of turned on me. The project leader let the police take me away without another word.

"I was so shocked, I could barely speak. No one took my great work history or reputation into account. Instead, they took the word of some newbie. And I couldn't believe Ian would betray me like that."

"I can," Kendric said with a small shrug. "Sounds like those coins are worth a lot of money."

"But at the expense of my life?" she asked.

"Unfortunately, yeah. What do you think he's going to do with the coins?"

"Sell them," Marlowe said. "He probably has already. He was only scheduled to be on the dig for a month, and at the time of my arrest, he had less than two weeks left. It was an internship for him, part of his master's thesis. It would've been fairly easy to smuggle them back to the States."

"Is there a big market for that kind of thing? I mean, how easy would it be to find a buyer?" Kendric asked.

"If you know the right people, probably not too hard," Marlowe admitted.

"And does he? Know the right people, I mean?"

"I have no idea. But considering his major, and the fact that he had connections enough to get on that dig to begin with, probably."

"So he planted the pills and called in the tip to the authorities, knowing how hard Thailand has been cracking down on the sale of drugs in their country," Kendric mused.

"I don't know for sure, but that's the only thing I can think of. He was frequently assigned to the evening crew, and he always seemed . . . I don't know the right word, but . . . hyped up, maybe? Yaba is basically a combination of caffeine and meth. I figured taking the pills kept him awake on the job. I'm sure you know, yaba pills are super cheap and readily available, and I'm guessing locals were probably more than willing to sell to him.

"But the police weren't interested in my side of the story. They wouldn't listen to me, no matter how much I begged. I told them about the coins and how Ian was stealing, but it was like I wasn't even speaking. They seemed to have no problem believing Ian when he said I was selling drugs. It was . . . awful," she finished lamely.

"We're not going to let him get away with it," Kendric said firmly.

Marlowe simply shook her head. "I don't care anymore. Honestly, I just want to go home. Can I tell you something?"

"You can tell me anything."

Maybe it was the darkness. Maybe it was how they were wrapped around each other. Maybe it was because she couldn't forget the look in his eyes when he'd said "I do" earlier, in such a reverent and intimate way. Whatever the reason, Marlowe found herself admitting something she'd never said out loud to anyone, not even her brother.

"I don't love being an archaeologist."

Just saying the words felt as if a thousand-pound weight had been lifted from her shoulders.

"I kind of fell into it, was too far along in my studies to change my major without losing a ton of credits. Tony was helping pay for my college, and I didn't want to disappoint him or cost him any more money. I also didn't know what else I might like to do, and I loved the history aspect." She shrugged.

"Anyway, I got my first job on a dig in Montana right after I graduated, and things just kind of steamrolled from there. I was a hard worker, minded my own business, didn't cause any trouble, and my supervisors just kept recommending me for other jobs. I ended up going to Egypt, Jordan, China, Turkey, Korea, and of course Thailand. Tony seemed so proud. So jealous that I was getting to see the world. But I was always homesick. I love meeting new people, experiencing new cultures, but . . . I honestly never really liked digging in the dirt."

She held her breath, waiting to see what Kendric would say. What he'd think.

She was startled when he started to laugh.

"I'm sorry," he said between chuckles. "I'm not laughing *at* you. But the idea of an archaeologist who doesn't like digging in the dirt? That's funny as hell."

Marlowe smiled. Her face was pressed against his neck, and he smelled so good. Like the herbal soap they'd used in the shower. And . . . male. It was warm in the hole, and she could feel herself beginning to sweat. Just as Kendric was. And somehow, the combination of his own musky scent with the soap he'd used was both comforting and a turn-on.

"I know. It's ridiculous," she agreed with a small shrug.

"So what now? I mean, when you get home?" Kendric asked.

"I . . . I'm not sure. I mean, when you're told you're going to live the rest of your life behind bars, you don't really think much about the future. It was all I could do to get by day to day."

"I'm getting you home," Kendric said earnestly. "You can do whatever you want. Live wherever you want. Be whoever you want."

"How did you end up in Maine?" she asked. He'd told her at some point in the last few days that he and his friends lived in the small town of Newton.

"When we were held captive, JJ decided he was done with the military. We played rock paper scissors to decide where to live once we were out, and what we'd do for a living."

"Seriously?" Marlowe asked.

"Yup. It was really to get our minds off the pain more than anything else. I was going to vote New York City, but I lost my round," Kendric said.

"I can't see you in a big city like that," Marlowe said. "I don't think I'd like it. I'm an introvert at heart, and having all those people around all the time . . ." She shivered for dramatic effect.

He chuckled. "Yeah, I'm not sure I would've either, but Maine has also been a bit hard for me."

"How so?"

"It's so . . . staid. Don't get me wrong. I love working with my buddies and meeting the people we lead on hikes on the Appalachian Trail. But I missed the excitement of the missions we went on in the Army."

"Which is why you're here with me now," Marlowe said, a little disappointed, though she didn't fully understand why.

"Yeah. I got connected with this FBI guy who works in certain government circles. He sets up rescue missions."

"And he somehow knows Tony."

"That's my guess."

"What do your friends think of what you do? Do they ever join you?" Marlowe asked.

"They don't know."

"Wait—*what*? What do you mean, they don't know?"

"I've been lying to them. Telling them I'm visiting a sick aunt," Kendric admitted.

Marlowe went up on an elbow and tried in vain to see through the dark. "Are you serious?"

"Yup."

"That's . . . that's the stupidest thing I've ever heard!" she blurted. "Kendric! Those are men you literally would've died for. You've been through things together that I couldn't even imagine. You decided as a team to quit the Army and start your own business. And you haven't told them? Why not?" Marlowe knew she was being rude, but she literally couldn't understand Kendric's reasoning.

"I don't want them to feel guilty that I've been feeling unsettled. That I needed more excitement."

Thank goodness he didn't sound upset with her for yelling at him. Marlowe tried her best to calm down. "They wouldn't have felt that way," she said with conviction. "I don't know them, of course, but from everything you've said, they would've supported you. Now, I'm guessing they won't be happy when they find out you've been gallivanting around the world, risking your life without letting them have your back."

"They won't," Kendric agreed. "Which is another reason why I haven't told them."

"How long did you say you'd be gone this time?" Marlowe asked.

"Two weeks."

"What's going to happen if you don't return?"

"They'll be worried. They'll try to track down my aunt, and when they discover she doesn't exist, they'll freak out. Probably call a friend of ours, a computer genius, and demand he find me. Tex will tell them where I am and what I'm doing. He'll probably get them in touch with my contact, who may give them even more details, and possibly link them up with your brother. Then they'll get on the first plane to Thailand to track me down personally. Their wives will be stressed out, and I'll feel guilty as hell about interrupting their lives and having to shut down Jack's Lumber while they're out of town."

"Holy crap. Really? Is *any* of that an exaggeration?"

"No."

"Kendric?"

"Yeah?"

"You really are an idiot."

He chuckled. "I know."

"I mean it. You have this incredible group of friends. People who have your back no matter what. You shouldn't have lied to them. If you need more excitement in your life, I'm sure they would've supported you. *They'll* probably feel guilty for holding you back. I'm sure they would've encouraged you to do what you needed to do."

"You're right."

Marlowe sighed. "So . . . if they find out, what happens when you get home? After you apologize and grovel for their forgiveness? Another mission?"

"I'm not sure," he said.

"Not sure about what? They'll forgive you, I know they will. That's what friends do."

"Oh, they will. They'll give me hell, and I'll be hearing about this for the rest of our lives, but that's not what I'm unsure about. I'm not sure I want to keep doing this. The rescue missions."

"Why not?" Marlowe asked. This man fascinated her. She felt as if she could ask him a million questions and still never feel as if she'd learned everything.

"I don't know. I'm proud of what I've accomplished, the people I've helped, but . . . I can feel myself changing. The adrenaline rush I've gotten from these missions fades faster and faster. It doesn't feel as exciting as it used to. And I'm not getting any younger."

"Oh please. How old are you?" Marlowe asked.

"Thirty-five."

"Really? Me too," she said with a smile.

"I know. And it's hard to explain, but I think I'm finally beginning to understand the appeal of living a quiet life."

"What changed?" she asked, genuinely curious.

"So many things could've gone wrong on this mission. I'm not saying this to scare you, but the fact that you're here in my arms, and not still in that prison, is literally a miracle. That in itself is enough to make me rethink attempting another harrowing mission.

"June and Cal are trying to get pregnant. Carlise and Riggs want a slew of kids. I can't imagine not being in Maine when my nieces and nephews are born, if I'm on some mission. And no, I'm not related by blood, but those kids *will* be my family. So . . . I'm thinking I can find other ways to satisfy that adrenaline rush. Maybe I'll build a zip line. Or a rock climbing wall. Something that will give me the excitement I need without having to risk my life quite so much."

"I think that's a great idea," Marlowe told him.

"But it means that people like you will be left hanging," he said warily.

"Kendric, you can't save the world. I mean, I know you'd try your hardest to do just that, but there will always be people who need help. There will always be jerks in charge of countries. Always be corruption. And there will always be other men and women like *you*, who do this sort of thing for a living. You've done your part. More than done it. In fact, I'm naming my first child after you. I pray I have a son first, otherwise my daughter's gonna be real pissed to be called Ken."

Kendric chuckled, and she felt his huff of breath against her scalp.

"No one's ever reached out after they were rescued to thank me," he admitted softly.

"Assholes," Marlowe spat out.

"Wow. I think that's the first cussword I've heard you say," Kendric said.

"I try not to swear, Tony kind of drilled it into my head that ladies don't cuss, but I think this situation warrants it. I'm sorry, Kendric. That's awful. I understand why someone might want to put such a scary situation behind them, but if not for you, they wouldn't be alive and able to forget in the first place. And I was serious about naming my firstborn after you. I've also already planned on sending Christmas presents, and flowers on our wedding anniversary, and random thank-you notes when you least expect them. Just a heads-up."

He laughed again. "I wasn't insinuating that I wanted or needed any thanks."

"I know you weren't, but seriously, that's whacked. I don't know the situations you've saved people from, but even if we don't get out of the country, and I get thrown back in jail, I'll always be grateful that you were willing to risk yourself to help me. And speaking of which . . ." Her tone became solemn. "If anything happens, you aren't allowed to get caught. Understand me? I'll willingly give myself up if it means you can get away. I can't live with myself if you end up in jail too."

"Not happening," he said firmly.

"Kendric, I mean it. I—"

"Not. Happening," he repeated almost angrily. "You really think I'd let you give yourself up so I can get away? I've never been that guy, and I never will be. You're under my protection, Marlowe. Hell, you're my *wife*, and I'm going to protect you with my last breath if need be. You *will* get back home."

"It's possible we aren't really husband and wife," she murmured.

"Funny, I remember standing in front of that officiant today, promising to honor and protect you for the rest of this life and beyond," he said dryly.

"All I mean is that I have no idea if it's recognized in the States. And I'm not going to hold you to it either way."

"Why not?"

Marlowe was at a loss for words. What was he saying? That he *wanted* them to be married for real?

The pang of longing that hit her was surprising. Despite barely knowing this man, she wanted him for her own. She wanted to meet his friends. See those children being born. Watch him fly down that zip line she was sure he'd build one day.

When she didn't respond, he said, "We're both getting out of here, Marlowe. You remember what I said about my friends? How if I don't get home when they expect, they'll track me down? Even if we do get caught and put back in jail, they'll get us out. Both of us."

"But they don't even know me."

"Doesn't matter. You're with *me*. That's all they need to know."

"Kendric . . . ," Marlowe said, words failing her. She'd never had anyone, other than her brother, throw down for her like Kendric was. And it felt good. Really good.

"Tell me about your brother. Are your folks still alive?" he asked.

Relieved he was changing the subject, because she was feeling a little too emotional, Marlowe gladly talked about her family. "Tony's five years older and has always watched out for me. Our parents died when he was nineteen, and I was fourteen. They were in a huge pileup on the freeway. He fought the state for the right to keep me with him. Put college on hold for a few years as we settled into our new normal. He's married now, with two kids. He still tries to boss me around, but it's hard when I'm not even in the country." She smiled as she thought about her bossy brother.

"He sounds amazing."

"He is. Overprotective and a worrywart, but without him, I don't know where I'd be today. What about your family?"

"My friends are my family," Kendric said. "My parents weren't . . . good. They didn't care much about what I did. They didn't even want a kid, they made that pretty clear, but it would've looked bad if they got rid of me. I went my own way when I graduated high school and haven't looked back."

"Do you talk to them at all?"

"No. But don't feel sorry for me. I'm sure they're living their lives, happy and free, and I have my family in Chappy, Cal, and JJ. And now their wives."

"Tell me about them?" Marlowe asked, then yawned.

"You're tired. You should sleep," Kendric said.

"Please?"

"Okay." His hand hadn't stopped stroking her lower back, and his touch made Marlowe want to purr. "Our business, Jack's Lumber, is named after JJ, because he had the idea to get out of the Army in the first place, and he's the guy who keeps us all in line. He was a leader on the battlefield, and he still is, now that we're out. April is our admin assistant that we hired a couple of years ago, and the two of them have a thing, but neither will admit they're attracted to the other. It's an interesting dynamic, and we're all just waiting for the fireworks when they finally give in and admit they were meant for each other.

"Then there's Carlise and Chappy. They met when she was trapped in his cabin in the mountains during a blizzard. She had a stalker who came to kidnap and kill her, but was saved by an avalanche and by hiding in an old, abandoned prepper's bunker."

"Um . . . *what*?" Marlowe asked. "Are you kidding?"

"Nope. And Cal and June are a real-life Cinderella story. Complete with a nasty stepmother and stepsister who hired a hit man to kill June, in the hopes that the prince would come running back to the stepsister to protect her."

"Oh my God! And they're all okay?"

"Well, the hit man managed to shoot June, and it was touch and go for a while, but she's tougher than she looks. She pulled through and is thriving now."

"Wow. And they still live in Maine?"

"Yeah, why?"

"Not in a palace in Liechtenstein? Will their kid be king or queen someday?"

Kendric laughed. "Not a chance in hell. Cal is like twentieth in line or something, and he wants nothing to do with ruling his country. But I suppose that, yes, their kids will be princes and princesses."

"So if they'll be your nieces and nephews, that makes you some sort of de facto royalty too, right?"

Kendric dug his fingers into her side, making Marlowe squirm and try to evade his touch as he tickled her.

"Not even close, woman!" he told her.

"Uncle! Uncle!" she cried through her laughter.

He stopped at once, smoothing his hand over her side where he'd tickled her. "Cal and June are truly something together. They got married when she was still in the hospital. I've never seen my friend so broken as when he wasn't sure if she would survive or not. They had a whirlwind courtship, and he'd do literally anything for her. As would Chappy for Carlise. Come to think of it, they also came together extremely quickly. Like, in just days. I suppose living the kind of life we have . . . when you know, you know."

Marlowe thought about that. Then immediately wondered what he thought about *her*. But she was too chicken to ask. She sighed and ended up yawning again.

"And now you really do need to rest," Kendric insisted.

"They sound awesome," she told him sleepily. "Your friends."

"They are."

"Kendric?"

"Yeah?"

"I'm worried about you."

"Me? Why?"

"You aren't sleeping enough. I want you to rest too. I'll keep the bogeymen away. I promised to protect you too today, you know." She was barely aware of what she was saying. The dark, the heat, and her full belly were finally catching up with her, and she was on the verge of falling into a deep slumber.

"I will," he said.

"Promise?"

"Yeah."

"Okay. You know what?"

"What?"

He sounded amused, but Marlowe didn't care. "I'm glad I was thrown in jail."

"Glad?" he echoed, sounding shocked.

"Yeah. Because if I hadn't been, I wouldn't be right here, right now. Safe. Married to you. Good night, Kendric."

She didn't feel his arms tighten around her, or the kiss he placed on her forehead, because she'd already fallen into a deep, healing sleep.

Chapter Six

Bob wasn't sure how long he and Marlowe had been in the "safe room" under the floor, but he was surprised to realize that he'd slept. *Truly* slept, for the first time in years. He hadn't woken up from a nightmare. Hadn't tossed and turned. From what he could tell, he hadn't moved throughout the last several hours.

Not that he could've moved much anyway, but he'd slept well, content to hold Marlowe in his arms. He knew he had her to thank. She was a minor miracle. *His* miracle . . . and it would be excruciating to give her up once they reached the States.

Pushing that thought to the back of his mind to deal with later, once they were both home, he took a deep breath, trying to clear his mind. He was hot and sweating, and he could feel the dampness of his clothes where Marlowe was plastered against him. Her skin was dewy where his hand rested on her lower back, but they were safe. That was all that mattered.

Just as he was about to sit up and figure out what time it was, and wake Marlowe so they could head out to their next destination, he heard voices. The spot under the floor was well built and kept out the light from the room above, but apparently it didn't completely keep out all sounds.

Something fell onto the floor right above their heads, making him jump and waking Marlowe.

She stiffened in his arms, and Bob hurried to reassure her. In a toneless whisper—because if he could hear the people above them, they could surely hear him as well—he said, "It's okay, Punky. We're safe."

She nodded against him, but every muscle in her body was tense. He could practically hear her thinking. She was probably plotting how she could give herself up to save him. When she'd suggested that earlier this morning, dread nearly overwhelmed him. There was no way he'd allow her to do such a thing. He'd die first.

The only other people he'd ever considered giving up his life for were his teammates. But he wasn't the least bit surprised that Marlowe was now at the very top of that short list. His feelings for the woman were getting deeper by the day.

It wasn't even hard to admit to himself. Especially after learning more about her before they'd fallen asleep. He liked everything he knew so far. And she was now his wife. Their marriage may or may not be legal back home, but he didn't care.

Marlowe's entire body trembled as the voices grew louder, and her fear cut through Bob like a knife. He hated that she was scared, but there was nothing he could do at the moment other than hold her tight.

He couldn't understand what was being said above them, but he did hear Marlowe's name more than once. Whoever was up there with their host was definitely looking for her. Bob prayed the woman wouldn't give them up.

He heard more words, then footsteps receding.

Ten minutes later, the footsteps were back—then the trapdoor above them was wrenched open.

Bob moved instinctively, shoving Marlowe against the wall and pulling out the knife he kept in a sheath at his waistband, all in the same motion.

But the only person waiting for them was the elderly woman. She frantically gestured for them to get out of the hole. She looked anxious and kept glancing over her shoulder.

"Go!" she said urgently. "Go now!"

Praying she wasn't double-crossing them, that the money Willis was paying her was more than she'd get for turning them in to the authorities, Bob stood and held out his hand for Marlowe.

"What's going on?" she asked as she swayed on her feet.

Bob steadied her and climbed out of the hole. Not giving her a chance to climb out on her own, he grasped her waist and lifted her up and out. "We're leaving," he said tensely.

"Are they waiting for us outside?" she asked.

"I don't know. But I'm thinking not." Bob had no idea *what* to think, but he wasn't going to heap any more worry onto Marlowe's shoulders. He kept a tight hold on her hand as he followed the woman out of the office, toward the back of the house. She went straight to a covered window, peering around a tiny sliver in the curtain before turning to them and pointing to the door.

He shouldn't have been surprised when Marlowe stepped toward the woman and gave her a long, hard hug, but he still was.

"Thank you," she told the woman.

She pulled back and stared at Marlowe for a moment, then held up a finger, asking them to wait.

Anxious to be on his way, Bob had to use all his self-control not to rush Marlowe out the door. But the woman was back in less than thirty seconds, holding a piece of paper. She handed it to Marlowe with a small smile.

Looking over her shoulder, Bob saw the document was written in Thai, but it had both their names—their real names—in the center of the form. The woman held out a pen to Bob. Nodding at it, then at the form. She pointed to a line at the bottom.

"I think it's our wedding certificate," Marlowe whispered. "She wants us to sign it."

Bob didn't hesitate. He took the pen and gently removed the paper from Marlowe's hand. He held it up against the door and signed his name on the line the woman had pointed to. Then he passed the pen to Marlowe and held her gaze for a heart-stopping moment. Praying she'd follow his lead.

He needed her name on that paper. It made what they'd done legal. At least in this country. And knowing he and Marlowe were officially tied together in at least one country in the world made the anxiety inside him about the future settle a bit.

Marlowe took the pen from him and copied his motions, adding her signature to the line below his own. "Kendric and Marlowe Evans," she whispered, reading their names that had been printed at the bottom of the form.

The woman said something else and smiled at them, before frowning once again at a noise toward the front of the house.

"It's time to go," Bob said, taking the paper, folding it up, and stuffing it into his pocket. He wished he could get it framed. Wished he didn't have to put even one crease in the document. But their time here was up. They needed to get out. Now.

Without complaint, Marlowe nodded and turned to the door. Bob took five seconds to bow over their host's hand and kiss it before nodding at her and opening the door.

Looking around, he saw it was once again dark, which was a huge relief. The scooter that had faithfully brought them this far was waiting. Praying it had been filled with gas, as it had at all their other stops, Bob climbed on, watching as Marlowe quickly donned the blonde wig once more. He'd forgotten about it until now, and he was more than thankful she hadn't.

It had saved them at the checkpoint in Bangkok, and he hoped it would continue to be a good luck charm.

Without looking back, Bob eased the scooter out of the yard, started it up, and raced down the dark alley.

The closer they got to the border, the more tense things seemed. Neither spoke much as they rode along the dark back roads, trying to avoid heavier traffic. They only had one more stop in Thailand, a safe house less than a mile from the border. So far, everything had worked out according to plan. But Bob knew more than most people that the second he let down his guard, that's when things could go awry. So the closer they got, the more on edge he became.

It was still dark when they neared another run-down house in yet another small village. Most of their safe houses had been little more than shacks . . . but for some reason, just looking at this one made the hair on the back of Bob's neck stand up.

He shut off the scooter, but didn't attempt to dismount.

"Kendric?"

Bob would never tire of hearing Marlowe say his name. "It's okay. Everything's fine," he said to reassure her. She sounded just as nervous as he felt. "This time tomorrow, we'll be in Cambodia."

He felt her nod against him. She was plastered to his back, her arms locked around him, as she had been for every second of the last few nights. The scooter might not be the fastest mode of transportation, but it got them where they needed to go, was able to travel on smaller roads and paths that a car couldn't. And it gave him an excuse to keep Marlowe wrapped around him.

"Come on. Let's greet our hosts and get some sleep."

His lips twitched at the huff of annoyance that left Marlowe's lips. "As if you'll sleep," she muttered.

She wasn't wrong. He didn't sleep much, the previous day not-withstanding. Definitely not deeply. And it was only partly because of the nightmares he couldn't seem to shake. He wanted to make sure Marlowe was safe. That no one sneaked up on them. The thought of her being taken back to that prison—and treated even worse because she'd escaped—was unbearable. A lack of sleep was a small price to pay to ensure her freedom.

Bob believed her story about what had landed her in this unbeliev-able situation in the first place. He'd made a mental note to find this Ian West and make certain he couldn't screw over anyone else ever again. He'd rue the day he decided to not only steal from the dig, but also set up one of the sweetest women Bob had ever met.

Taking a deep breath, he said, "Hop off, Punky."

She immediately swung a leg over the seat, and Bob couldn't help but remember the first time she'd tried to stand after riding behind him. She'd definitely gotten the hang of the bike since then.

He climbed off himself, then reached for her hand. It was instinctive. Natural. Every day, as soon as they were done riding, they reached for each other. Held hands as long as they could. Neither had brought it up; they'd just fallen into the routine.

Pushing the scooter with one hand and holding on to Marlowe with the other, Bob headed for the back door of the dwelling owned by their latest contact.

It opened before he knocked, and a man stood there with a frown on his face. A woman peeked out from around him.

"In," he said gruffly, opening the door farther.

For a moment, Bob hesitated. He wasn't sure what it was about the man that made him so uneasy, but just like when he'd seen the small dwelling, his gut instinct flared to life.

He was about to turn away, to tell Marlowe they'd find somewhere else to hole up for the day, when she yawned.

Studying her for a moment, even in the dark he could see the deeper shadows under her eyes. She was exhausted. And while he had no doubt if he told her they were going to continue on, she'd not let one word of complaint cross her lips, he didn't want to do that to her. She'd already been through so much.

"Hang on a little longer and you can get some sleep," he said, trying to shove his unease aside.

"I'm good," she said, lifting her chin as if to challenge him.

Bob simply smiled and squeezed her hand before following the man inside. He left the scooter propped against the house and prayed it would still be there later. This far from the city, and away from the possibility of better-paying jobs, it was obvious people were struggling.

The couple led them through a cold, dark kitchen and a room with a low table, two wooden chairs, and nothing else, and finally into a bedroom at the front of the house. There was a pallet on the floor, a few threadbare blankets, a couple of broken crates that held what Bob thought were clothes, and some worn shoes against the wall.

The man nodded at them, then turned and left, closing the door behind him.

Bob sighed. It wasn't as if he expected another hot meal and shower—the fact that they'd gotten both at the older woman's house was a bonus, not an expectation—but he knew the people helping them get across the country were being paid generously to do so. Even a bit of rice would have been appreciated.

"It's okay," Marlowe said, as if she could read his mind. "I'm not hungry. Just tired."

"We've got a few protein bars left," Bob said. "You can eat one of those."

She nodded, then looked at the bed with a small grimace.

"Over here," Bob said, well familiar by now with her reluctance to sleep on anyone else's bed. He steered her over to the wall, eased the backpack off her shoulders, then sat, pulling her down with him.

To his satisfaction, she sat right next to him, so close her thigh touched his own and their shoulders brushed. He dug through the backpack and brought out a protein bar and handed it to her.

"Are we safe here?" Marlowe asked after taking a bite.

Bob's first inclination was to say yes. To reassure her so she wouldn't worry. But she wasn't stupid. She'd never asked that question at any of the other places they'd stopped. Something about the couple's greeting had struck her as wrong, just as it had with him.

"We should be," he settled on saying.

She stared at him with big brown eyes for a long moment before nodding.

"I should've done this before now, but I need you to do something for me," Bob said, keeping his voice low.

"Anything."

God, this woman. The longer he was around her, the more he wanted to keep her for himself. "I need you to memorize this phone number. If anything happens, you call it. Tell my friends who you are and that you were with me. They'll help you."

"Chappy, Cal, and JJ, right?" she said softly.

Relieved she wasn't going to argue with him, Bob nodded. "Yeah. Chappy's real name is Riggs. Riggs Chapman. Cal is Callum Redmon, he's the Liechtenstein prince, and JJ is Jackson Justice. We all work at Jack's Lumber, named after JJ. The number is 555-824-8733. The last four numbers spell the word *tree*—555-824-8733. Repeat it back to me."

She did.

"Again," Bob insisted.

She recited the numbers again without hesitation.

"Good. If anything happens, find a phone and call. During business hours, someone will answer. Probably April. But even on nights and weekends, a service forwards any emergency calls to her cell. My friends will help you." It was important to Bob that Marlowe understand she had someone else to turn to, should anything happen to him.

"Don't do anything stupid," she said earnestly. "Don't sacrifice yourself for me. I couldn't bear it if you got caught making sure I got away."

Bob wasn't going to promise anything. Somehow in the last week, he'd fallen hard for this woman. He believed in her innocence, and nothing was going to stop him from getting her across the border. There was no guarantee the Thai authorities wouldn't come after her even when they were in Cambodia, but he was pretty sure with Willis's connections, they'd be able to get out of the country before the two governments could work together to stop them.

When he didn't respond, Marlowe sighed. "Fine. *I'll* just have to make sure you don't do anything stupid."

Bob couldn't help but smirk at that.

"Here," she said, holding out the half-eaten protein bar. "I've had enough. You finish that up. I'm going to nap. But Kendric?"

"Yeah, Punky?"

"Maybe we can head out a little early? Would it matter if we left when it was still light outside? Now that we're so close, I can't wait to get out of Thailand."

Yup. She was definitely as uneasy as he was. They just had to hope their hosts didn't sell them out. "Yeah, I think we can do that."

"Good." She reached up and scratched her head. "I hate this wig," she mumbled, but didn't move to take it off. "I know it's super important, but I still hate it. There's a reason I keep my hair short."

He put his arm around her shoulders and pulled her against him. She snuggled in immediately, wrapping an arm around his chest and pushing the other behind his back and holding on tight.

He turned his head and kissed her forehead. "Sleep, Marlowe."

She nodded and sighed. A minute or two went by before she said, "You slept today."

Bob frowned. "What?"

"At the woman's house. You slept. I woke up and you were out. Like, *really* out. I was worried for a moment, but then I realized what was different. You were sleeping hard. You really needed it."

"It's you," he whispered.

She lifted her head and stared at him with big eyes. "Me?"

"Yeah. It's as if my subconscious knew I was safe with you, that you'd protect me while I was asleep."

"I will," she said fervently. "I dare anyone to try to touch you while you're sleeping."

Bob grinned. She was adorable. He put his hand on her head and gently eased it back down to his chest. "Down, girl. We're good. Close your eyes and get some sleep. We'll head out late this afternoon and hopefully get across the border right when it gets dark."

"I'm afraid to believe that I might just get home," she whispered against him.

"You will. I promise."

Marlowe hugged him tight and nuzzled his chest. Just minutes later, she was asleep.

Bob's heart swelled as he held her close. He'd always felt protective with the people he was sent to rescue, but *nothing* compared to the feelings coursing through his veins at the moment.

Marlowe didn't deserve what happened to her. The same was likely for some of the other women who were incarcerated with her. He wasn't a proponent of drug use, but enduring a life sentence for a few ounces of pot or a couple of yaba pills wasn't right either.

He'd get Marlowe to safety, and he only hoped any other innocent prisoners still at large were able to hide. To continue to evade the police, with or without someone's aid. That they'd be able to start their lives again.

Sometime later, Bob jerked awake. Glancing at his watch, he was surprised to see he'd actually dozed for a good while. It was now afternoon, and while he'd promised they could get an earlier start today, it was still a couple of hours before he felt they could safely continue their journey.

He scooted down until he was lying on the hard wooden planks of the floor, moved their backpack under his head, and adjusted Marlowe in his arms, more than content to let her use him as a pillow.

He was staring at the ceiling, going over the trickiest part of their escape in his head—getting across the border undetected—when he heard a sound that made his gut clench.

Their hosts were in the other room, arguing. They were trying to be quiet, but it was obvious they were having a heated disagreement about something.

The hair on the back of Bob's neck stood up as he listened.

They were in a very poor area, like so many others they'd passed through. He wanted to trust Willis's network, and an argument didn't necessarily mean anything in regard to him and Marlowe. But he understood how tempting it would be for their hosts to turn them in for the reward money, no matter how much Willis had paid them.

Bob had also been a Special Forces soldier long enough to trust his instincts. And his instincts were telling him to get the hell out of this house. *Now.*

He sat up, shaking Marlowe as he did. "Punky, wake up. We need to leave," he whispered.

To her credit, she didn't ask why. Didn't complain about more sleep, or moan about any aches and pains she might have from sleeping on the floor. She silently got to her feet, put the backpack on, and looked to him for direction.

Elsewhere in the house, the voices had stopped. Bob quietly strode to the door and opened it a crack, looking out. Not seeing anyone, he gestured for Marlowe to come closer. She was at his side immediately.

"We're going to go out the front door," he whispered. "I'm guessing our scooter is probably long gone. We're going to have to go the last bit on foot." He glanced down at her shower shoes with regret.

"It's fine. We've got this," she whispered back.

Damn, he adored this woman. When the going got tough, she didn't break. Unbelievably, she got even stronger. "Come on," he said, reaching for her hand. "We're just two tourists out for a walk. We don't want to bring any more attention to ourselves than we'll already do because we don't fit in here."

"Do you think they called the police on us?" Marlowe whispered.

Bob pressed his lips together and nodded. He had no proof, but from the moment they'd arrived at this house, his gut had told him something was off. If they *had* notified the authorities, he wasn't sure why they'd waited so long. They could have had the police waiting for him and Marlowe upon their arrival. Based on the argument he'd overheard, he could only guess maybe one of their hosts hadn't been so eager to betray them.

Whatever the reason, he was kind of surprised it hadn't happened before now. The lure of a double payout was too much for some people to resist. And looking at the poverty most of their hosts lived in, he could hardly blame them.

He cautiously left the bedroom, thankful now that it was at the front of the house, and took the few steps to the front door. Closing it behind them as silently as he could, Bob quickly ushered Marlowe down the street, remaining on high alert. After a few blocks, they cut between two run-down homes, then traversed a long alley.

Suddenly, he heard sirens from a police car.

The sound seemed to echo around them before Bob pinpointed its location—in the direction they'd just come from. Again, there was no proof the police were actually coming for them, but for Bob, it was confirmation that his instincts were likely correct. The couple had notified the authorities.

"Easy, Punky," Bob crooned as he continued walking at a brisk pace through the small town.

"Should I take the wig off?" Marlowe asked. "I mean, they didn't see me without it, so they'd probably describe me to the police as having long blonde hair."

Shit, he should've thought about that. Bob nodded. "Yeah, give it to me," he said, holding out the hand that wasn't clutching hers.

She quickly ripped the wig from her head and handed it over.

Bob couldn't stop the grin from forming. "I bet that felt good."

"No, it felt *great*," she countered, returning his smile.

The next rubbish bin they passed, Bob threw away the offensive wig that had kept her safe for days. Marlowe ran a hand over her head, making her short black hair stick straight up. The hair at her temples and the back of her neck was wet with sweat, but he still hadn't seen anyone as beautiful as this woman in a very long time.

"Stop staring at me," she murmured with a self-conscious huff.

"Can't help it. You're radiant."

She rolled her eyes. "Such a sweet talker. If I had known that earlier, I wouldn't have said yes."

"Yes, you would've. I'm irresistible," Bob teased. He was well aware how much danger they were still in as he continued to lead them away from the house where the police likely expected to take them both into custody. But keeping Marlowe calm was more important than ever right now. Panic caused mistakes. And they couldn't afford even one misstep. Not when they were so close to the border.

"And your ego is huge," she said with a smile, letting him know she was kidding. "But I suppose you have reason to be a bit egotistical. I mean, you did break me out of prison, get us through that roadblock, and get us this far."

"You helped," he insisted. "Without your levelheadedness and willingness to sleep on floors, and *under* floors, and do whatever's necessary to stay under the radar—like wear that uncomfortable wig and marry a bum like me—we wouldn't be as well off as we are now."

"Are we well off?" she asked seriously. "I mean, I know you said we're near the border, but what if there's an extradition policy and they're waiting for us on the other side? Or what if Thai police follow us across and grab me?"

"Don't borrow trouble," Bob warned. "We'll figure things out as we go. Just as we've been doing."

"Okay."

"Okay," he agreed.

They walked through the town, sticking to the alleys and between homes as much as they could. They continued to hear sirens, and Bob guessed the police were now searching for them. The sun was hours from setting, which would make it that much more difficult to get to the border undetected. Bob further suspected the police were well aware they'd try to cross into Cambodia, and therefore would have the road that ran parallel to the border fence well patrolled.

About twenty minutes later, they reached an area of isolated, run-down-looking shacks beyond the edge of town, with plenty of space between each. Bob stopped behind the one closest to the surrounding jungle and pulled Marlowe into a crouch beside him.

"This next part's going to be tricky," he said.

Marlowe nodded and pressed her lips together.

"There's about two hundred yards of jungle, then a rural road, then another fifty or so yards of scrub brush and trees before the border. From the intel I was given, there's a chain-link fence running along the border, with barbed wire across the top. There are no trees close to the fence for cover, of course, so once we get there, we're going to have to move as fast as possible."

He was impressed all over again at Marlowe's ready acceptance of the situation he described.

"Once you get to the fence, start climbing and don't look back, no matter what. Understand? When you get to the top, be *extremely* careful. Aside from the police, the main thing we have to worry about out here is infection if you happen to cut yourself."

"Infection, and not being shot in the back as we're climbing?" Marlowe asked dryly.

"They want you back alive," Bob said bluntly. "They'll want to make an example of you. Make sure foreigners are aware of their zero-tolerance policy for drugs. Your only job is to get up and over that fence, then run like hell. There's a farm about a mile in from the border. That's your goal. The owners are expecting us."

"Our goal," she said with a frown when Bob stopped talking.

"What?"

"That's *our* goal. I'm not leaving you, Kendric. Don't ask me to. I won't do it. If the Thai authorities want to make an example of me, they won't hesitate to arrest you for aiding and abetting. Hell, they'll probably plant drugs on you for good measure. We're doing this together or we aren't doing it at all. To love and protect, for better and worse . . . remember?"

Marlowe would've made a hell of a soldier. Bob was proud to have her at his side. "*Our* goal," he repeated softly.

"I'm serious." Marlowe scowled. "Without you, I won't make it. I won't know where to go or what to do. The only reason I've made it this far is because of you. I'm not leaving you."

Bob clutched her shoulders and stared into her eyes. "You'd make it. I have no doubt. You're smart. And stubborn. And resourceful. But I give you my word that I'll do everything in my power to get us both over that border. Okay?"

"Okay." She took a deep breath. "I'm ready. Piece of cake, right?"

"Right," Bob echoed. He couldn't stop himself from leaning forward and kissing her lightly on the lips.

Marlowe grabbed his shirt when he started to pull away. She stared at him for a beat before blurting, "I want you."

Bob blinked in surprise—but exhilaration coursed through his veins. "I want you too," he admitted.

"Good. Then when we both get across that border, we'll take a shower, find a soft bed of some sort, and make love before sleeping for hours."

"Sounds like heaven," Bob said.

"Yeah."

They stayed crouched, staring at each other for another long moment, before Bob took a deep breath of his own. "The sooner we go, the sooner we can find that bed," he whispered.

"Let's do this." She squeezed his hand.

They stood up, and Bob muttered, "Fast walk across the field toward the trees. No running, it'll bring attention to us if anyone's in these shacks. When we're in the trees, we'll make our way to the next road, wait until the coast is clear, then make a break for the border."

"Got it," Marlowe said a little breathlessly.

Bob imagined her adrenaline had kicked up a notch. Sirens sounded not too far from where they stood, and it was now or never.

Without another word, he stepped out into the narrow strip of field behind the shack, holding Marlowe's hand and praying harder than he had in years. He had more to lose this time. Just the thought of Marlowe being hurt or taken back into custody was as terrifying as anything he'd ever experienced in his life. Including being a POW.

But he'd get her into Cambodia—or die trying.

Chapter Seven

Marlowe's skin crawled. And not just because of the tropical bugs she was constantly brushing off her arms. The feeling of being hunted wasn't a comfortable one, and she had no doubt she and Kendric were merely steps ahead of the authorities.

They'd made it into the jungle without drawing anyone's attention, as far as she knew, but getting through the trees was much harder than either of them had expected. The thick vegetation and thorny bushes were relentless. There were pockets of wet, swampy ground that tried to suck her shoes off at least twice. They'd lost time as Kendric had fished her shower shoes out of the muck. She'd wanted to leave them, but he'd refused, saying there was no way she could walk through the thorns and foliage without something protecting her feet.

Marlowe knew he was right, but she hated that she was slowing them down. The closer they got to the border, the farther away it seemed. Fate wouldn't be so cruel as to let them get so close, only to have them captured now, would it?

They finally made it to the edge of the road beyond the jungle, a one-lane strip of asphalt in the middle of the trees. Kendric had told her that to their left, about eight miles or so down the road, was one of the many official checkpoints leading into Cambodia. In front of them were fifty yards of more trees, more pricker bushes, shoe-sucking mud holes . . . and a fence topped with barbed wire.

"Ready?" Kendric asked in a low, urgent tone.

Marlowe nodded, even though she wasn't remotely ready. She desperately wanted out of Thailand, but for some reason, she had a sudden feeling they weren't going to make it. She wanted to hide out in the trees for another day. Wait until those damn sirens that had been going nonstop faded into silence.

"Here we go," Kendric said in an upbeat tone as he stood and held out his hand. Marlowe grabbed it, and he hauled her to her feet.

They weren't even halfway across the road when they heard shouts to their left.

"Shit! Go, go, go!" Kendric ordered as he shoved her ahead of him toward the trees.

Five seconds. That's all it would've taken to get across that road unseen. But of course, a roving patrol had to come along at exactly the wrong time.

Her heart beating out of her chest, Marlowe ran. Her shoes flew off, but she didn't even notice. Their only goal was getting to the fence, then up and over it.

Kendric stayed at her back, his hand touching her as they ran. She had no doubt he could've gone a lot faster, but he refused to leave her side. He had her back, and nothing she could say or do would make him go on ahead of her. She knew that better than she knew her own name.

Determination welled up inside her. She wouldn't do anything to get this man caught. She owed him her freedom. Her life.

She loved him.

The thought should've been outrageous, even scary, but instead it centered her. She loved him already, despite just knowing him for days, and there was no way they'd made it through everything they had, only to be caught now.

Pressing her lips together, she did her best to block out the sounds of someone crashing through the trees behind them and yelling something in Thai.

"There it is," Kendric panted.

Looking up, Marlowe saw the fence. It looked huge and foreboding. The curls of barbed wire at the top made her wince; they were almost as tall as she was. How the hell were they going to get across that?

She hit the fence hard—and was surprised when she felt it give under her weight.

"Up, Marlowe. Start climbing!" Kendric said.

Instead of heeding his order, something made her look down. When she'd run into the fence, it swayed more than she thought it should've. She fell to her knees and started digging the dirt and leaves away from the chain-link.

"Marlowe! What are you doing? We need to get over this. Now!"

But she knew she'd never get over that barbed wire. Not without shoes. Not at her height. She frantically dug faster.

She heard a noise behind her, and glanced over her shoulder to see two men coming at them from the trees.

Their time was up.

Kendric didn't even hesitate: he charged the men, meeting them head on.

It was an eerie fight. No one said anything. All Marlowe heard were grunts and groans as the three men did their best to subdue each other.

Torn between continuing to free the bottom of the fence—she was getting close, she could feel it—and helping Kendric, she ultimately stood. Shrugging off the backpack, she looked around for something she could use to help him fight.

"Go, Mar!" he yelled as he struggled with the men. "Damn it, *go!*"

She continued to search her surroundings. She *wasn't* leaving without him.

The two men were some sort of security. From what she could see, neither had a gun, which was a huge relief. The last thing she wanted was either her or Kendric being shot when they were so close to freedom.

Just when she was feeling utterly frantic, she finally spied a large tree limb. Running toward it, she blanked her mind from anything but what she needed to do.

By the time she turned back to the fight, Kendric had incapacitated one of the men, who was lying on the ground, moaning. But it looked like he was losing the battle with the other one.

The security officer had pulled a knife and was doing his best to slice Kendric to ribbons as they fought. Marlowe hovered as close as she dared, waiting for an opportunity to strike.

Her chance came when Kendric grabbed the man's knife arm, and they seemed to come to a brief stalemate, each trying to force the other's hand.

Rushing up behind the officer, Marlowe swung the branch as hard as she could. She was smaller than the man, but more determined than ever to end this.

The branch hit him on the side of his head and immediately shattered into hundreds of splinters as it made contact.

For a moment, the man stood stock still, his eyes wide with shock. Then he crumpled to the ground in a heap.

Marlowe stared, equally shocked. Crap! Had she killed him? That hadn't been her plan. It was bad enough she was thrown in jail for having drugs; murdering someone would surely get her the death penalty.

"Come on," Kendric said, grabbing her hand and twirling her around, back toward the fence.

Snapping out of her stupor, Marlowe once again went to her knees. "Help me, Kendric!" she cried. "It'll be easier to go under than over!"

For a moment, he hesitated, but then he was next to her on his knees, frantically digging as best he could with his bare hands. With his help, it wasn't long before there was a small space under the fence.

"Go!" Kendric exclaimed, pushing her to the ground. He wedged the backpack so it was holding up the part of the fence they'd pried from the dirt. It was going to be a tight fit for her, and Marlowe wasn't sure Kendric would be able to fit at all. But he didn't give her a chance to protest. He grabbed her calves and pushed her forward.

She slithered and squirmed on her stomach, and with Kendric's help, she was suddenly on the other side.

Not pausing to kiss the ground or rejoice that she was actually in Cambodia, Marlowe twisted toward him. "Your turn."

He looked at her, then up at the top of the fence, then behind him at the two men, who'd begun to stir. She had a moment to be glad that she hadn't killed the man with the tree branch, but then panic set in.

"Kendric! Come on!"

"I'm not going to fit," he said with a small shake of his head.

"Yes, you will!" Marlowe cried, truly panicking now. "You have to try!"

She was more relieved than she could say when he lowered to his belly.

"Give me your hands!" she ordered. "I'll pull."

He ignored her and did his best to squeeze under the fence.

He was right. He wasn't going to fit.

"No, no, no!" Marlowe chanted under her breath as she fell to her knees next to his head and began digging once more. She flung dirt behind her as she frantically tried to deepen the hole. Tears fell from her eyes, unnoticed as she worked.

The security officer Kendric had knocked out was now on his feet, stumbling toward him.

Sobbing, Marlowe grabbed Kendric's shirt and pulled as hard as she could. But all she managed to do was pull the material up to his armpits and practically strangle him.

He grunted as he kicked out at the man, who was trying to grab hold of his legs to pull him backward.

Screaming in rage and terror and frustration, Marlowe wrapped her arms under Kendric's armpits and used all her strength to hold on to him, to pull him onto the Cambodian side of the border.

One second, she and the security guard were having a tug-of-war contest, and the next, she landed on her ass in the dirt—with Kendric half in her lap.

For a moment, she and the security officer were both frozen. Staring at each other. Then he let out a series of what Marlowe could only assume were swear words.

She looked down and saw that Kendric had rolled to his back. He was lying there motionless, a grimace on his face.

"Kendric?" she asked, putting a hand on his shoulder.

He took a deep breath, and when he opened his eyes and met her gaze, she couldn't read the emotions she saw there.

"You did it," he whispered.

For some reason, Marlowe shook her head in denial.

"No, you did," he insisted. "I wasn't getting under that. No way in hell. I didn't fit. I shouldn't have made it through, but with your refusal to give up . . . here I am." He sat up, pulling his shirt back down to cover his torso, and yanked her against him.

Marlowe snuggled into him, not caring that they were sitting in the dirt. That the security officers were both yelling at them now, threatening them with all sorts of awful things, no doubt, if they didn't come back to the other side of the fence.

Marlowe and Kendric ignored them. She buried her face in his neck and straddled his waist. He held her so tightly, it almost hurt. But she wasn't going to complain. In fact, she never wanted to let him go again.

They didn't sit there for long. It was inevitable that the security officers would call for backup and soon the area would be crawling with more cops. Probably some with guns. And Marlowe wasn't willing to take the chance that they'd be shot through the fence.

They got to their feet and took their first steps away from the border, their arms around each other, the other men shouting in their wake.

"The backpack!" she said, looking behind them.

"It's not important," Kendric said. "We can find new clothes and food. We don't need it."

Marlowe nodded and turned her back on Thailand. She couldn't ever go back, she knew that, but it wasn't as if she'd *want* to go back. In fact, all she wanted to do was get home and never leave the States again. She'd had enough of traveling.

They stumbled along together, her without shoes and Kendric hurting from the slashes he'd received from the knife fight and the punches he'd taken. They went into a line of trees, and it was a huge relief not to be able to see that damn fence. They were leaving Thailand behind once and for all.

They could still hear the security guards shouting, but they kept putting one foot in front of the other.

"Shit," Kendric said as they exited the trees.

Marlowe stared at the canal in front of them. It was about ten feet wide, which wasn't too bad, but the banks on either side were steep, and there was no way to go around it that she could see.

"We're going to have to go through it," Kendric said. "Look, over there." He pointed to a speck in the distance. "See that house? That's our destination. It's a farm. Our next stop."

"But Kendric . . . the water . . . it's gross," Marlowe said. And it was. The water was brackish and a dark-green color. Flies and other insects were buzzing around the surface, and she swore she could see feces bobbing in the water as well.

"Yeah," he agreed. "But we can clean up when we get to the farm."

Marlowe wanted to protest. Insist there was no way she was getting anywhere near that water. But if she wanted to get home, she had to do what she had to do.

She took a deep breath, straightened her shoulders, and nodded.

"That's my brave Punky," Kendric said. He reached out and ran the backs of his fingers down her cheek.

That almost broke Marlowe. She wanted to fall to the ground in a heap and cry. She wasn't brave in the least. Her face was probably red and her eyes swollen from the crying she'd already done when she thought Kendric wasn't going to make it under the fence, her muscles hurt, she was shaky from the adrenaline dump, and her feet hurt from walking without shoes. But the last thing she wanted was to be a burden. She'd keep going because she had no choice.

To her surprise, he leaned over and picked her up, holding her against his chest with one arm under her knees and the other at her back.

"Kendric! What are you doing?"

"There's no sense in both of us getting all gross in that water. I'll carry you."

"I can walk," Marlowe protested, even as she tightened her hold around his neck.

"I know. Please, let me do this," he said softly.

She studied him for a beat, wanting to argue. But something about his expression had her nodding.

"Hold on. I'm going to need one hand to brace as I go down the bank on this side," he warned.

Marlowe nodded again and held on tightly as he slipped down the bank. She heard the slight splash as he entered the canal, but between Kendric's height and the relatively shallow depth of the water—it stopped a few inches above his knees—she stayed well above the water line.

He began wading through the disgusting-smelling water. Looking around, she saw that it *had* been poop she'd seen from above. A fresh pile of cow manure floated past them as Kendric strode toward the bank on the other side, which was far steeper. It was obvious he wasn't going to be able to climb out with her in his arms.

Just as Marlowe was preparing herself to stand up in the nasty water, Kendric surprised her by heaving her upward—and she landed precariously on the sloped bank on her hands and knees. His hand went to her ass, and he held her steady. "Climb up, Punky. I'll brace and push from down here."

She wasn't sure it was going to work, but she didn't hesitate to start crawling toward the flat ground several feet above her. In the end, it didn't take long for her to make it to the top, especially with the final hard shove Kendric gave her. She flew upward and barely kept herself from face planting into the dirt.

Marlowe turned around in time to see Kendric attempting to heft himself up and over the bank—until the dirt crumbled under his weight and he fell backward into the nasty water.

He popped up and grimaced, wrinkling his nose in distaste. He was soaking wet but didn't say a word. Just moved to his left about eight feet, to a section of the bank that hadn't been disturbed, and within seconds, he was beside her.

Marlowe wanted to hug him. To thank him. To tell him how scared she'd been. How proud she was of him. How worried she was about how they were going to get out of Cambodia—but he held up a hand.

"No, don't touch me, Punky. That water was disgusting. We need to hose off. Get clean. Then I'm going to hold on to you so tight, you'll bitch that I'm making you claustrophobic."

"Not a chance," she told him with a small smile. "Feel like a hike? Through the hundred-degree heat and the bugs that want to eat us alive, to that farm where the owners may or may not greet us warmly?"

He chuckled, then got serious.

"What?" she asked when he didn't say anything.

He shook his head. "*You.* I've admired my fair share of women because of their looks. Or because they made me laugh. Or because they were brave in situations that would've brought others to their knees. But you . . . you put them all to shame, Punky. I know we've done everything so far because it was necessary, but I've never been prouder of anyone in my life. Happier to have anyone by my side, to share my name with, than you."

"Kendric," Marlowe whispered, overwhelmed.

"Right. Not the time or place, because I'm covered in Cambodian cow shit and who the hell knows what else, and I can't hold you or kiss you. But don't think I've forgotten our conversation from earlier. About our plans for tonight."

"I haven't either."

"Good. Come on. Let's get this done."

He held out his hand, and Marlowe didn't hesitate to take it with her own. There was a film of gunk on his skin, but she ignored it. His strong, warm hand was her anchor. With him by her side, she could do anything. Survive anything. They were a team. She'd never felt that way about anyone in her life. Now she couldn't imagine not waking up in this man's arms every day. Not hearing his chuckle. Not seeing his smile. Not holding his hand.

She had no idea what the next few days would bring, but she prayed they were through the worst of their journey. That from here on out, things would be smooth sailing, and they'd soon be on a plane back to the United States. Kendric's contact had gotten them this far—that last couple of traitors notwithstanding. She had to trust that things would continue to work out as planned.

Chapter Eight

Later that night, Bob sighed in frustration. The owner of the farm had expected them, but he wasn't happy with the attention their illegal crossing of the border had brought to his doorstep. The Cambodian authorities had shown up shortly before Bob and Marlowe, inquiring if the man had seen two American fugitives from Thailand on his property. He said he hadn't, and after a quick search of the premises, they'd gone on their way.

That meant Bob and Marlowe had to lie low for the evening before continuing their journey the next day. Which wasn't any different from the preceding days . . . except their situation seemed more dangerous now. It was even more risky to stay in one place for long. They were also still too close to the border for Bob's comfort, but they needed to rest and regroup.

Marlowe needed shoes, and he was hurting from the fight. The knife-wielding security guard had made contact several times, and he had half a dozen shallow gashes in his arms that needed tending. His back was also throbbing. Bob knew exactly what had caused that particular pain.

That damn fence.

Marlowe had dug the prongs out of the ground and slipped under them without too many issues, but he hadn't been so lucky. The rusty old metal had dug into his skin as he'd tried to squirm under the fence, gouging into his skin. Even without seeing the damage, Bob knew it wasn't good—especially after falling into that disgusting canal.

But there was literally nothing he could do about his injuries. They wouldn't stop him from making sure Marlowe was safe. Willis had arranged for them to fly out of Phnom Penh International Airport. It was the biggest airport in the country, and not too far from where Willis had contacts who would expedite them through security and get them to Tokyo, where they'd catch a plane back to the East Coast of the US.

They were currently in the farmer's barn, in an empty stall between two others holding oxen, which the owner probably used to plow his fields. Instead of a hot shower, they'd been offered a hose on the side of the barn, but at least the water was cleaner than the muck he'd fallen into earlier.

He'd done his best to hose off thoroughly, knowing infection was a serious risk after his cuts were exposed to that canal. Once Marlowe had rinsed herself as well, the farmer gave them a bowl of fried rice to share, a sheet and two towels, and then quickly left the barn. It wasn't the warmest welcome, but they were alive and together, so Bob was grateful.

He'd hung his shirt and pants over the edge of the stall to dry—as much as possible in the damp climate—and Marlowe had done the same. There was still plenty of light in the sky when she finally appeared in the entrance of the stall after using the hose to clean herself. At the sight of her, it was all Bob could do to remain sitting.

He'd spread the sheet out on a thick bed of hay and draped his towel over his lap. He made sure to keep his back to the wall, because the last thing he wanted was Marlowe freaking out over the ragged gouges. From what he could tell, blood still trickled slightly from the wounds, and he probably needed a few stitches, but that would have to wait.

For now, he wanted to hold Marlowe . . . to show her how deep his feelings ran . . . even if he couldn't say the words. He refused to hold her back or make her feel obligated toward him if she didn't feel the same.

"I . . . this is a little weird," she blurted as she stood uncertainly in front of him. She had the towel wrapped around her body, but Bob could still see a lot of leg and thigh. He swallowed hard and held out his hand.

He couldn't help but feel pleased when she immediately came to him. He helped her sit, then reached for the bowl of rice. Scooping out a spoonful, he held it to her lips.

"I can do that."

"And hold on to that towel in a death grip at the same time?" he asked with a small grin.

She rolled her eyes, shrugged, then leaned forward and opened her mouth.

He slipped the spoon between her lips and couldn't take his eyes off them as her tongue came out and licked some of the grease that had been left behind on her lips.

"Good?" he asked.

"Honestly? Yeah. It's delicious."

"I'm always starving after an adrenaline rush," he told her before spooning up another helping and holding it out to her. They shared the rice until they'd finished it all, and Bob put the bowl off to the side.

The animals in the barn shuffled around, making quiet noises. The fact that they were calm made Bob feel relatively safe. He lay back, ignoring the pain it caused his back and careful not to dislodge the towel from over his crotch, and held out his arm. "Come here, Punky."

She moved into his arms as if she'd done it every day of her life, instead of merely the last few days. Her head rested on his shoulder, and when she adjusted her body to lie more comfortably, the towel around her slipped, allowing him to feel her bare skin against his own. He shivered.

Marlowe lifted her head. "Are you okay?"

"Actually, yeah. I'm perfect," he told her.

They lay like that for a long time, listening to the sounds of the animals around them, feeling more relaxed than they'd been for a week.

Bob knew they weren't home free—he wouldn't relax completely until they were standing on US soil—but they were a hell of a lot closer than they'd been in days.

"What are you thinking?" she whispered. Her arm was draped over his stomach, her fingers absently caressing his side, and Bob was surprisingly comfortable on the borrowed sheet, despite lounging on hay. It was still hot and humid, but having Marlowe practically on top of him felt . . . right.

"Honestly? Just how much I'm enjoying this."

"Yeah," she agreed. After a moment, she added, "I feel as if I've known you for years . . . Is that weird? I mean, I know it's probably just the intense situation we've been in, being on the run and hiding out, but I've never felt as comfortable with someone as I am with you. I'm not trying to pressure you in any way, or trying to get you to say something similar, I just . . . wanted you to know."

She'd summed up what he'd been feeling almost perfectly. "I never say anything I don't mean," he told her. "I don't agree with people just to be polite, and I've never been accused of being politically correct. April doesn't let me answer the phone or emails back home, because she knows I don't have the patience to be nice when people are being jerks. So trust me when I tell you that there's *nowhere* I'd rather be right this moment than right here with you. In Cambodia. In this smelly stall. With you in my arms."

Marlowe's arm tightened as she gave him a hug. Her head lifted, and he gazed into her beautiful brown eyes. "Kendric?"

He smiled. She had a habit of doing that. Saying his name before asking a question or telling him something. "Yeah?"

"I lost a bunch of weight over the last month. So my boobs aren't anything to write home about. And I need about ten hot showers in order to feel completely clean again . . . but I still want you."

This woman slayed him. She had more bravery in her little finger than most people had in their entire bodies. He tightened his arm around her waist and rolled until she was lying on her back beneath him. His own towel had slid off, and they were both completely naked. His cock was already rock hard against her inner thigh.

His back gave a twinge as he moved, but he ignored it. At the moment, his entire attention was on Marlowe.

"You are the most beautiful woman I've ever seen, Punky. You've held up amazingly well over the last week . . . hell, the last month. And I'd have to say that your boobs are the best tits in the world, simply because they're *yours*." He leaned up a little farther and slowly ran a hand down her body. From her neck to her shoulder, down her chest—briefly touching the nipple that had hardened and was practically begging for his mouth—over her belly, and ending by brushing against her outer thigh.

"As for your body? You fit against me as if you were made to be here. Therefore, it's perfect."

"Kendric," she whispered, clearly overwhelmed.

"I've been with a few women since I got out of the Army, but I've never wanted any of them more than I wanted to breathe. I slept with them because I was restless. I'd have been just as happy going skydiving to burn some nervous energy—which explains why it took me too much time and concentration just to get off. But with you? I want you so badly, Marlowe, it's all I can do to control myself and not blow right here and now."

"Then take me. I'm yours," she said, running her hands up and down his arms.

She *was*. His, that is. He had a marriage certificate in the pocket of his pants that said so.

Their names at the bottom of the form flashed in his brain. Kendric and Marlowe Evans. He'd never thought he'd get married, but now he was borderline obsessed with the idea. She was his, just as he was hers.

Then another thought struck him—and he closed his eyes in frustrated anger.

"What? What's wrong?"

"I can't protect you," he blurted.

She frowned in confusion. "Kendric, you've been protecting me just fine for a week."

She was so cute. "No, Punky. I don't have any condoms. I can't protect you from getting pregnant."

"Oh. Um . . . okay, this is awkward, but . . . we're adults, right? We can talk about this. I haven't had my period for a while. I guess it's because of stress, or maybe because I wasn't eating much and lost a bunch of weight. I'm thinking that I probably can't get pregnant right now even if I wanted to. So . . . it's okay."

It wasn't okay. Bob hated the thought of her body basically shutting down its normal functions because she wasn't getting the nutrients she needed. "We can wait," he said, even though the words almost physically hurt. He wouldn't do anything that might put this woman at risk.

"I want kids," she blurted. "And I mean, I've *always* wanted them. That's what I *really* want to do—be a stay-at-home mom. It's not a popular opinion, and of course I had to work to support myself. But being a mom is the only job I've ever truly wanted. I want to watch my kids grow up. I want to be there when they go off to school and welcome them home in the afternoons. I want to learn how to cook, and maybe sew, and honestly, I don't even mind housework.

"What I'm saying is that if—and that's a huge if—I get pregnant from being with you, I . . . I wouldn't be upset about it. I'm thirty-five. Not getting any younger. And I wouldn't ask for anything from you. I wouldn't bug you for money, or support, or anything you don't want to give."

"If you had my child, I'd want to be a part of his or her life," Bob warned. "I wouldn't be that asshole father who didn't support his kids—or their mother."

They stared at each other for a long, drawn-out moment.

Abruptly, he chuckled. "Look at us, married one day and planning our family the next," he drawled.

She giggled. "It's ridiculous."

"Is it?" he asked without thought. For some reason, nothing about this situation felt ridiculous.

"No. It feels right," Marlowe finally whispered.

And there she went again. Being braver than he could ever imagine.

"Make love to me, Kendric. Please. Whatever happens, happens. Tomorrow, the Cambodian authorities could find me and drag me back to Thailand. We could be bitten by a rabid mosquito. Mauled by a feral ox. I don't know. All I know is that if I don't get a chance to feel you deep inside of me, at least once, I'll regret it for the rest of my life."

She was right. They had this moment, and he'd been thinking about making love to her nearly every minute since he'd said "I do." And even before, if he was honest. Since that kiss.

She was his wife, and he was her husband. Everything he'd done in his life felt as if it had led to this moment. She was his reward.

Bob's head lowered without another thought. He kissed her gently at first. Telling her without words that he'd keep her safe. Would make sure nothing happened to her. That he'd treat her with care.

But apparently care wasn't what Marlowe wanted. She immediately fisted his hair, tilted her head, and thrust her tongue into his mouth. Their tongues dueled and caressed, and Bob felt himself panting as he pulled his head back to take in some much-needed oxygen.

Her hand snaked down his body, and she wrapped her fingers around his cock.

"Holy crap," he muttered as she touched him with firm, confident strokes. He grabbed her wrist and pulled her hand away. "Any more of that and there won't be any lovemaking at all, because I'll be done," he warned.

"You're young," she said with a smile. "You'll recover."

But Bob didn't want to come anywhere but deep inside her body. He needed to claim her in the way that men had been claiming their women for centuries. It was old school and a little caveman-ish and a lot careless, but he didn't care. At the moment, in this barn, after everything they'd been through, he was going to take whatever she was willing to give. Was going to claim this woman as his own.

He leaned down—wincing as the wounds on his back protested—and clamped his mouth around one of her nipples. She hadn't lied; she was small. But her nipples were extremely sensitive. She arched her back and let out a small cry as he suckled her. One of her hands returned to his hair as she held him against her chest.

Bob licked and sucked. And while he was loving what he was doing, he needed more. A hand snaked down her body, and his fingers brushed through the curls between her thighs. She moaned again and opened her legs for him, giving him access to her most private parts.

She was soaking wet already, and Bob's heart rate sped up. She wanted him. She wasn't with him out of a sense of gratitude. She truly wanted him, as much as he wanted her.

Bob wanted to take his time. Wanted to worship her body from head to toe. But his dick had other ideas. A spurt of precome escaped from the tip. He was on the edge. Needed to make this woman his in the most primal way.

He came to his knees over her and gripped her inner thighs, opening her even farther. Then he fisted the base of his cock and scooted forward. His gaze was locked on her pussy.

"Yes," Marlowe half moaned, half pleaded from under him. Her hands went to his thighs and her nails dug in . . . even as he suddenly hesitated.

Instinctively, Bob knew making love to her would change his life. He'd never be able to let her go. He'd be one of "those" guys. The ridiculous mushy ones who called and texted their women fourteen times a day to make sure they were all right. A man who bought her flowers for no reason. Who shook his head and just smiled when she spent too much money.

Who worshipped the ground she walked on.

And he didn't care.

She had him wrapped around her little finger already, and she didn't even know it.

"Kendric?" she whispered a little uneasily.

Shit, his hesitation had made her question herself. He reached for her hand and brought it back to his cock. He sighed as she wrapped her fingers around him. Her touch felt good. Too good.

"You do it. Put me inside you," he said in a low growl.

"It's been a while for me," she admitted a little shyly.

"I'll go slow," he said immediately.

He saw her nod, then bite her lip as she stroked him before pushing his hard dick down and notching him to her opening.

Bob saw stars. Literal fucking *stars*. Heaven was waiting. All he needed was one hard thrust to experience it. But he'd go slow if it killed him.

Marlowe was tight. And even though she was wet, her body wasn't letting him inside very easily.

It took every ounce of control he had, but Bob refused to do anything that might hurt her or make this experience, their first, anything but life changing and pleasurable.

He braced himself on one hand and used the other to seek out her clit. She jerked under him at the first touch of his finger on the sensitive bundle of nerves, but her body relaxed enough for the head of his cock to slip inside her a little bit farther.

"Oh!" she exclaimed.

"That feel good, Punky?" he asked, already knowing the answer, but wanting to hear more of her husky words.

"Yes! So good. More, Kendric."

Anything she wanted, she'd get. Bob continued to stroke her clit, reaching down every now and then and using her own natural lubrication to ease his way.

It wasn't long before her hips were rocking toward him, begging for more. With each movement, he was able to slip farther and farther inside. Bob didn't know if she even realized she was moving.

Before long, her hips were thrusting up and down, and she was basically taking *him* from below.

It was one of the most sensual and erotic things Bob had ever experienced. He held himself still over her as he did his best to keep his hand on her clit and continue to stroke. Her eyes closed and her head flew back as she concentrated on the pleasure that was building.

Bob was loving this. Couldn't wait for her to explode around him.

As he watched her take her pleasure, something registered in his brain. Stalks of hay were in Marlowe's hair. He'd rolled them right off the sheet, and she was lying on straw. The same straw some animal was probably standing on earlier in the day. Which was unacceptable.

Without pulling out of her, Bob clamped his hands on her hips and rolled them again. If anyone was going to be lying on the rough straw, it would be him.

Marlowe jolted and looked down at him from her new position. Her legs were spread around his hips and his cock was halfway inside her.

"Take me, Marlowe Evans," he said gruffly, holding her waist tightly. "As hard and deep as you want." He moved a hand between her legs once more and realized he had better access to her clit in this position. Not giving her a chance to feel awkward about being on top if she was unused to it, he stroked her hard and fast.

She froze over him and arched her back. Her nipples were hard on her chest, and she was panting within seconds. "Kendric," she cried as she finally moved her hips, trying to keep his fingers where she wanted them.

He stared at his cock. He wasn't inside her fully, and he so wanted to slam her down against him. But that might hurt her. So he clenched his teeth and let her have complete control over their lovemaking.

She tilted her head down and looked at where they were joined— then gasped. "You aren't even all the way in," she blurted, reading his mind.

He smiled. "I'm big," he said with no ego whatsoever. "Only take what's comfortable for you."

Marlowe blew his mind by looking him in the eyes and saying, "I want all of you." She wiggled over him, rocking forward and back, and the next thing he knew, all of her body weight was on him, their pubic hair meshed . . . and she'd taken him fully inside.

They both groaned, and Bob felt his cock twitch inside her body. She felt fucking *amazing*. Wet, tight, and so goddamn hot, she was practically scalding him. And he never wanted to leave.

His fingers moved on her clit, and suddenly he needed to feel her come on his dick. Needed to feel her muscles spasming around him. It became his goal in life.

She jerked in his grip, both outwardly and inwardly, and Bob's balls let loose another long spurt of precome deep within her body.

"Holy crap, Kendric! You feel so good. I'm so full!"

"Come for me, Marlowe. Come all over my dick. Let me feel it. I've got you, let loose, baby."

He didn't really know what he was saying, just that he wanted to reassure her. That he'd catch her as she fell. He stroked her clit harder. Her hips began to undulate faster, but she didn't come off his cock even an inch. She kept him stuffed inside her as far as she could get him.

His balls pulled up, preparing to release their load. Gritting his teeth, Bob held on by a thread. She felt too good. His emotions were overflowing with everything he felt for his woman—including love.

He stared up at her face in wonder as she got closer and closer to the edge. Her fingernails dug into the bare skin of his chest. He didn't feel the sting of the knife cuts he'd gotten earlier. Didn't feel the coarse straw irritating the wounds in his back. All he could feel and see was Marlowe.

Suddenly, every muscle in her body tightened, and she held herself still on top of him. She was on the verge. All she needed was a nudge and she'd be flying.

Bob pinched her clit between his fingers and was rewarded with a strangled scream from his woman; then his cock felt like it was in a vise as she flew over the edge.

~

Marlowe couldn't breathe. She couldn't see. She couldn't think. All she could do was feel as she had the most intense orgasm she'd ever experienced. She had no idea how long she was out of it, but when she finally opened her eyes and looked down at the man she loved under her, she was smiling.

"That was the most beautiful thing I've ever seen. Thank you," Kendric said reverently.

She should be thanking *him*. "Did you . . . ? I'm sorry, I should know, but I was too busy soaring through the stars and didn't register anything that was happening around me . . . or in me," she added with a small shrug.

His smile widened. "No. I was too busy watching and feeling your pleasure."

Marlowe felt her cheeks heat with a blush.

"What do you need from me to come?" she asked boldly. She was a woman determined to satisfy her man. Not a sixteen-year-old kid experimenting with sex for the first time.

"Not much. I'm so on the edge it's not even funny," he said a little sheepishly.

Experimenting, Marlowe tightened her inner muscles, squeezing him tightly deep within her body, and was rewarded by his fingers gripping her hips and a groan escaping his lips.

She slowly lifted a fraction, then lowered herself once more.

"Yes, just like that. Slow and steady," he told her, practically panting.

Smiling, loving the power she apparently had over him, Marlowe lifted off him once more. She stopped, hovering, surprised at the rush of wetness she felt seeping out of her body.

"Holy shit, that feels incredible!" Kendric gasped. He moved a hand between them and stroked the part of his cock that was outside her body, brushing against her sensitive lower lips as he did.

"We're soaked," he said unnecessarily. "I feel you on my balls. It's amazing. I want more. Move, Marlowe. As long as it's not painful for you."

It didn't hurt. Not at all. Yes, he was big and it had taken a bit for her to be able to take him all the way inside her, but now? She was slick and relaxed from her orgasm, and she wanted everything he had to give her.

She hadn't lied earlier. She did want children. She didn't think making love tonight would produce a child, not with everything else going on with her body, but if she *did* get pregnant, she'd love their baby with every ounce of energy in her.

She began to move. Up and down. Squeezing her inner muscles as she bottomed out on him, wanting him to experience what she had.

"Marlowe . . . yes! You feel so good. You have no idea."

She loved how out of control he sounded, the way he was babbling his every thought. Needing more, wanting his complete surrender, Marlowe began to move faster. Soon the sound of their skin slapping together echoed throughout the barn as she rode him hard.

Just as her thigh muscles began to shake from exertion, Kendric clamped his hands around her hips and pulled her down on top of him. He was so far inside her, it almost hurt. He groaned, his hips jerking as he came.

It was the most intimate thing Marlowe had ever done. The look on Kendric's face was almost one of pain as he filled her. She was still staring at his face when his eyes popped open and his hand moved. He roughly began to tweak her clit once more, and she jerked in surprise.

"One more," he demanded. "I need to feel you come around me again."

His touch was almost overwhelming, but in a good way. She tried to squirm away for a moment of relief, but he held her tightly. "Kendric," she moaned as the pleasure rose within her much faster than it had before.

"That's it. Squeeze me, just like that. I can feel your muscles fluttering on my cock. You feel so unbelievable. If I could live inside you, I would. As much as I love filling you with my seed, I love this even more. Feeling your pleasure from the inside. It's incredible, Marlowe."

His words cascaded over her like a warm tropical waterfall. She couldn't stop herself from undulating against him, on his cock, as he brought her closer and closer to the edge. She wasn't the kind of woman who had multiple orgasms during a sexual encounter. Hell, many times she never even had one. But she was quickly approaching the edge for the second time, and this one felt even more intense than her first.

"You're *mine*, Marlowe. You took my name. Now you're taking my cock. It's yours. All of me is yours. Do it, Punky. Let go. I'll catch you."

The practical part of her had a feeling he was saying the things he was because they were in the throes of sex. Really *good* sex, but once their endorphin high was gone, reality would set in and he'd probably be embarrassed at the things he'd proclaimed. But for now, she let his words settle in her soul.

A little scream left her throat as he pushed her over the edge. She trembled and shook in his grip, and she heard him moan under her.

When she could breathe again, she felt boneless. Kendric lowered her onto his chest, still buried deep inside her body. She could feel their combined juices leaking out from between their bodies, and she had the thought that she was glad she didn't have to sleep in the wet spot. He held her against his chest and stroked her back with his big hands.

"Holy crap," she mumbled when she felt as if she could speak again.

He chuckled under her, and Marlowe could only smile at the intimate way she felt his laughter because she was draped over him.

"That was amazing. Seriously. I've never felt that before."

Marlowe lifted her head and frowned. "Really?"

"Nope. I take care of the women I sleep with, but I've never been inside one when she came."

Marlowe supposed she should feel weird about her man talking about sex with other women, but since he was basically saying she'd given him an experience he'd never had before, and because she was the one he was still buried deep within, she wasn't concerned.

"I'm gonna want that again," he warned. "Probably every time you come. That going to be a problem?"

It was her turn to laugh. "Did you seriously just ask that?" she said as she lowered her cheek back to his chest.

"I wasn't sure if you thought it was weird or anything," he defended.

"Anytime you want to make me come, you just go right on ahead," she teased. She felt his cock twitch inside her and couldn't stop the grin from forming on her face. He didn't seem as if he was in any hurry to move. He simply lay under her, letting her use him as a pillow as he stroked her back, her arms, her hair.

"Kendric?"

"Yeah?"

She hadn't missed the way he'd called her Marlowe Evans when they'd been in the middle of making love. She wanted to be his wife for real, more than she wanted almost anything in the world, but she was well aware that their situation wasn't normal. It was incredibly intense, and they'd been relying on each other in ways that some couples never would. She couldn't hold him to anything once they got back to their real worlds.

"Do you really think we're going to make it home?"

"Yes." His answer was immediate and almost forceful. "I'm going to get you home, Marlowe."

She sighed. Was it weird that she almost didn't *want* to go home now? Probably. She knew things between her and Kendric would change when they left.

"It'll take three or four days to get to the airport," Kendric told her. "Once there, I'll get a hold of my contact, and he'll arrange for us to have passports, in fake names if he deems it necessary, once he sees what's going on with Thailand and your situation. We'll be home in less than another week."

"That's good," she said, her reply sounding a little weak to her own ears.

"What's wrong?" he asked, completely in tune with her feelings.

"I just . . . I want to go home, don't get me wrong. But . . ." Her words tapered off.

"You can tell me anything," he reassured her.

"I've gotten used to having you around," she said, trying to lighten her tone so her words didn't feel quite so serious.

But Kendric didn't laugh. Didn't make a joke. Instead, he said, "Look at me, Marlowe."

Taking a deep breath, she lifted her head so she could see his face.

"I want to see you when we get back. I don't know how it'll work, since I'm ready to settle down in Maine for good and you'll be wherever you'll be. But I don't want us to lose touch."

Her heart sped up. What was he saying exactly? She was too chicken to ask him outright. "I want that too."

"Good," he said, sounding relieved. "I want you to meet my friends. They're going to love you. They'll probably try to convince you to move to Newton. If you're not careful, April will have rented an apartment for you before we can even get home."

Marlowe rested her head back down on Kendric's chest and used her fingers to trace little circles on his skin. She didn't think she'd mind living in Newton. It sounded like the kind of town that would be safe for raising kids. She'd had more than enough adventure to last her a lifetime. "My brother is going to love you too," she told him.

"I'm looking forward to meeting him," Kendric said.

Unexpectedly, tears sprang to Marlowe's eyes. She wanted this. Lying in Kendric's arms, talking, sharing. But she was smart enough to know nothing was ever this easy.

He'd have to deal with his friends being upset for not telling them about his missions. And while he might say he was ready to settle down, she wasn't sure that was exactly true. He'd go back to Maine and inevitably get bored once again. How could she compete with the adrenaline rush he got while saving others? She couldn't.

The thought of him going who-knows-where and putting himself in danger wouldn't be something she could stomach. Not when she'd experienced firsthand how dangerous his missions could be. Asking him to stop wouldn't be fair to Kendric, though. He was who he was, and she'd never want to hold him back.

The truth of the matter was that being with her would be boring. She wanted a slow and easy life from here on out, and this man would never do well with slow and easy. He was born to help others. To live on the edge.

"Are you crying? Did I hurt you? Shit!" he exclaimed, trying to move from under her.

But Marlowe clutched him to her and shook her head. "No! You'd never hurt me. I'm just feeling emotional. You know, everything's catching up with me." She hated the small lie, but it wasn't completely untrue.

He relaxed under her once more, and his hands returned to stroking her back. "You're okay, Punky. You're safe. We'll head out in the morning. I think it's at least a little safer to travel during the day, now that we're out of Thailand. We'll get you some shoes, some clean clothes, and when we get to the airport, I'll get a hold of my contact and get us out of here."

She nodded and closed her eyes once more. He was still buried deep in her body, and Marlowe had never felt as safe as she did at that moment. Even though they were in a barn, and she still longed for a real shower and soap, she was more content than she'd felt in a very long time.

"I should move and clean us up," he muttered.

But Marlowe gripped him tighter. "No. It's okay."

He chuckled. "I can see someone isn't going to want to sleep in the wet spot, huh?"

His words made it seem as if they had a future together. More nights of making love and deciding who would sleep where. "Sex without a condom is messy," she said after a moment.

"I hadn't realized just how much," he said, still completely relaxed under her.

Marlowe lifted her head once again. "Really?"

"Really. I wasn't ready to be a father before."

His words lay heavy around them. She wasn't sure of the connotations in that statement. That he wasn't ready before, but he was *now*? She sighed. "I don't mind the mess," she said after a minute. "I mean, I'm not sure I'd like walking around feeling your come leaking from between my legs, but this? Lying here with you still inside me? It's . . . intimate."

"Yeah," he agreed.

She felt him hardening again, and she grinned against his chest.

"Marlowe?"

"Yes?" she replied, feeling excitement and arousal ramp up inside her once again as he filled her.

"Are you sore?"

"No."

"I want you again," he said bluntly.

"You can be on top," she told him a little shyly as she sat up on him once again.

But he shook his head. "No. I don't want your skin touching the hay."

She frowned down at him. "Why not?"

"Because it's scratchy. And dirty."

"And that's okay for you but not me?"

"Yup."

"That's not fair," she protested.

Kendric merely shrugged. "Don't care. To love and protect, cherish and honor, respect and nurture. That's what I promised, and I take my vows seriously."

Marlowe's heart melted.

"Besides, I know you like being on top. And I like you there. Take me, woman. I want to fill you up again."

She rolled her eyes. "You really are bossy."

"It's good you're learning this now. Move, woman. Please."

So she did.

~

Hours later, Marlowe woke slowly in Kendric's arms. The animals were stirring around them, so she had a feeling the owner of the farm would make an appearance soon. They needed to get up, get dressed, and start heading south for the airport.

But she couldn't make herself move. She was still lying on top of Kendric, although they'd managed to get half the sheet draped over themselves after the last time they made love. They'd both come again and had spent at least an hour talking about their lives. Their hobbies and their likes and dislikes, and Kendric had told her more stories about his friends and some of the missions he'd been on while in the Army.

He'd also told her more about Newton, the town in Maine where he lived. Her mouth watered at hearing about Granny's Burgers. She was fascinated by his friend who was a prince, and mentally shuddered at the thought of having to go to Liechtenstein to meet the king and queen and have some sort of formal, very public wedding ceremony, like Cal and June would be doing at some point.

She couldn't help but think that her own ceremony had been perfect. Just her and Kendric. She'd treasure the memories of their host pouring water over their hands to bless them, of Kendric saying "I do." And even though they'd spent their wedding night stuffed in that tiny space in the floor, it was one of the best experiences she'd ever had.

She was plastered against Kendric right that moment just as tightly as she'd been on their wedding night, but this time they were both naked and replete from their multiple orgasms. Marlowe was feeling mellow.

But when Kendric jerked violently under her, she was immediately on alert.

"Cal! Where's Cal?"

"Shhhh, it's okay," Marlowe soothed.

"Chappy! Are you all right? Please hang in there!"

"They're safe," she told him, smoothing her hand down his chest, trying to calm him.

Kendric had told her that he didn't sleep well, that he had nightmares, but up until now, she hadn't thought much about it since he'd rarely slept at all on their journey. Apparently he'd let down his guard enough for his brain to go into REM sleep, and he was now having one of those nightmares he'd mentioned. Her heart broke for him.

"Marlowe! Run! Go, go, go!"

She blinked. He was dreaming about *her*? It broke her even more, knowing that helping her escape had provided new material for bad dreams.

"Get your hands off her! No! Marlowe! I'll get you out! I promise! Don't give up! I'll find you!"

"I'm right here, I'm safe," Marlowe tried again, but Kendric wasn't hearing her.

He sat up, dislodging her from his chest as easily as if she wasn't even there. "I'm coming! No, get off her! Marlowe! Don't touch her, you bastards! Nooooooo!"

The last word was more of a wail, and Marlowe was desperate to wake him now. To stop whatever was happening in his head. She climbed onto his lap, straddling him and putting her hands on his cheeks. "Kendric! Wake up! I'm right here. No one is touching me. We're safe and in Cambodia. Please wake up!"

For a moment, she thought it wasn't working, that he was still stuck in whatever horror he was dreaming about—but then he blinked and his gaze found hers.

"That's it. You're okay. We're both okay. Wake up for me. I'm right here."

"Marlowe?" he croaked.

"Yeah, it's me."

"Shit," he breathed, lowering his head until his nose was buried in her neck. "Are you all right?"

"I'm fine. Do you want to talk about your dream?"

"No."

His response was immediate and firm.

"Okay. But you're good. We're both okay."

He abruptly lay back, and Marlowe let out a surprised squeak. He held her tightly against him as he kept his eyes closed and breathed hard, obviously trying to shake the aftereffects of his nightmare.

Marlowe continued to stroke him, reassure him that she was fine, that he was too, and that it was only a bad dream.

Finally, he quietly mumbled, "I hate dreaming. *Hate* it."

"It's why you don't let yourself sleep much, right?" she asked.

Kendric nodded. "Ever since I was a captive, I've had nightmares. I've talked to psychologists and therapists and even a few sleep specialists. They all say the same thing. That they'll eventually fade away. But it's been years, and they're still just as vivid as they were right after we were rescued."

"It's because you care so much," she said firmly. "If you didn't, you wouldn't be so worried about your friends."

"I never remember much about the dreams. Just that I'm frantic and trying to get to my friends and can't," he admitted. His eyes opened and looked up at her. "I've never come out of them as fast as I did just now, though. Usually it takes me hours to feel like myself again. But with you here . . . touching me . . . it helps."

It felt good to know she could help him at least a little. "Good."

They lay there for a few minutes before Kendric sighed. "We need to get up. I don't want the farmer seeing your butt."

119

Marlowe giggled. "Well, I don't want him seeing yours either," she countered.

"Don't think it's my butt he'd be interested in," Kendric told her with a smirk.

"You never know. It's a damn fine butt," Marlowe protested.

"How do you know? You didn't see it last night. You were too busy admiring my cock, and sitting on it."

Marlowe felt herself blushing. "Whatever."

He laughed. Loudly. "God, you're adorable. Take the towels and clean up with the hose. I'll make do with the sheet, and we'll be on our way. I'll talk to the farmer about shoes for you, and we'll stop at the first shop we find and get you some clothes."

"You're too good to me," she blurted.

"No such thing," he returned. Then pulled her down and kissed her gently. "Thank you for last night. You gave me a gift I'll cherish forever."

"I didn't give you anything," Marlowe protested.

"You gave me *you*," he said. He stood with her in his arms, set her on her feet, and handed her the towels that had been pushed to the side the night before. "Go on before the farmer gets here."

She nodded and wrapped one of the towels around her body before turning to head out of the stall. She looked back once and saw Kendric's gaze was still glued to her. He hadn't moved to get dressed. In the soft predawn light peeping through the slats in the barn, she admired his form right back. He was so muscular, looked as strong as the trees he talked about cutting up back home in Maine. It was hard to believe she'd spent the night with him. That he wanted her. But it was obvious by his growing erection that he definitely hadn't been with her out of pity.

She gave him a small smile and left the barn, heading for the outdoor spigot. As much as she wanted to go right back to bed with Kendric, she felt grubby, and they really did need to get going. Being this close to the border made her nervous. As if someone would burst in at any moment and drag her back to prison. The sooner they made their way south to the airport, the better she'd feel.

Chapter Nine

Four days later, Bob knew he was in big trouble. His wounds hadn't gotten any better with time. In fact, they were infected, and any kind of touch to his back sent radiating waves of pain throughout his body. He wasn't eating, because he couldn't keep anything down, and was getting weaker and weaker by the day.

At first, he'd tried to keep his pain a secret from Marlowe, but she wasn't stupid. She knew immediately that something was wrong. It wasn't until two days ago that he'd had to admit what was wrong, when she'd wrapped her arm around him after he'd stumbled as they were walking—then jerked away from her and couldn't stop the moan of pain from leaving his mouth.

She'd insisted on lifting his shirt and taking a look at his wounds, and her horrified inhalation told Bob all he needed to know. She'd wanted to find a doctor, but he'd refused. He needed to get her home. He'd lived through infections before, lived through beatings and torture, and come out of both just fine. He could muddle through until he was back in the States.

But in the last twelve hours, Bob knew he wasn't going to make it home.

Every step was torture. Every movement felt as if he was right back in that cell overseas and his captors were slicing their knives deep into his skin.

He'd managed to get him and Marlowe to the small room in the back of a shop near the airport, the last place Willis had arranged for them. Then he'd fallen to the floor . . . and hadn't been able to get up again.

Marlowe had been amazingly strong over the last few days, encouraging him, doing her best to clean the wounds on his back with what she could find, but the infection raging through his body had won.

"Kendric?" she cried frantically as he lay face down on the floor.

"I'm okay," he mumbled, knowing he was lying through his teeth. "Just gotta sleep an hour or so. Then I'll call Willis and we'll go."

"All right. You sleep. I'll be right here," she told him.

That was the last thing Bob remembered before he passed out.

⁓

Marlowe paced the room. It was small, only large enough for her to take about five steps from wall to wall. She'd known Kendric was hurting, but wasn't aware of exactly how bad things had gotten. He'd hidden his pain well. Even though she'd seen his wounds two days ago, he hadn't let her clean them since. When he'd passed out, and she'd lifted his shirt to see how bad the damage had become, she'd almost fainted herself.

The gouges in his flesh were a mottled green, enflamed red around the edges, and leaking pus. And they smelled awful. His skin was hot to the touch and puffy from the infection. He needed medical assistance immediately, but she had no idea how to provide it without one or both of them getting arrested.

Panic set in as she paced. She didn't think about how close she was to getting home; all she could think about was the man she loved lying on the floor. He'd gotten them all the way to the airport, and now she seriously wondered if he was going to die. His breathing was fast and shallow, and she was scared to death that she was going to lose him.

She had no idea how to get in touch with his contact, Willis. Kendric had stopped along their journey, using pay phones and paying shopkeepers to use their personal cells, but he hadn't shared the man's number. She'd dug out his wallet and knew they were out of money. She had no idea how he'd planned to get a hold of Willis to arrange for their passports and flights, but it didn't matter. He was in no shape to do anything more than lie on the floor at the moment.

Marlowe chewed on her thumbnail and thought over the last four days. How he'd gotten hurt climbing under that fence, then carried her through that foul-smelling canal. She'd stayed dry, but the feces-filled water had obviously gotten into his wounds. When they were in the barn, he'd lain on his back on the bare straw so she'd touch it as little as possible. Again, more germs had probably infected the wounds then.

They'd festered as they'd journeyed south—and he hadn't said a word about it. Probably because he didn't want her to worry. Well, fat lot of good that did. She was worried now. Petrified, in fact.

And she had to do something. But what? She had no money, no identification. Didn't speak the language. She was a damn fugitive.

Every now and then, Kendric would moan or mumble, but otherwise he was totally out of it. It was terrifying, and Marlowe knew she had to get help for him. She had nothing of value that she could use to barter with someone to use their phone. All she had was the clothes on her back. Literally.

Kendric moaned again, and she stopped pacing to study him.

A plan formed in her mind. She hated to do it, but she literally had no choice.

She knelt next to him on the floor and reached for his arm. She quickly unfastened the fancy watch he was wearing, which they'd used to get them through Thailand and Cambodia. It had a GPS and a compass . . . and she hoped Kendric wouldn't be too upset with her for taking it to barter for use of a phone.

Feeling sick inside, and worried about Kendric, and nervous about going out by herself, Marlowe took a deep breath. She had to do it. She was literally the only one who could help him. It was very likely he'd die of sepsis if he didn't get antibiotics and fluids.

"I'll be back really soon," she told Kendric.

He didn't move.

"You got us this far, and I'll get you the rest of the way home. You're going to be fine, hear me, Kendric?"

Again, he didn't answer. Marlowe couldn't help but think back to a few days ago when he'd seemed so strong and larger than life. When he'd made love to her. When he'd made her feel beautiful for the first time in years.

She'd do anything to make sure her rescue didn't end in his death.

Her resolve strengthened, Marlowe leaned down and kissed him on the forehead before standing and heading for the door. She opened it and looked back one last time. Kendric was breathing way too fast, and she hated how vulnerable he looked lying there on the floor. Taking a deep breath, she turned and headed out to get him some help.

An hour later, she was hot, sweaty, frustrated, and as nervous as she'd ever been in her life.

The shop where she and Kendric were hiding was her first bust, followed by countless others. But she'd finally found a business owner near the airport who was willing to let her make a long-distance call on his shop phone, in exchange for Kendric's watch. She was never so glad that Kendric had made her memorize the phone number of his business as she was right that second.

She wasn't sure of the time difference, but figured it had to be about the same as it was when she was on the dig site in Thailand. Maine would be around eleven hours earlier than it was here . . . she hoped. Because that meant someone should be in the office. She carefully dialed the number, 555-824-8733, and held her breath.

"Hello, Jack's Lumber. How can I help you?"

For a moment, Marlowe was so relieved that someone answered, she couldn't even speak.

"Hello?"

"Hi, sorry! I'm here!" Marlowe blurted. "I'm calling for Chappy, Cal, or JJ. Please, it's an emergency."

"I'm April, their assistant," the woman on the other end of the phone said. "Can I ask who's calling?"

This was it. It was almost surreal to be talking to April, a woman who Kendric had talked about a lot. Someone he admired, and who he and his friends relied on.

"My name is Marlowe Kennedy, and I'm in Cambodia with Kendric Evans. He needs help, bad, and he made me memorize this phone number just in case, and I really need to talk to one of his friends."

To April's credit, she didn't ask questions that would waste more time. She simply said, "Hold on, please," then apparently put the phone against her chest or something—and yelled extremely loudly for her employers.

"Chappy! Cal! Jack! Get in here! Right now! It's an emergency!"

Glad that she was taking her call seriously, Marlowe waited what seemed an eternity before April came back on the line.

"I'm going to put you on speaker, hon. Everyone's here. Tell us what's going on."

Taking a deep breath, Marlowe did just that. "Again, my name is Marlowe, and I'm in Cambodia with Kendric. I'm an archaeologist who was on a dig in Thailand. I was accused of something I didn't do and ended up in prison. My brother works in DC, and he has a lot of connections, and I guess he got a hold of someone named Willis, who works with Kendric. He came to Thailand and got me out of prison, and we've been on the run. We managed to make it into Cambodia, near the airport, and were supposed to fly back to the States soon. But Kendric got sick."

Marlowe's voice hitched, and she forced herself to keep going. "I don't know how to get a hold of this Willis person, we don't have any money, Kendric is unconscious, and I'm scared to death he's going to die! Please, he's talked so much about all of you. Will you help him?"

"Marlowe, this is JJ. You know who I am?"

"Yes," she said, wiping away the tears that had fallen from her eyes as she'd been speaking. "You're Jackson Justice. You were the one who

125

decided to get out of the Army and play rock paper scissors to decide where to settle once you were all out."

"Holy shite, she *does* know who we are," muttered a man with a British accent.

"You're Cal Redmon, from Liechtenstein," Marlowe babbled. "You suffered the most as a POW because of those asshole captors, and Kendric admires you so much, you have no idea."

"I'm scared to hear what Bob said about *me*," a third man said.

Marlowe sighed. "And you must be Chappy. If you really want to know, he thought you were crazy for marrying a woman you'd known for days, who was trapped in your cabin during a snowstorm, but now he thinks you and Carlise were meant to be and he's very happy for you."

"You're in Cambodia?" JJ asked, redirecting the conversation.

Marlowe took another deep breath. "Yeah, near the Phnom Penh International Airport. Please don't be mad at Kendric! He lied to you about the sick aunt, and he's been working with Willis because he's been . . . unsettled . . . there in Maine. He loves it," she said quickly. "Loves working with you guys and the weather and everything, but he said he needed more. So he's been working with Willis to help rescue people overseas.

"But I think he's officially done with that. He told me more than once while we were trying to get to the airport that he thinks he can fulfill his need to help others in a different way. Maybe working with a rope rescue group or something. He loves all of you so much, he'd be devastated if you kicked him out of the business and stopped talking to him," she said, before realizing she was babbling again.

"Relax, Marlowe, we aren't kicking him out," JJ said.

"Although we *are* going to have words," Chappy said sternly.

"Can't believe the bloke didn't tell us what he was doing. What a wanker," Cal added.

"Will you help him?" Marlowe asked anxiously.

"Of course. Tell us where you are and what's wrong with Bob," JJ ordered.

Marlowe did her best to describe where they were staying. She couldn't remember the actual name of the shop, mostly because it wasn't in English, but she told Kendric's friends that it sold a variety of groceries, then described all the other shops around it. She went on to give them the highlights of her escape from the prison, and how she and Kendric had barely made it across the border.

"He scraped his back on the fence and then waded through really nasty water. We slept in a barn afterward, which I don't think helped. The scrapes are really gross now. Red and green, puffy, and there's a lot of pus coming out of them. I've cleaned them as best I can, but it's not helping. He's been delirious and in and out of consciousness.

"I don't care what happens to me, but please, *please*, can you come and get him? I'm afraid to bring him to a hospital, not that I know how I would even physically manage that. The Thai and Cambodian authorities are looking for us, and I can't let him go to prison for helping me. He did nothing wrong—"

"Did *you?*" Chappy interrupted.

Marlowe closed her eyes. "No," she whispered. "I swear. I don't use drugs. I don't sell drugs. I didn't have anything to do with the yaba pills that were found in my stuff. I'm pretty sure it was my coworker who planted them. I caught him stealing artifacts from the dig site. Ancient coins. And I think he turned me in so he could get away with it."

"Holy crap," April whispered.

"Who?" JJ asked sharply.

"Um . . . his name is Ian West," she answered, not sure why he wanted to know so badly. She closed her eyes, shaking her head as she added, "It doesn't matter. *Please.* I seriously don't care about myself. I'll go back to prison if that's what it takes to get Kendric help. He can't die. He can't! I'd never forgive myself."

Marlowe finally opened her eyes and saw the shopkeeper frowning at her. Her time on the phone was going to come to an end soon, and she needed these men to believe her.

"Can you give us a second to talk?" JJ asked.

His words didn't reassure Marlowe. "Yes, but . . . I don't know how much longer I'll be able to talk. The shopkeeper whose phone I'm using is looking impatient."

"It'll just take a minute. Do *not* hang up. Understand?" JJ ordered.

"Yes."

"Good. April, mute us for a second."

There was a beeping noise, and Marlowe expected to hear music or silence . . . but instead, she could still hear Kendric's friends. Whatever April had pushed, it wasn't the mute button.

"I can't believe Bob's been lying to us all these years!" Chappy exclaimed. "If he was bored, all he had to do was tell us. We would've gone with him on these rescue missions!"

"I think he knew that, but he probably also saw how happy we were to be here," Cal replied.

"None of that matters right now. We have to figure out how to get him out of Cambodia and to a hospital," JJ said urgently.

"Do you think the airport's been alerted? That he'll be blocked from leaving the country?" Chappy asked.

"I don't know. But it's a possibility. I need to figure out who this Willis person is and see what he had planned for their extraction," JJ said.

"What do we do about the woman? She's probably for sure on a watch list. It's not as if she can waltz into the airport and breeze through customs," Chappy observed.

"I can use my family's connections and get Bob out without too much of an issue," Cal said. "You guys know my parents pushed hard to get you three added to their unofficial-official list of people the royal family are willing to aid, after what you did for me when we were POWs. But that's not going to help this Marlowe woman. I mean, the royal protection extends to our direct relatives, of course, so Carlise and June are covered. But Marlowe isn't any relation. She's going to be on her own unless we can figure out how to help her."

"If you can get a plane headed to Cambodia," JJ said, "I'll see what I can dig up about her brother and Willis. There *had* to be a plan to fly her out. A fake ID and passport. It'll just take a while to figure it out and get the ball rolling again."

Marlowe's stomach rolled at the thought of being left behind to fend for herself, but she'd do it if it meant Kendric would get the help he needed. Still, she couldn't help but say "Excuse me?" when there was a lull in the conversation on the other end of the phone.

"What the hell, April? I thought you put it on mute?" JJ grumbled.

"I thought I did too! It's a new phone, I must've pushed the wrong button."

Marlowe wasn't quite so sure. Something in the other woman's tone made her think she'd left the line open on purpose. But she didn't have time to dwell on it.

"I'm sorry, but I heard what you were saying. And please don't think I'm going back on what I said earlier, about getting Kendric out and leaving me here. I'm not. I mean, that's fine. But . . . Cal, what you were talking about . . . Does it make a difference if I tell you that Kendric and I are married?"

There was dead silence on the line, and Marlowe panicked momentarily, thinking they'd been cut off. Then Chappy said, "Holy shit! Really?"

"Yeah. I wouldn't lie about that," Marlowe told them.

"Looks like he's moved as fast as we have," Cal said, sounding almost amused. "How did that happen? Because I know for a fact he wasn't married when he left here two weeks ago."

"We were on our way to the border, and at one of the safe houses, there was a woman who was old fashioned or very religious or something. She'd agreed to hide us for the day, but she didn't realize we were a man and a woman. I think she thought Marlowe was a guy's name. Anyway, the hiding space was tiny, and she refused to let us stay there together unless we were man and wife. We figured it wasn't a big deal, so . . . we agreed."

"You have any proof?" JJ asked.

"The lady gave us a marriage certificate before we left that night. It's in Thai, and probably isn't recorded yet or whatever," she felt compelled to point out. "And we only did it to avoid looking for another safe place to stay."

"Bob doesn't do *anything* he doesn't want to do," Chappy said. "He could've figured out something else instead of getting married if he'd really wanted to."

At the man's words, Marlowe's toes curled in the cheap shoes Kendric had found for her. She *had* been surprised at how quickly he'd acquiesced to getting married, but she'd figured he was even less interested in finding them another place to hide out for the day.

"I'm still wrapping my head around the fact that first Chappy, then Cal, and now *Bob* were all forced to share beds with women they ended up married to," April said, sounding quite happy for her friends and employers.

"That's that, then," Cal said, ignoring April's comment. "You and Bob are married, which means my people can get you both back to the States without fuss. Stay put, Marlowe. We'll come to you."

"Really? Soon?" Marlowe asked.

"Well, not me specifically," Cal said. "We're too far away to get there as fast as it sounds like Bob needs us to. Liechtenstein is closer. I'll make a call after we hang up. My people will have identification and passports for you and Bob, and hopefully there won't be a problem with customs. With the royal family vouching for both of you, it shouldn't be an issue."

It sounded too good to be true to Marlowe, but she wasn't going to complain. "Okay."

"Go back to Bob and stay put. They'll find you. I'll make sure a doctor is with the extraction team, and Bob'll get the help he needs on the way to Maine."

"Maine?" Marlowe asked in surprise. She figured they'd go to Cal's home country.

"Yeah. I'm guessing the favors I'm calling in will be enough to get you out of Cambodia, but they aren't going to want to harbor a fugitive in their country . . . political shite, you understand."

Marlowe wasn't sure she did, but she mumbled her agreement anyway.

"We'll fly you both into Bangor and get Bob to a hospital right away," Cal told her. "Your job is to keep him alive until my countrymen and women can get there. Got it?"

"Yes." Her response was firmer now. She was so relieved, she could cry. But she held back the tears. She couldn't fall apart now. She had to get back to Kendric.

"You did good, Marlowe," JJ said quietly. "Thank you for calling."

"Thank *you*," she said with a small shake of her head. "I didn't know what else to do."

"I can't wait to meet—"

The line abruptly went silent as April was speaking, and Marlowe looked over to see the shopkeeper had cut the connection.

He said something in rapid-fire Khmer, the official language of Cambodia, obviously letting her know her time was up. Marlowe handed the receiver back to him and thanked him in English, then quickly turned and headed out of the shop. She needed to get back to Kendric. Now that she knew help was coming, she felt cautiously optimistic.

That feeling lasted until she entered the room where Kendric was still lying on the floor. He hadn't awakened while she'd been gone. If anything, he seemed worse. His breathing was shallower, and when she lifted the sheet she'd placed over him, the wounds on his back looked even angrier than before.

"You have to hang on, Kendric," she whispered as she walked over to the last bottle of water he'd procured for them before he'd been too weak to do anything else. She poured some of the precious water onto a clean corner of the sheet and did her best to wipe away the green pus from his wounds. They needed stitching, and she'd kill for some antibiotic cream, but all she could do was try to clean out the wounds and wipe away the nasty infectious pus.

"Your friends are coming," she told him, ignoring the tears that dripped from her cheeks. "Please hang on. They're on their way. And we get to fly on a royal plane. Isn't that cool?"

She tried to get him to drink some of the water, holding his head up to make it easier, but she wasn't sure she was successful.

She kept talking to him. For hours she rambled, speaking until her voice was hoarse. She needed him to know that he wasn't alone, hopefully make him keep fighting the infection raging throughout his body.

Marlowe wasn't sure when to expect their rescuers. She didn't even know how they'd find them, but Cal seemed to think they wouldn't have any trouble locating them using the info she'd provided. She trusted Kendric's friends. She knew they'd help him.

She hoped Kendric wouldn't be too upset with her for telling them his secret about what he'd been doing behind their backs. But ultimately it didn't matter if he was mad. If he decided he never wanted to see her again. As long as he was alive and healthy, she'd deal with the consequences of her actions.

She'd done everything she could. Now all she could do was wait . . . and pray.

Chapter Ten

The extraction from Cambodia went surprisingly smoothly.

Four men and a woman showed up at the door of Marlowe and Kendric's room a very stressful sixteen hours later, and immediately got to work moving Kendric from the floor to a stretcher. The woman barked out orders in what sounded like German as she got an IV line started in Kendric's arm. She paused to lift the sheet and look at his back, made a concerned sound in her throat, then covered him up and gave more orders to the men.

Marlowe found herself following along behind their rescuers as they loaded Kendric into a van. They shuttled her inside, then raced off toward the airport.

The driver bypassed the main terminal and instead went to a smaller building. He flashed his identification at the man stationed at a security hut, and it seemed to Marlowe that they barely even slowed down. They drove straight to an airplane with the Liechtenstein flag painted on the side, and everyone jumped out of the van and began to assist with the stretcher.

The next thing Marlowe knew, she was walking up the stairs and into the luxurious plane.

The doctor was hovering over Kendric toward the back, while two of the men locked the stretcher into place to make sure it didn't move around when they took off.

"Please, have a seat," a woman said from next to her in accented English, making Marlowe jump. She hadn't even seen her approach.

"We'll be taking off as soon as the doctor gives the word," she went on. "Would you like something to eat? Or drink?"

Marlowe was extremely thirsty, but the thought of putting anything in her stomach right now made her nauseous. "No, thank you. I'm fine. When . . . how . . . don't we have to go through customs or something?"

The woman smiled. "It's been taken care of. I met with the authorities and showed them your passports."

She handed over two dark-blue passports that said *Fürstentum Liechtenstein* at the top. Under some sort of crest was the word *Reisepass*. In a daze, Marlowe opened one and saw her picture, one that she recognized from her American passport, which had been seized by the Thai authorities . . . and the name Marlowe Evans.

The other passport had Kendric's name and picture in it.

She looked up at the woman. "I don't understand," she whispered.

"Your husband is an unofficial member of the royal family, by decree." She shrugged. "It is not technically a legal passport, and they will be confiscated before you deplane, but it was the fastest way to get you out without a lot of hassle." She winked. "From what I understand, Thailand is looking for a Marlowe Kennedy, not Marlowe Evans. If you could please have a seat, we'll be in the air soon."

Marlowe sort of fell into the nearest seat. She was in shock. Cal had come through in a huge way. She wanted to cry in gratitude, but her eyes were already puffy and she didn't feel as if she had any tears left.

Twenty minutes later—after they were in the air, and Marlowe felt as if she could breathe, *truly* breathe, for the first time in a month and a half—she unsnapped her seat belt and made her way back to where Kendric was lying.

The doctor was writing in a chart, frowning as she approached.

"Will he be okay?" Marlowe asked.

The woman responded in accented English. "I believe so, yes. But it was a good thing we got there when we did. He's very sick. The infection had spread to his organs."

Alarm filled Marlowe. "But he'll be all right?"

"We've got fluids going, and a heavy dose of antibiotics. He needs stitches to close those wounds in his back, but that can't be done until the infection is under control. I've cleaned his injuries, including the wounds on his arms and hands. Knife?" she asked.

Marlowe nodded.

The doctor gave her a reassuring look. "We just have to wait for the antibiotics to do their thing. He'll be up and around in a few days."

"Really?" Marlowe said, hope coursing through her veins.

"Yes. He is young and strong. I am confident he will be fine."

Marlowe's knees almost gave out from under her, and she reached a hand out to brace herself on a nearby seat.

"Sit," the doctor ordered. "I should look you over too."

"No," Marlowe said with a shake of her head. "I'm fine."

"To be blunt, you do not look fine," the doctor said. "You are too skinny, and your cheekbones are sunken in. You are clearly dehydrated, and you could have an infection as well."

"I'll be okay once I've had a few good meals," Marlowe insisted. "Kendric's the one I'm worried about."

The doctor frowned but didn't push. "All right. But you should drink some water. Rehydrate. Eat something."

"I will," Marlowe promised, not entirely sure she *could* eat anything. But now that she knew Kendric was going to be okay, she'd at least have something to drink.

～

Several hours later, Marlowe felt as if she was going to drop. The flight to Maine was over eighteen hours long, and they still had eleven to go. While she was exhausted, she couldn't sleep. She was too worried about

Kendric. He hadn't woken up, and even though the doctor said he'd be okay, Marlowe couldn't rest until she'd spoken to him. Seen for herself that he was on the road to recovery.

She was sitting next to his stretcher when he made a whimpering noise in his throat. Marlowe immediately stood up and took his hand in hers. "Kendric?"

He didn't respond, but began to twitch as he lay there.

"Stand back," the doctor ordered.

But as soon as Marlowe let go of Kendric's hand, he began to thrash on the stretcher. "Marlowe!" he yelled.

The strength and volume of his shout made both her and the doctor jerk in surprise.

"Marlowe!" he shouted again. "Where are you? *Marlowe!*"

"I'm here," she said, but one of the men had taken hold of her arm, preventing her from returning to his side. "Let go of me!" she seethed, struggling to get out of his grasp.

"He's agitated," the doctor insisted.

"No shit!" Marlowe exclaimed, not caring how upset she sounded.

"Let her go! No! Marlowe, I'm coming!"

Kendric was now trying to push himself off the stretcher, and the doctor was attempting to hold him in place, which just seemed to agitate him more.

"He's going to pull out his IV if he doesn't stop. Come hold him down while I sedate him," the doctor told one of the men.

"No! Let me try to calm him down. Please!" Marlowe begged.

The doctor looked at Kendric, then at her, then back to her patient. Finally, she sighed and stepped back. "Let her go," she told the man holding Marlowe.

As soon as she was free, Marlowe raced back to Kendric's side. She grabbed his hand and put the other on his shoulder. "I'm here, Kendric. You're okay. I'm okay. Relax."

His eyes were open, but they stared into space, obviously not seeing much of anything. "Punky?"

"It's me. I'm here."

"Don't leave me. Don't ever leave me!"

His words made her heart turn over in her chest. "I won't. I'm right here."

Even though Kendric was out of it, he turned onto his side and tugged her closer.

"Wait, no—" the doctor began, but Marlowe was already moving. She climbed onto the stretcher and plastered herself to Kendric's front. His arm wrapped around her, clutched her to him with an iron grip.

The doctor said something in German, and Marlowe had a feeling it was probably a good thing she couldn't understand the language. She held her breath, praying she wouldn't be forced to move. Here in Kendric's arms, she felt better than she had in hours.

"Try to keep him calm," the doctor said after a moment, grabbing the sheet that had fallen to the floor during Kendric's struggles. She draped it over them both.

Closing her eyes, Marlowe sighed in relief.

And just like that, her eyelids felt impossibly heavy. She couldn't keep them open a second longer. She felt as if she was right where she belonged. In this man's arms. He'd held her like this often during their escape from Thailand, and it was where she felt the most safe.

She marveled that she could soothe him, the same way he calmed *her*. He was quiet now, his breathing slower, and thankfully his skin didn't seem quite as hot as it had been earlier. Marlowe prayed that meant the antibiotics were doing what they were made to do . . . healing the man she loved from the inside out.

Marlowe kissed Kendric's chest, then snuggled deeper into him. "Love you," she whispered.

She hadn't thought she'd said it very loud. Or that he'd even understand the words. So she was shocked when Kendric replied just as quietly, "I love you too."

Tears sprang to her eyes once again. She'd thought she was all cried out, but apparently she was wrong. Kendric wasn't exactly in his right mind, but she'd still treasure his words for the rest of her life.

She fell asleep seconds later. A deep, healing sleep, a result of too many hours of worry, stress, and terror that one or both of them would be caught and hauled back to Thailand and locked up.

~

A couple of hours later, Bob opened his eyes and tried to make sense of where he was. He didn't recognize his surroundings and racked his brain to try to figure out what the hell was going on. The only things he *did* recognize were the woman in his arms—her scent, the feel of her body snuggled against him—and, unfortunately, the pain in his back.

"Are you awake?" a female voice asked.

Jerking in surprise, and holding back a moan from the pain the movement caused, Bob twisted his neck to look over his shoulder. A woman he'd never seen before was standing behind him, spreading some sort of salve on his wounds.

"Yeah," he croaked.

"Good. Your wife was worried. I told her you'd be fine now that you were getting treated, but she wasn't convinced."

Bob put his head back down. He felt extremely weak, but the longer he was awake, the more his mind cleared. The last thing he remembered was arriving at the room Willis had arranged for him and Marlowe to hunker down in until he could arrange for their identifications and a flight out of Cambodia.

He could tell the plane they were on definitely wasn't a commercial bird. The woman treating his wounds had a German accent, and there were a few men scattered in the seats. They were wearing official-looking uniforms . . . and he suddenly recognized where he was.

"This is one of the royal planes from Liechtenstein," he said. "I recognize the flag on the backs of the seats."

It wasn't really a question, but the woman behind him answered anyway. "Yes. Your wife called your friends. Prince Redmon set things in motion for us to extract you. We are on our way to Maine, where the prince and the others will most certainly be waiting for you."

"What? How?" Bob stuttered.

"I do not know. I was called to the plane and briefed on your condition on the way to Cambodia. You will have to ask your wife when she wakes up what happened before we arrived."

Bob closed his eyes and tightened his hold on Marlowe. His wife. Damn if that didn't sound good. "Were there any issues getting us out?"

The doctor chuckled. "None. No one would dare mess with the royal family. You had the proper documentation, forged of course, and Liechtenstein passports."

Bob's head was spinning. Cal had somehow gotten him and Marlowe passports from his home country? Holy crap, the man had more pull than he'd expected. He owed him. Huge. Even though he knew Cal wouldn't let him do a damn thing to thank him.

"You would not calm until she climbed onto the stretcher with you," the doctor told him. "As soon as she did, she basically passed out. I don't think she's gotten any sleep recently. You should take better care of her."

Bob took the small rebuke to heart. He'd messed up. Big time. He'd known his wounds were infected, and yet he'd hidden that fact from Marlowe because he didn't want her to worry. He figured he at least had time to get back to the States before he'd have to worry about medical care. He'd obviously been wrong. By the time he got them to the room by the airport, he'd been in big trouble.

How exactly had Marlowe gotten them rescued? Everything was a big blank in his head, and he hated it. But he wasn't going to wake Marlowe to ask her. She was deadweight against him and obviously needed the sleep.

"You should get her checked out too. She's tiny. And she did not eat. I *did* get her to drink some water, but she needs much more."

Bob nodded, then inhaled sharply as the doctor probed one of the wounds in his back.

"Sorry," she said, not sounding particularly apologetic. "These need stitching, but the infection needs to come out first. I'm draining them now. There's some pain meds in your IV, but if you need more, let me know."

What she was doing hurt like hell, but Bob didn't ask for more narcotics. The pain was a result of his stupidity. Besides, he'd been through worse when he was a captive. "I'm good," he told her.

When the doctor was done with his back, she fussed with his IV for a moment, nodded at him, then walked around the stretcher to sit in one of the seats toward the front of the plane, giving him and Marlowe some privacy. Before walking off, she'd told him they had about three more hours to go before landing in Bangor. He'd clearly been out for a long time.

When they arrived, Bob had a feeling he'd have to answer to a lot of people. He needed to make sure Marlowe's brother knew she was safe and call Willis and update him, and he'd most definitely have to talk to his friends. Try to explain the secret life he'd been living.

He ran a hand over Marlowe's head, and was surprised when she stirred. He moved his hand to her nape and tightened his hold, supporting her head as she leaned back to look up at him.

"Kendric?"

"Yeah, Punky, it's me."

She immediately burst into tears, burrowing her face in his chest and crying all over him.

Figuring it was a release of the tension over whatever had happened while he'd been unconscious, Bob did his best not to panic. He simply held her tightly as she sobbed.

Before long, she sniffed and leaned back once more. "You're okay." It wasn't a question.

"I am," he assured her anyway.

"I was so worried."

"I'm so sorry—" he started, but she shook her head.

"Nothing to be sorry about," she told him.

Bob was relieved Marlowe hadn't tried to get up, to leave his embrace. He wasn't sure he would've been able to let her go. She felt perfect right where she was. As if she was meant to be in his arms.

He'd tried halfheartedly to resist his feelings for this woman as they fled Thailand and traveled across Cambodia, knowing he and Marlowe would eventually part ways. But even without knowing the details of how he'd gotten to be on this plane, his feelings had changed yet again. Or more honestly, deepened.

She'd taken care of them both while he was out of it. She'd managed to get them out of Cambodia safely, and he was even more proud of her than he'd been before, which was saying a hell of a lot, since he'd already been overwhelmed by how she'd dealt with everything.

"Want to tell me how we ended up on a royal Liechtenstein plane on our way to Maine?" he asked.

And his Marlowe, being her usual self, didn't hesitate. She told him everything.

How scared she'd been, how she'd taken his watch and traded it for a phone call. How she'd called Jack's Lumber and talked to his friends and April. How the doctor and the royal officers had shown up and whisked them to the airport and onto the plane. She told him about the forged passports and how the doctor insisted he was going to be all right.

And she admitted that she'd told his friends about what he'd been doing behind their backs, in order to explain who she was and how they'd come to be in their predicament.

She didn't leave anything out, and by the time she was done explaining, Bob felt a mixture of shame that he'd let her down so badly and immense pride at how well she'd coped.

"I should've given you Willis's number," he said softly when she was done.

"Yeah, but what's done is done," she said with a small shrug.

Her ability to forgive was astounding. His screwup could've resulted in her being thrown back into prison.

"Kendric, stop," she scolded, reading his mind. "We're okay. You're going to get better, and we'll be back home soon. Although I *am* mad at you about something."

Bob wasn't surprised. There were a lot of things she should be mad at him about. "Yeah?" he asked.

"You should've told me you were hurt from crawling under that fence. Especially after you went into that disgusting water," she huffed out, rising onto an elbow on the stretcher. "That was stupid. And not something I'd expect from a former Delta Force operative," she scolded.

"But it was something a man would do for his wife. For the woman he cares about. And this has nothing to do with me being stronger, or a man, or even a former soldier. In the moment, all I could think about was trying to protect you. Doing anything and everything to keep you safe."

Marlowe stared at him for a long moment before taking a deep breath. "I need to tell you something."

Bob tensed. What hadn't she already told him? Had she been hurt while getting them help? "What?"

"I love you."

It took a moment for her words to sink in. Before he could say anything, she went on.

"I'm not telling you that to try to trap you into anything. But these last twenty-four hours . . . when I thought you might die . . . it was awful. And I realized how much I care about you. If you'd died, I'm not sure I would've survived it. So I had to tell you how I feel. But I don't expect you to do anything about it. Or say anything. I just want you to know how amazing you are. And how good you make me feel. That's . . . that's all."

Bob's heart felt as if it was growing like the Grinch's did at the end of *How the Grinch Stole Christmas*. He'd thought this woman was brave before, but now he knew without a doubt that she was ten times braver than he'd ever be.

"It's a good thing you feel that way, since I feel the same."

She stared at him for a beat before blinking. "Really?" she whispered.

Bob vowed to never let a day go by without telling this woman how much he loved her. "Yes, really. I love you, Marlowe Evans. More than I ever thought I could love *anyone*."

"Holy crap."

He smiled at that. "It's also a good thing we're already married, because if we weren't, I might be bugging my friends to find a priest or officiant or whatever it's called to come to the hospital."

"I'm still not sure our ceremony was legal," she said with a small smile.

"I have a wedding certificate in my pocket that says differently," Bob said. "At least, I hope it's still in my pocket."

Marlowe nodded, and he relaxed.

"We'll have another ceremony when I get out of the hospital, just to be sure. But our anniversary will always be that day we said our vows back in Thailand."

Marlowe lowered herself and went back to snuggling into his chest. "It feels unbelievable that something good came out of my visit to Thailand. I mean, it's not a bad country. It's beautiful, in fact. There's so much history, and most of the people are so welcoming and openhearted."

Bob took a deep breath. His Marlowe had been mistreated horribly, and yet she still had the ability to be kind and generous toward the people of Thailand.

"Can we send money to that woman?"

He knew exactly who she was talking about. The one who'd insisted on them being married. "Yes. I'll get Willis on that."

"Good. Kendric?"

He smiled. He'd almost lost that. Hearing her say his name before asking a question. It was one of the million tiny things he already loved about her. "Yeah?"

"Don't scare me like that again. From here on out, if you get even the smallest splinter, I want you to tell me about it. I was so scared."

Bob tightened his hold on her. "I will. I promise."

She nodded. Several minutes went by, and he thought she was asleep again, but then she said, "I'm sorry I had to tell your friends about the rescuing-people thing."

"I'm not," he reassured her. "It was time. I didn't like lying to them, and honestly, the thrill of doing those missions has officially worn off. I like helping people, but I'm done putting myself in harm's way like that."

"Good. That's what I told them. I even told them what you mentioned to me in Cambodia. That you might see about getting on a rope rescue team or volunteer with a search and rescue group or something. You'd be amazing at either. Not that you aren't great at the tree business or leading hikers on the Appalachian Trail, I'm sure."

"I know what you meant. And while I'm looking forward to seeing what the possibilities are for my future, I've got something else to occupy my time now."

She looked up at him. "You do? What?"

"You."

He saw her eyes watering before she closed them.

"That is, if you want that. I want you to move to Maine with me, Punky. Live with me. I'll teach you to cook if you want, or I'll do all the cooking. You'll love Carlise and June, and April too. We'll find something for you to do if you want to work. Or if you want to keep traveling, I'll come along and be your bodyguard or something."

Her eyes opened at that. "No!" she blurted, then took a deep breath. "I don't want to travel anymore. I'm content staying home."

"Okay. All I'm saying is that whatever you want to do, we'll make it happen."

"I want to be with *you*," she whispered. "Have a family."

Bob's heart lurched. "Yes," he said fervently.

They smiled at each other.

"Does your back hurt?" she asked.

"No," he lied.

Marlowe rolled her eyes. "Whatever. So much for confessing every splinter."

Bob grinned. "You still look tired. We have a couple more hours before we land. Sleep, Punky."

"I'm not tired anymore," she said, but a huge yawn belied her words.

Bob chuckled. "Right. I hear you."

"Okay, maybe I'm a little tired. But just another hour. I want to have time to look presentable when I meet your friends."

"You're already presentable," he told her.

She rolled her eyes again. "I'm a mess," she said unselfconsciously. "My hair is probably sticking up everywhere, I stink, I'm dirty. I need to clean up before we land. I don't want your friends thinking you're with a wild jungle creature."

"You're *my* wild jungle creature," Bob said with pride. "And I love you exactly how you are."

She seemed to melt into his arms. "I love you too," she said shyly.

Bob palmed the back of her head and kissed her forehead gently. "Sleep, Punky. I've got you."

"I know you do," she replied, then promptly fell into a deep sleep.

Bob held her tightly. Lying on his side was uncomfortable, but he didn't move even an inch. This woman had literally saved their lives . . . and she loved him. Two things that he wouldn't have thought possible when he'd met her two weeks ago. Now she'd agreed to move to Newton with him. To have a family. He couldn't be more content than he was right that moment.

Chapter Eleven

Marlowe woke up groggy and confused. She opened her eyes and saw that she was still on the stretcher with Kendric, but they were being wheeled into a huge building, which could only be the hospital in Bangor.

"Hey . . . we . . . *what*? Kendric, you didn't wake me up," she scolded.

He chuckled. "I tried. You smacked me and told me to give you another ten minutes," he told her.

"I did not!" Marlowe said, horrified.

"All right, you didn't. But you were sleeping so soundly, I didn't have the heart to wake you up. You slept through the transfer to the ambulance and the ride here."

Marlowe turned her head left and right, and she saw three men walking alongside the stretcher as the automatic doors in front of them opened.

"Oh crap," she said under her breath, bringing a hand up to her hair to try to smooth it down at least a little.

But Kendric caught her hand in his and brought it to his lips. "You look fine."

Marlowe shook her head. She didn't. She'd seen her reflection in the mirror in the small bathroom on the plane, before she'd crawled into Kendric's arms. She was a mess. And she really *had* wanted to at least try to clean herself up before she met his friends. But it was too late now.

She lifted her chin. She had to make the best of the situation. It was what it was.

She and Kendric were wheeled down a hallway and into a room. The three men crowded in as well. She shifted in Kendric's grasp, and he squeezed her tight for a moment, as if he wasn't going to let her go, before leaning forward, kissing her forehead, and finally releasing his grip.

She swung her legs off the edge of the stretcher and hopped to the ground—and promptly would've fallen flat on her face if one of the men hadn't caught her arm.

"Easy," he said.

"Marlowe?" Kendric asked in concern.

"I'm fine. Just a little dizzy from getting up too fast," she reassured him. Then she turned to his friends and held out a hand to the man still clutching her elbow. "Hi. I'm Marlowe."

The man grinned. "Chappy."

"And I'm JJ," another guy said.

Marlowe shook his hand, then turned to the last man. She hadn't thought about what she was going to say when she met Cal face to face. Now, overwhelmed, she couldn't help throwing herself into his arms and giving him a tight hug.

The man chuckled and hugged her back.

"Thank you," she whispered. "Thank you so much."

"That's my line," Cal told her quietly. "You have no idea how much the guy on that stretcher means to me. What he's done for me. Getting you both out of Cambodia and back home was only the tip of what I owe him."

"Shut the hell up," Kendric said irritably from behind her. She smiled at Cal as the man released her, while Kendric continued, "You don't owe me crap, and you know it. I'm thinking I'm the one who owes *you* now."

"We can argue about who owes who later," JJ cut in. "I want a doctor to look at those wounds of yours. See what the next step is in making sure you're healed, so we can get you back on the job. While you were off caring for your *sick aunt*, we've been taking up the slack. There was a huge windstorm while you were gone, and we've been slammed."

Marlowe could tell by his expression that JJ was kidding, but she still felt guilty.

"About that," Kendric started. "I—"

JJ held up his hand. "Not now. We'll talk about it later, when you're healed up and home. For now, just know that we're good. All of us. Got it?"

Kendric nodded, and Marlowe was so relieved she felt light headed.

A man in a white coat strode into the room then and introduced himself as Dr. Galloway. He greeted Kendric and was all business when he asked him to turn onto his stomach so he could see what he was dealing with.

"Chappy, will you please take Marlowe . . . somewhere else?"

"What? Why?" she protested.

"Because he doesn't want you to have to watch what comes next," Chappy said, putting his hand on the small of her back. "It's going to hurt, and he's going to want to whimper and moan and cry like a little girl, and he can't do that if you're here."

Kendric rolled his eyes and shook his head at his friend in exasperation.

But because he didn't actually contradict him, Marlowe guessed there was at least some truth to what Chappy had said. She wanted to stay with him, but even *she* wasn't sure if she could look at his back again. She was queasy enough as it was.

"I'll take her down to the cafeteria and get her something to eat," Chappy said.

"And maybe find somewhere she can shower and get a change of clothes?" Kendric asked.

"That too," he agreed.

Marlowe walked toward Kendric and leaned over the stretcher. The doctor was waiting not so patiently behind him, but she didn't care. It felt weird telling him that she loved him in front of all the strangers in the room, so she simply kissed him gently on the lips. "As soon as you're in a room, I'll be there."

"No room," Kendric said firmly. "I want to go home."

Marlowe frowned. She straightened and said sternly, "You'll do whatever the doctor tells you to do. And if that means staying here for the next month, that's the plan."

The guys all chuckled, even Kendric. "Usually I'd do whatever you wanted, Punky, but not this time. I want to go home."

When Marlowe was ready to argue with him some more, he stopped her before she could get a word out. "Besides, you'll be there to make sure I don't do anything stupid. Right?"

She felt all gooey inside. "Yeah," she whispered.

"Right. Then go with Chappy. Eat. Shower. Change. By the time you're finished, the doc should be done torturing me, and we can go home."

"Okay," she said meekly.

"Okay," he agreed. Then he looked up at Chappy and gave him a nod.

Marlowe felt Chappy's hand at her elbow, and she let him lead her out of the room. It felt wrong leaving Kendric, but he was in good hands. There was no chance someone would burst into the room and haul him away to a dark prison cell somewhere. They were both safe . . . and it felt unbelievable.

≈

"Talk to me," Bob ordered JJ. He was lying on his stomach as the doctor cleaned out and stitched his wounds. The heavy dose of antibiotics he'd gotten on the way to Maine was already working extremely quickly. While he wasn't infection-free, the doctor thought it would be all right to sew the worst of the wounds shut.

Marlowe was right. The doctor didn't want to send Bob home, but he wasn't budging on that. He'd have Marlowe with him, and he had no doubt she'd hover and do whatever the doctor ordered. At the slightest indication that something was wrong, or if he wasn't healing as fast as she thought he should, she'd have his butt right back at the doctor's office.

Having someone watching over him—no, having his *wife*, who loved him, hovering and being worried about him—felt incredible. While healing from his injuries after being held captive, he'd had no one. Other than his friends, who were dealing with their own injuries. He'd been on his own, and he really hadn't minded in the least. Now, knowing just how much he'd missed out on had him anxious to soak up every ounce of Marlowe's love and concern.

While the doctor had given him a local anesthetic, Bob could still feel the pinch and slight sting as the man worked on his back. He needed a distraction, and talking with JJ and Cal would do just that.

"Tell me how pissed you guys are. Tell me what Marlowe said when she called. Tell me how the hell I'm here right now."

"I'm not pissed," JJ said. "I'm not," he insisted, when Bob gave him a skeptical look. "I'm more hurt than anything else. You should've told us. Should've told *me*. I would've understood."

Bob shook his head. "I'm not sure *I* understood," he told his best friend. "I was completely fine with moving here and starting the business. I still am. But after a few months, I got restless. Antsy. I needed more."

"More what?"

"Excitement. The adrenaline rush I got when we were on missions. At first, it was great. I'd leave, do what I needed to do, be back within a week. I got paid well, you guys were safe here in Maine, and I was helping others. But now . . ." Bob's voice trailed off.

"Now?"

"More things went smoothly than not on this mission . . . at least until the end there. Willis's plan to break into the prison worked, even if it was insane. Marlowe got out, I met up with her, and we made our way across the country. But with every day that passed, the more time I spent with Marlowe . . . something changed."

"You love her," Cal said, speaking up for the first time.

"Yeah. Love actually seems like such a tame word for how I feel about her. She's strong. And brave. And resilient. She did as I asked and didn't complain even once, even though she was under tremendous stress and had every right to. When that woman in Thailand suggested we get married, I let Marlowe believe she was talking me into it, but honestly? I didn't even blink."

"It's a bloody good thing that you are," Cal said. "It would've been nearly impossible to convince my people to get her out, considering she was a wanted woman, without her being connected to you legally."

"Thank you for that again," Bob said with feeling.

"You're welcome. And if you thank me again, I'm gonna get pissed." Bob grinned at his friend.

Cal rolled his eyes. "Shite. Now you're going to thank me every bloody day just to irritate me, aren't you?"

"Probably." Bob turned his gaze back to JJ. "Talk to me now about Willis. And Ian West. And her brother."

"What about them?"

"Don't do that. I know as soon as you heard their names from Marlowe, you were all over it. You've had a day and a half to look into them. Tell me what you found out."

JJ sighed. "Fine. I tracked down Willis. He was relieved to know you two were safe. When he didn't hear from you about the plans for getting on a plane, he started to get concerned."

"Yeah, I screwed up and didn't give Marlowe any of his info. I didn't think she'd need it."

"But you made her memorize the number to Jack's Lumber," JJ said.

"If anything happened, I knew you guys would take care of her. And you did."

"Of course we did, you arsehole," Cal said.

The men all chuckled.

"Right. And her brother?"

"He's aware that she was flown here. I'm guessing he's going to be making a trip to Maine sooner rather than later," JJ said.

Bob wasn't surprised. He was glad, actually. If it hadn't been for Tony getting a hold of Willis, he never would've met Marlowe, and she'd still be rotting away in that prison in Bangkok. "And Ian West?"

"That situation is a little trickier," JJ hedged.

Bob braced as his friend continued.

"He arrived back to his home in Boston nearly six weeks ago."

"Really?" Bob asked in surprise. He'd figured the man would probably want to come back to the US to off-load the coins, but if he'd gotten back weeks ago, that meant he hadn't even completed his monthlong obligation on the dig. Instead, he'd left shortly after Marlowe had been arrested.

"Yup. Apparently, he had a family emergency and had to leave Thailand."

"Yeah, right. Family emergency, my ass. He wanted to get back here to sell the damn coins he stole from that dig," Bob seethed.

"I've got Tex looking into figuring out how he's planning to off-load them. It's not like he can take out an ad on social media or in the newspapers," JJ said.

"And we're not messing around this time. We dragged our feet with June's situation. Got complacent. That's not happening again," Cal said firmly.

Bob nodded. They really had screwed the pooch with the situation with June's stepmother and sister. They'd had a good idea the sister's "stalker" was a ruse, that she and her mom would do anything to get Cal's attention—and his money. But they hadn't expected them to go so far as to hire someone to kill June. No one would make that mistake again, including Tex.

"So what's he finding?"

"Nothing yet, but he's scouring the dark web for any mention of ancient coins for sale. He promised he'd be in touch soon. He wants to make up for what happened to June, even though we keep telling him that wasn't his fault," JJ said.

"If West finds out Marlowe isn't in that prison in Thailand anymore, he could panic. Do something stupid—like contact the authorities. Technically, Marlowe's still a fugitive," Bob said, voicing the concern that had been rattling around in his brain for a few days, ever since they'd made it into Cambodia and the chances of them getting back to the US had increased exponentially.

"We know. We're not going to let your wife out of our sights," Cal told him firmly. "She'll either be with you, or with one of us while visiting our women, or she can hang out at the office with April. No one's touching one hair on her head. No way."

Bob relaxed a bit at hearing his friend's declaration. Cal, more than anyone, knew how it felt to have someone he loved almost taken from right under his nose.

"She needs to know what's going on, though," JJ warned. "To make sure she's aware of her surroundings at all times."

Uneasiness swept through Bob. Not because he wanted to keep anything from Marlowe, but because he wasn't sure how she'd react. He had a feeling she wouldn't be cowed by her former coworker. She'd want to stop him. Make sure he didn't profit from the theft of the priceless artifacts she'd caught him stealing. "I'll talk to her when we get home," Bob told his friends.

"She's gonna need stuff. Does she live near her brother? Will he bring any of her things up?" JJ asked.

Bob shrugged. "I don't know. She was gone so often on digs, going from one country to the next, she doesn't currently have an apartment stateside, just a storage locker with most of her things."

"I'll look into that," JJ said. "In the meantime, April will help her out."

"June too," Cal immediately agreed. "And you know Carlise will want to be in the thick of things."

"Expect to have visitors soon, brother," JJ said with a small grin. "April and the others weren't happy to be left back in Newton. They wanted to come with us to Bangor. But we thought it might be good not to overwhelm you and Marlowe from the get-go."

"Thanks," Bob said. But deep down, he wouldn't have minded if the women had come. He wanted Marlowe fully merged into his life, and with his friends, as soon as possible. He wanted her to get to know Carlise and June and April. Because he had no doubt they'd all hit it off without any issues.

Then he thought of something else. "I need a favor."

"Anything."

"Name it."

And that was why he loved these guys so much. "Marlowe can't cook. I'm not disparaging her, it's just a fact. She'll tell you that herself. And I'm not sure how much I'm going to want to be on my feet the next few days. Can you guys arrange to have some meals delivered? Don't go overboard," he warned. "But Marlowe needs to gain back the weight she lost while in prison, and I'm not sure ramen, SpaghettiOs, and chicken nuggets will be the best thing for her right off the bat."

His friends laughed.

"Consider it done. We'll make sure you guys have some healthy meals until you're back on your feet," JJ said.

"Appreciate it. One more thing," Bob said. "For the record . . . those pills weren't hers. Ian set her up."

Cal looked pissed, and JJ's lips pressed into a tight line.

"I can't believe you even felt the need to say that," Cal said with a shake of his head. "We know you wouldn't have taken the job at all if you thought she was guilty of the charges. We know you, Bob. You might have been a wanker and gone behind our backs, lied to us about a sick aunt, and pretended to be happy when you weren't, but you aren't the kind of person who sticks his neck out for a liar and a drug dealer."

Even though his words were harsh, Bob sighed in relief. "Thanks, Cal."

"Whatever. Stop thanking me," he said, turning for the door. "I'm gonna go call June so she stops worrying."

When he was gone, Bob turned to JJ. Cal seemed certain Marlowe wasn't selling drugs . . . but JJ hadn't said a word. "So? Do *you* believe that she wasn't involved?"

"Of course. All I had to do was take one look at the way she clung to you on that stretcher to know she's innocent."

Bob tilted his head as he stared at his friend. "Yeah?" he probed lightly.

"Yeah," JJ confirmed. "Like Cal said, we *know* you, Bob. You wouldn't have married her, wouldn't have risked your friendship with us, risked your damn life, if you weren't completely sure she hadn't done what she was accused of. And the way you held on to *her* told me everything else I needed to know. You love her, and that says it all for me."

Bob's throat got tight. He didn't deserve such loyal friends. "I didn't understand Chappy and Cal. Didn't get how they could've fallen so hard for their wives in such a short time. But from the moment I laid eyes on Marlowe, she was under my skin. The longer I was around her, the harder I fell. When that Thai woman said we had to be married before she'd allow us to stay in her home? I was secretly glad. *Excited.* She means the world to me, JJ. And I hate that the man who put her in prison is still out there. Living free with no consequences."

"He'll pay for what he did," JJ said firmly. "We'll make sure of it."

Bob inhaled sharply and bit back a groan when the doctor probed one of his wounds deeply.

"Sorry," Dr. Galloway said. "The Liechtenstein doctor did a good job of cleaning these wounds, but I just want to make sure all the infection is scraped out before I close this last gnarly slice."

"I'm gonna go check on Marlowe and Chappy. And let April know what's up. You need anything?" JJ asked.

Bob wanted to tell him that, yeah, he needed Marlowe . . . but he merely shook his head. "Don't forget about me. I want to go home today," he warned. "Don't play games with me on this, JJ. Please."

"I hear ya. We'll get you home, don't worry."

"Thanks."

"I'm glad you're all right," JJ said, putting his hand on Bob's shoulder briefly. "I admit that when Marlowe told us where she was, where *you* were, I was shocked. But my mind immediately turned to how we were going to get you home. You're my brother, Bob, and to steal a Navy SEAL saying, a brother doesn't leave a brother behind. I'll be back up later to check on you and to make sure the discharge papers are in the works."

And with that, one of his three best friends in the world left the room.

Bob lowered his head and rested his cheek on his hand as the doctor finished cleaning and stitching his back. He'd had a close call. He knew that more than most people. It was only thanks to Marlowe and his friends that he was home and on the mend.

Some people would look at his wife and dismiss her as weak. Because of her size, because she was a woman, but he knew better. She was stronger than just about anyone he knew. And he'd spend the rest of his life making sure she knew how capable she was. That she felt loved down to her core.

He also made a mental vow to ensure Ian West paid for what he'd done. For setting up Bob's woman and getting her thrown into jail for what would have been the rest of her life. As long as the man suffered no consequences for his actions, he'd likely do it again. Steal a country's heritage right out from under their noses, and if caught, throw some other innocent man or woman under the bus.

Well, that wasn't happening as long as Bob was alive. Ian West would rue the day he hurt Marlowe. Period.

≈

Marlowe felt like a completely different person after the long hot shower she'd had at the hospital. Chappy had patiently stood guard while she'd scrubbed every inch of her body three times and washed her hair twice.

Then he'd led her to the cafeteria and wouldn't let her leave until she'd finished the entire plate of food he'd bought. He'd taken her to the gift shop next, standing there with his arms crossed, again not budging until she'd picked out a T-shirt, socks, and a ridiculously comfy pair of slippers for herself, and a shirt for Kendric. He'd easily scrounged up a pair of scrub pants for her, and she had to admit she felt one hundred percent better by the time they met back up with Kendric.

The doctor discharged him—with a frown and two full pages of discharge information, which Marlowe promised to follow to the letter. And the ride to Newton in Cal's fancy SUV was eye opening. She'd never sat in a car seat as comfortable or felt leather so soft.

But by the time they arrived at Kendric's apartment, it was obvious he was in a great deal of discomfort. Marlowe had no concept of what time it was, other than it was nighttime because it was dark outside. Her internal clock was completely messed up by all the international travel and the sleep she'd had while on the way to Maine.

JJ, Chappy, and Cal helped get Kendric into his apartment and onto his bed. JJ said something about being back in the morning with food, but Marlowe barely heard him as she was more concerned about making sure Kendric was settled.

It wasn't until everyone had left and it was just her and Kendric in his room that she had a moment to reflect on everything that had happened.

"Punky? Come here," he said, holding out a hand.

He was on his belly in his huge bed, wearing only a pair of boxer shorts. Bandages covered the wounds on his back.

She walked over to the bed and sat next to him.

"Are you okay?" he asked.

Marlowe blinked in surprise. "Yes, why? I should be asking you that."

"Because you've been through a lot recently. I feel as if you haven't had any say in what's happened to you in a very long time. And I don't want you to think you're stuck here. Or that you have no other choices. My cell phone should be around here somewhere, I never take it when I'm on a mission. It probably needs charging, but you can call your brother and get him to come pick you up at any point. I think he's already planning on coming up to check on you, but you can speed that up if you want."

"You think I want to leave?"

"Do you?" Kendric countered.

For the first time, Marlowe felt uneasy. Was this his way of *asking* her to leave without having to come right out and say it? Did he regret saying he loved her? Had he simply been grateful for her help, and now, back with his friends and safe at home, in a familiar setting, he'd changed his mind?

"Shit. I don't like that hesitation," he muttered. He went up on an elbow and didn't quite hide the wince from the pain the movement caused. "For the record, I want you here. With me. In my bed. As my wife. I love you, Marlowe. So much it scares me. I don't want you to leave, but I'd never force you to do *anything* you don't want. If you want to go stay with your brother for a while, get your bearings, I won't stand in your way."

"I don't want to go," she said quickly, relieved beyond what she could express in words. "I love you too, Kendric. I think I have since you first appeared out of nowhere when I got outside that prison."

"Good. Just one more thing then, before we get some sleep."

"Yeah?" she asked when he didn't continue.

"I need you to find our wedding certificate and pin it to the wall where it belongs."

Marlowe grinned, and butterflies swam in her belly. She immediately stood and went out to the other room, where Cal had dropped the bag containing their clothing. Kendric had also been given a clean pair of scrub pants to wear home. The T-shirt he'd worn in Cambodia had been discarded before they'd even boarded the plane, but the pants were inside the bag. She reached into the back pocket and pulled out the folded and battered piece of paper. She unfolded it as she walked back to the bedroom, where Kendric was waiting for her.

He watched as she did her best to smooth out the wrinkles and looked around for something to pin it to the wall.

"There's a bowl of tacks on my dresser," Kendric said.

Marlowe laughed. "Do I dare ask why?"

"No."

She chuckled again. She really didn't care why her husband had a random bowl of thumbtacks in his bedroom. Picking up a red one, she pointed to an empty space above the headboard. "There?"

"Perfect."

She didn't think twice about putting a small hole in the document. Later she'd get it framed, and the hole would add just a little more character to the already ragged document.

"Perfect," Kendric said. "Now, come to bed."

He held out a hand, and Marlowe hesitated for only a beat before reaching for the hem of the T-shirt she had on. It had a silhouette of Bigfoot with a mountain next to him and the word **MAINE** in big block letters underneath. It had made her smile when she'd seen it in the gift shop, and she hadn't been able to resist.

She dropped it onto the floor and shoved the scrub pants over her hips. She wasn't wearing a bra. She'd tossed the prison-issue bra while still in Cambodia, and she didn't really need one anyway. When she climbed under the covers next to her husband, he immediately turned onto his side and gathered her into his arms. They both sighed with contentment.

"I don't think I'll be able to sleep without you ever again," he murmured into her hair. "Before meeting you, I can't remember the last time I didn't wake from a nightmare. It's a miracle. *You're* my miracle."

Marlowe didn't bring up how he'd screamed for her on the plane, or in that farmer's barn in Cambodia. She didn't like remembering the desperation she'd heard in his tone. If it helped him sleep, she'd spend every night for the rest of her life right where she was.

"Welcome home, Punky," he said softly.

She sighed with contentment. She *was* home. For most of her adult life, she'd felt as if she were a dandelion seed blowing in the wind. Not having a place to settle, always going with the flow, from one job to another. But being in Maine, with Kendric . . . it was like she was finally where she was meant to be.

She felt his lips on her temple and smiled, snuggling into him even more. Having his bare skin on hers felt divine. Made her think about their tryst in that barn in Cambodia. Made her remember how he'd felt inside her. How he'd made her come.

She wanted that again. But for now, she reveled in the feeling of being safe. And loved.

Chapter Twelve

Bob felt almost like his old self again. The past week and a half had been spent getting to know Marlowe without the pressure and stress of being fugitives on the run. They'd slept in, watched TV, visited with their friends, and spent three days with her brother, who'd shown up the day after they'd arrived in Newton.

It was obvious how close brother and sister were. They'd heard Tony's side of how terrified he'd been when he'd learned of Marlowe's imprisonment, and how he'd done everything legally possible to get her out. When that hadn't worked, he'd turned to Gregory Willis. Apparently, the FBI agent had seen the advantage of Tony owing him a favor in the future. And, coincidentally, Willis also had a friend who'd been incarcerated for political reasons in Beijing in the past, and it had taken two years of negotiations to get him home. Turns out, he was especially sensitive to someone being locked up abroad for something they didn't do.

The reunion between Tony and Marlowe was emotional, and everyone who'd witnessed it—basically all Bob's friends, who'd also been visiting at the time—had been thoroughly moved.

The atmosphere changed a bit when Tony found out that Marlowe and Bob had gotten married while overseas.

The man wasn't happy at first, assuming Bob had taken advantage of his sister's desperate situation. Bob had managed a few minutes to sit down with him privately and reassure him that in no way would he ever

Susan Stoker

hurt his sister. That Marlowe was his first priority. His sincerity must've
gotten through to the man, because when he left to go back to his job
and family in DC, he'd shaken Bob's hand and told him to look after
Marlowe. It felt like approval, which meant the world to Bob.

His stitches had already been removed, and while he was stiff and
a little sore, and still needed to take the antibiotics he'd been prescribed
for at least another ten days, he felt pretty damn good.

Marlowe was putting on some of the weight she'd lost, with the
help of Carlise, June, and April. The three ladies had been awesome,
coming over every day, bringing delicious meals, then staying to get to
know Marlowe. Watching her click with his friends' women had made a
warm feeling bloom deep inside Bob. He wanted everyone to get along,
because if they did, the chances that maybe Marlowe would want to stay
increased. And Bob really wanted her to stay.

He hadn't talked to her about Ian yet, but after a conference call
with Tex, he knew it was time. Tex had finally found a post on a dark
web auction site for the coins Ian was trying to sell, and it seemed there
were some interested buyers. He'd also informed Bob and his friends
that Ian was still in touch with a couple of locals who were on the dig
in Thailand.

Without having to be told, Bob knew that meant someone could
mention Marlowe's escape to Ian—if they hadn't already. And that
would make the man justifiably nervous.

Marlowe needed to be brought up to speed, so she could watch her
back and have a say in what happened next.

He hated to bring up bad memories, as it seemed she was settling
into life here in Newton extremely well, but it had to be done. He just
hoped the news wouldn't scare her back to her family in DC.

The more time Bob spent with Marlowe, the more he *wanted* to
spend with her. And it wasn't about sex, although he was looking forward to getting the all clear from his doctor to make love to her again.

No, it was about waking up with her snuggled next to him. About
teaching her how to cook, and laughing together when her attempts

were complete failures. It was about watching Marlowe get to know his friends and their women, and seeing her blossom with her newfound freedom.

He also hadn't realized just how lonely he'd been until Marlowe. Maybe that was the reason he'd felt so unsettled since leaving the service, always looking for ways to stay busy. Even though his days were much the same as they'd been before he'd gone to Thailand, they felt much more fulfilling now. He was looking forward to a future he hadn't thought possible.

Bob had asked JJ to come over when he spoke with Marlowe about the situation with Ian West, and he was making sloppy joes for lunch in preparation for his friend's arrival. Marlowe was currently in the living room speaking with Tony on the phone. He could hear her reassuring her brother that she was fine. That no, she wasn't bored, and everyone she'd met had been welcoming and extremely nice.

The fact that she didn't feel the need to talk to Tony behind closed doors, didn't mind if he overheard her side of the conversation, was just another thing that made him feel closer to her.

Eventually she hung up and wandered into the kitchen. She hopped up on one of the barstools around the small island and rested her chin in her hand. "I feel bad," she said.

"About what?" Bob asked.

"That you're the one who's injured, and you've been doing all the cooking."

"Do you *enjoy* cooking?"

She looked surprised. "Um . . . not particularly. You know that."

"Then why should you?"

"Because you were hurt. Because I want to help out around here. Because I don't want you to think I'm taking advantage of you in any way."

Bob couldn't help but chuckle. "I was hurt, but I'm fine now." *Fine* might be a stretch, but with every day that passed, Bob felt more and more like his old self. "And you *do* help around here," he went on. "You folded all our clothes yesterday, changed the sheets on our bed, and you put all the dishes away. And as far as taking advantage of me goes . . . you aren't. Not by any stretch of the imagination. I love having you here, Punky. I never thought much about living with a woman, but you make it so incredibly easy."

"Kendric," she complained softly. "You need to stop being so nice."

"Why?" he asked, genuinely wanting to know. He stopped stirring the meat and turned to look at her.

"Because."

"That's not an answer," he chided gently. "And I'm never *not* going to be nice to you. I want to spoil you. Look after you. Make your life as easy as I can make it."

"Can I do the same for you?" she asked with a tilt of her head.

"Don't you know? You already are. I've been a bachelor a long time. Done my own cooking and cleaning. Washed my own clothes. Mopped my own floors. Woke up alone, went to bed alone. Having you here? Sharing the daily chores? Lying in my arms when we sleep? It feels amazing. I'll do whatever I have to in order to keep you happy."

"I am," she said without hesitation.

"Me too," he agreed. Then he walked around the island and stood in front of her chair. Thanks to the high stool, her head was just about level with his own. He took her face in his hands and leaned in. "It's been more than a week. How are you feeling? And be honest. You had that nightmare last night . . . Want to talk about it?"

Marlowe took his wrists in her hands and met his gaze. "I'm good, Kendric. I mean, yeah, I have moments where it feels surreal that I'm here. Safe, free. But honestly, I feel more settled and secure than I have in a very long time. I used to stress about what job I would be assigned to next. Where in the world I'd be. But knowing that next week I'll wake up in the same place I am now . . . it's a relief."

Her words settled in Bob's soul. "Good."

"What about you?" she asked. "Have you been dreaming? I mean, I've been sleeping hard most nights, and I don't want you to hide your nightmares from me. I want to help you if you're having them."

He hadn't thought about it until right this moment, but Bob was amazed to realize that he couldn't remember having one nightmare since he'd gotten home. Oh, he'd had dreams, but they involved either Marlowe and him naked together, pleasing each other, or faceless children running amok as he and his friends watched with tolerant and loving glances.

"I'm not," he said in awe.

"You aren't what?" Marlowe asked with a frown.

"Having nightmares. I haven't dreamed about being a captive since we got home."

She stared at him with wide eyes. "Really? You aren't lying about that to try to make me feel better?"

"Yes. And no, I'm not lying."

"That's awesome," she said with a huge smile.

"It's you," Bob told her. "Something about holding you in my arms, having you by my side, seems to calm the demons in my head."

He wasn't surprised when Marlowe shook her head. "It's not me," she insisted.

"You can think that, but you're wrong," he said firmly.

"Well, I'm glad either way," she told him. "But I also don't want you to hide them from me. If you have them, you have them. We'll deal. Okay? Don't be embarrassed or anything."

Bob wasn't sure he could be embarrassed about anything around this woman. "Same goes for you. I know how awful nightmares can be. They can wipe you out and make you feel as if you didn't get any sleep. That happens, we'll take a nap or something so you can feel rested."

She smiled at him. "Okay."

"Okay." Then Bob leaned down and touched his lips to hers. They both moaned as the chaste kiss quickly bloomed into something more. Bob's hand speared into her short hair and held her still as he deepened their kiss. Her fingers curled into his chest as she gave as good as she got.

165

When the doorbell pealed through the apartment, both of them jerked in surprise.

Bob pulled back and stared at his woman for a long moment. She licked her lips, which were plump from their kiss. The doorbell sounded again.

"We should get that," she said.

"Yeah," Bob agreed, but he didn't move.

She smiled, then bit her lower lip.

"Tonight," he growled. "Tonight, I'm going to show you how proud I am that you're my wife. How happy I am that you're here. How much I appreciate everything you did for me when I was out of it."

"Did you talk to the doctor?" she asked, her eyes gleaming with interest and lust.

"No. But I know my body," he said. When she frowned, Bob ran a thumb over her bottom lip. "I'll be careful."

The bell rang again, over and over, as if JJ was officially tired of waiting for them to open the door.

Bob would keep his friend outside forever. Marlowe's response was more important right this moment.

"Okay," she said shyly.

Possessiveness swept through Bob's body. His dick immediately hardened at the thought of being inside this woman once again. Of coming home.

"Okay," he agreed. Then he leaned down and kissed her again— keeping it short this time—before running his fingers over her cheek, then stepping away to answer the door.

"Keep your pants on!" he yelled as he reached for the knob.

As expected, JJ was standing on the other side of the door, grinning like a lunatic. "About time," he told his friend.

"Whatever."

"Smells good," JJ said as he entered.

His comment reminded Bob that he needed to finish up their lunch. He shut the door behind JJ and headed back to the kitchen.

One part of him didn't want to have this conversation. He'd prefer to take care of Ian West himself, without any involvement from Marlowe. But that wouldn't be fair. And she could protect herself better if she had all the same information they did.

Not that Ian had made any indication that he was going to seek her out, but Bob didn't want to take the chance.

The three of them made small talk as he prepped their lunch, and Bob couldn't take his eyes off Marlowe. She had a way of making everyone around her feel comfortable. As if they'd been friends their entire lives. He'd seen it happen with Carlise, June, and April, and she was doing it now with JJ.

When they finished their sloppy joes, Bob took their dishes to the sink and left them there soaking, and they all headed to the small living area. Bob sat next to Marlowe on the couch, and JJ took the armchair to their right.

"Have you heard from Ian?" JJ asked Marlowe, getting right to the heart of the reason why he was there.

Her brow furrowed. "No. Why? Is he okay? What's happening with the coins?"

Bob wasn't surprised she wanted to know if he was all right. Even after all the man had done to her, she still didn't have it in her to really wish anyone ill.

"He's fine," JJ said.

"Darn," Marlowe muttered.

Bob couldn't stop the bark of laughter that left his lips. So much for him thinking Marlowe was as sweet as pie. Even JJ chuckled.

"Sorry, that was rude," Marlowe said with a shrug. "But seriously, what he did was awful. Not only did he steal from our dig site, he got me in serious trouble when he thought I might tell on him."

"Well, he's home in Boston, still living in his parents' house," JJ said. "But our sources indicate that he's trying to sell the coins and has a potential buyer."

"No! We can't let him get away with that!" Marlowe protested.

"We're working on making sure those coins don't end up in someone's personal collection," JJ said.

"How?" she asked.

He frowned. "We know he's had some interest from a few people on the dark web, but the offers have been made through third parties, from people who are very good at covering their tracks. But not good enough. Our guy, Tex, has been able to get in touch with two people who put in bids, and when they realized their real identities had been discovered—and the authorities notified—their interest waned, of course."

"But there are others who still want to buy the coins? For how much?" Marlowe asked.

"Yes, and the top offer at the moment is one million each."

"Three million dollars? Holy crap!" Marlowe exclaimed. "I knew they were worth a lot, but I didn't expect them to sell for *that* much."

"Yeah."

"So . . . how are we going to stop the sale from going through if we don't know who the buyer might be?" she asked.

JJ sighed. "We're working on that, with the help of our guy. The FBI is working on it too. But there's a major issue with trying to make Ian turn in the coins instead of selling them, and it involves you."

"Me?" Marlowe asked.

"Yes. The issue is that any trouble we cause for Ian, he can turn around and cause for you right back."

"What do you mean?"

"He can tell the authorities that you're an escaped convict from Thailand, Marlowe. If he finds out you're involved in trying to stop the sale of those coins, he can potentially get you thrown back in prison—unless there's solid proof that he planted those drugs in your tent."

"Can we go to the press?" Marlowe asked. "I mean about the coins? Give them an anonymous tip?"

"Maybe. Although I'm not sure the story will get the publicity we want or need in order to spook the buyer enough to halt the sale."

"Yeah, coins aren't sexy," Marlowe agreed. "It's a problem for many of the digs I've been on. People are eager to offer grants when what we're digging for is interesting and exciting enough to gain worldwide attention, but when it's a bunch of random bones, or shards of pottery, or just a few coins, it's often not worth their time or attention."

No one said anything for a full minute.

Then Marlowe quickly straightened. It was obvious she had an idea—and somehow, Bob knew he wasn't going to like it.

"What if I called him? Told him that I know it's him who got me arrested and I want in on the sale to keep my mouth shut?"

"What?" JJ and Bob asked at the same time.

"I mean, I could tell him that if he doesn't return those coins, I'll go to the authorities and the press. Make the coins so hot, no one would dare buy them. Not only that, no one would hire him to work on their digs ever again. He'd be blackballed. I realize he can get me in trouble if he knows I'm no longer rotting away in that prison in Thailand, but if I can somehow get him to admit that he not only stole the coins, but planted the drugs in my tent, that should be enough to get me off the hook, right?"

"No," Bob said.

At the same time JJ muttered, "That's not a bad idea."

"What? No!" Bob said more forcefully. "I don't want Marlowe talking to that asshole ever again. And we're talking three million dollars. That's a lot of money, and people get weird and desperate when that much is at stake."

"Kendric," Marlowe said gently, putting her hand on his knee.

But the sight of Marlowe when he'd first met her was stuck in his head. How skinny she was. How despondent. She was a far cry from that woman now, and he didn't want to do anything that might put her right back in that headspace.

And even *talking* to Ian could make him go to the authorities and inform them that he'd been contacted by an escaped convict. The threat of being extradited back to Thailand could bring on more nightmares like the one she'd had last night. Her whimpering had broken his heart, and all he could do was hold her and whisper over and over that she was safe.

He didn't even want to *think* of how much they'd both suffer if she was returned to prison.

"We don't know West. Yes, he's young, but he's not *that* young. And if you call him up and try to blackmail him, he could react violently," Bob said.

"And if I don't, he'll sell those coins, they'll be lost forever, and we won't have any proof that he stole them in the first place," Marlowe countered. "He'll probably steal from another archaeological site again because he's greedy, and he obviously has no morals if he didn't think twice about sending me to prison for the rest of my life! Not only that, I *need* to clear my name. I won't be able to get on with my life if I don't. The threat of going back to prison will always be hanging over my head if I don't get Ian to admit that he planted those drugs in my bags."

Bob felt as if he was going to puke. He couldn't deal with Marlowe being in danger. And if she contacted Ian, she'd be intentionally putting herself at risk.

But . . . he knew she had a point. And he hated it.

If he ever wanted a normal life with Marlowe, didn't want to look over their shoulders for the rest of their lives, they had to deal with those drug charges.

"We can get Chief Rutkey and his officers involved, so it's official," JJ added.

"I can call him and have it all recorded. If I can get him to actually admit he's got the coins, that should give the authorities enough for a search warrant so they can find them, right? Maybe if I rile him enough, I can even get him to admit to setting me up in the first place. That he put those drugs in my bags to get rid of me, so I wouldn't rat him out."

Just the thought of her talking to Ian West made Bob so crazy with fear, he clenched his teeth together until his jaw ached. He needed a minute to process the fact that Marlowe actually wanted to put herself in such a dangerous situation.

Without a word, he walked to the balcony door, wrenched it open, and stepped outside.

He heard JJ and Marlowe talking quietly in the room behind him, but all he could do was grip the railing and stare out into the trees as his mind spun.

Several minutes passed, and when Bob heard JJ's voice behind him, he wasn't exactly surprised.

"I know this isn't ideal—" his friend started out.

Bob spun around and spat, "Not ideal? My wife confronting the man who had her thrown in prison without a shred of remorse? You've got to be kidding me!"

"The alternative is that we do nothing, and rely on Tex and the FBI to try to track down the buyer. There's no actual proof West even has those coins, so the police can't search his place. But as I pointed out, the second this asshole realizes she's in the States, he can go to the police, turn her in. Get her rearrested. And this time, her brother might not be able to use his political connections and money. Might not find another reckless former Special Forces soldier who thinks he's invincible to go in and break her out of jail."

"Are you seriously trying to guilt-trip me into using my wife as bait?" Bob bit out.

"I don't like the thought of Marlowe talking to that asshole any more than you do."

"Right. But you'll still use your disappointment against me to make it happen. Are we really doing this now?" Bob asked, more pissed than he was before.

"I guess so," JJ said, his voice even and just as hard as Bob's.

"Fine! I went behind your back. I worked with the FBI to go into foreign countries and rescue Americans who'd gotten themselves in trouble. And I was damn good at it. Do I regret lying to you and the others? Yes. Would I do it again if I hadn't found Marlowe? Again, *yes*.

"I love it here. I love what we've built. But for years, it wasn't enough for me. I was unsettled, and maybe as reckless as you accused me of being, but the demons in my head *wouldn't stop*! I haven't slept for shit since leaving the service, and when I was on a mission, I was too focused to think about my past. About what happened to me and my friends. The adrenaline and danger kept me amped up enough that I could forget, just for a while.

"Then I went to Thailand and met Marlowe. And the risks I'd been taking suddenly seemed stupid. I was also tired. Tired of lying to my best friends. Tired of being alone. And the nightmares hadn't stopped. Going on missions wasn't helping, not in the long run.

"If you can't forgive me for going behind your back, I understand. I won't like it, but I get it. But encouraging my *wife* to put herself in danger just to get back at me isn't cool, Jackson. What if this was April? Would you be as stoic or calm if I suggested we put *her* in the middle of an op as fucking bait?"

A muscle in JJ's jaw ticked as he stared at Bob.

"Right. You wouldn't," Bob went on, answering his own question. "You'd be just as pissed as I am right now. I don't know what's going on between the two of you, but there's no way you'd just sit back and let April put herself in danger. Even if it was the best way to solve the problem. Even if you knew she was brave and strong and so damn selfless, it makes you feel like an ogre in comparison just being around her."

Bob swallowed hard, then took a deep breath and said in a low voice, "I can't lose her, now that I've found her, JJ. I *can't*."

"You won't," he said, stepping out onto the balcony and putting his hand on Bob's shoulder.

"You can't promise that. Neither can the cops. No one can. We don't know this West character. All we know is that he has no problem throwing others under the bus to get what he wants. He knew what would happen when he called in that tip about the drugs," Bob said. "He knew Marlowe would be taken to prison. And he didn't give a shit. He had her arrested *for life* just so he could return to the States with those coins."

"We won't do it then," JJ assured him. "We'll find another way. And for the record," he said, sighing deeply, "I'm not surprised you were doing what you were doing. I knew you were never completely sold on moving to Maine. Hell, you suggested New York City. That's a far cry from Newton. I just figured you'd either settle in time or come to us with your concerns. That doesn't mean I'm not hurt that you went behind our backs to work with Willis.

"Damn it, Bob—you're one of my best friends. We've been to hell and back together. I *hate* knowing you were out there, in dangerous situations, without us to have your back. I'm not mad about what you were doing, just sad that you felt as if you couldn't talk to us about it.

"And as far as you not sleeping goes . . . why didn't you say something? You think I don't have nightmares? That Chappy doesn't? That Cal doesn't relive what those fuckers did to him all the time? You aren't the only one with PTSD. We could've talked about it. It probably would've been good for all of us. But what's done is done. We're moving past it. Got it? We'll find you a new therapist and see if we can't get those demons out of your head once and for all . . . without you having to go to the ends of the earth and putting yourself in danger in the process."

God, Bob loved this man. He took a deep breath. "I wouldn't mind talking with you and the others about what we went through sometime, getting it all out on the table, but I think I've finally found the cure to my nightmares."

"Yeah? What's that? You aren't drinking, are you? Or taking medication?" JJ asked worriedly.

Bob snorted. "No way. It's Marlowe. Somehow, holding her at night . . . she keeps them at bay."

The look of longing on JJ's face was so fleeting, Bob almost thought he imagined it. Almost.

"I'm happy for you. Both of you."

"Thanks."

"So . . . no more missions with Willis?" JJ pressed. "We can find something else that fulfills that need within you. I don't know what, but we'll figure it out. As a team."

"No more missions," Bob agreed. "I'm finally ready to slow down."

"Good. Now, about that phone call . . ."

Bob tensed once more.

JJ dropped his hand from his shoulder and took a step back. "Talk to Marlowe before making any decisions. Listen to her side of things. She was put into a situation where she was completely helpless. No one would listen when she said she was innocent—she was as much a captive as we were, Bob. And even more than proving her innocence . . . I think she needs to take her power back.

"I swear on my life that if we do anything involving Marlowe, she'll be covered at all times. Who better to have her six than four former Delta Force operatives? One phone call. If West doesn't take the bait, we'll figure something else out. Maybe let him sell one of the coins and get him that way. But there's no need for him to know about you, where she is, or that she's working with the cops."

"He'll suspect," Bob couldn't help but say.

"Of course he will. But I have faith that Marlowe can convince him otherwise. I think she needs to do this," JJ said.

Bob closed his eyes. He hated that his friend was right. And he did have faith in his wife. If anyone could pull this off, it was probably her. But that didn't mean he liked it. "I'll talk to her," he told JJ.

"Good. Now, I have to get going. Jack's Lumber won't run itself. We got a call from a woman this morning who had three trees fall on her property during the last windstorm. One barely missed hitting her house, and another is blocking her driveway. She needs them chopped up and removed."

Bob frowned. "You need my help?"

JJ chuckled. "No. You might think you're Superman, but you're still healing. When you finish up the antibiotics and are back one hundred percent, I'm gonna work your ass off. Force you to take all the calls to make up for your stupidness."

"That's not a word," Bob told him.

JJ flipped him off and headed back into the apartment.

Bob followed him and saw that Marlowe wasn't in the living area.

"She went into the bedroom to give us some privacy to talk," JJ said, obviously seeing Bob's concern. "She's a good one. You couldn't have found a better match."

"I know," Bob said. He'd flown halfway across the world to rescue Marlowe, and had ended up being the one rescued instead.

"Call me later. If you decide to try the phone call, I'll set up a meeting with the chief. The four of us—sorry, five—can sit down with him and discuss details."

"I will. Thanks, JJ." Bob wasn't sure what he was thanking his friend for. Maybe because he'd forgiven him. Because he understood. Because he was empathetic. Because he truly believed JJ wanted the best for him.

"You're welcome. But it has to be said—don't do this shit again. We're friends, Kendric. The four of us have been through too much together. You're like my brother. If you need something you aren't getting, you have to speak up."

"I will."

"Good." He was at the door before he turned. "And that stuff about April? You were right. I wouldn't be happy if she put herself in danger. But things are . . . complicated between us."

"Then uncomplicate them," Bob replied.

"It's not that easy. I wish it was. Now go talk to your woman. She needs your support. Later."

JJ was closing the door before Bob could even open his mouth. The fact that his friend had admitted there was something between him and April at all was a step, but Bob wasn't sure if it was a step forward or backward. All he could do was wait and see, and be there for JJ if his friend needed him.

He turned the bolt on the door and headed for his bedroom. He and Marlowe needed to talk about her crazy plan. And once that was done, he wanted to make love to his wife in his—no, *their*—bed.

Nothing was going to keep him from worshipping the woman he loved. From showing her that even if they strongly disagreed on how to handle the situation with Ian, he would never stop loving her.

Chapter Thirteen

Marlowe sat on the edge of the bed in Kendric's room and bit her thumbnail nervously. He'd been so upset by her suggestion. And while she understood that meeting with Ian could be dangerous, she needed to make sure he couldn't steal any more artifacts, couldn't put any other archaeologists in such life-changing danger.

And she needed to clear her name.

She had no doubt she could get Ian to talk. Even if he suspected she was working with the cops, he'd still want to know what she had planned. He was also arrogant enough to think he could outsmart her—but he was wrong.

For now, Marlowe was more concerned about Kendric. He hadn't been able to look at her before storming out to the balcony. She'd wanted to go out there to soothe him, try to talk to him, but JJ had said it would be better if he went.

So now she was stressing. She'd heard the two men come in from the balcony, then the front door shut. Was Kendric still mad? Would he give her the cold shoulder? Would he yell and insist that she was being an idiot?

She didn't think so, but then again, she hadn't known him all that long. Definitely not long enough to know how he reacted when he was really pissed. She wasn't afraid of him; Kendric would never lay a hand on her in anger. But she didn't know if he'd give her the silent treatment or flat-out refuse to even consider her suggestion. Either of which would hurt beyond belief.

She heard a noise at the door, and her head flew up. She didn't have time to do more than stand before Kendric was there, pulling her close and wrapping his arms around her, holding her tight.

She sighed in relief. She wasn't sure what his mood was, but the fact that he was touching her, holding her, she hoped was a good sign. She buried her nose where shoulder met neck and inhaled deeply. He always smelled so good. Even when they'd been sweaty and dirty while trekking across Thailand and Cambodia, his scent always seemed to calm her.

After a moment, he pulled back. "We need to talk."

Ugh. No wonder guys hated when women said those words. They sounded so ominous. But Marlowe nodded. They *did* need to talk.

However, instead of talking, he reached for the hem of her shirt.

Too surprised to protest, she lifted her arms and let him pull it over her head. His actions were quick and methodical, not sexual in the least, but it had been so long since they'd been intimate, just standing in front of him half naked made her nipples tighten and her core begin to weep.

His lips twitched when he noticed her nipples, but he didn't pause as he unzipped her jeans and pushed them over her hips. Marlowe let him undress her, standing stock still as he removed her underwear as well.

When she was completely nude, he nodded to the bed behind her. "Climb in."

Feeling off kilter, Marlowe gladly got under the covers and watched as her husband removed all his clothes as well, then joined her.

He immediately pulled her into his arms, and Marlowe smiled as she snuggled into him.

"Much better," he sighed. "I'm not happy about this," he continued without beating around the bush. "I don't want you talking to the asshole who got you locked up."

"I know," Marlowe told him, and she did. If Kendric had his way, he'd make sure she never had to talk to *anyone* who'd ever done her wrong in the past. She knew that as well as she knew her name. But she needed to do this.

"I trusted him," she said quietly. "There weren't a lot of Americans on that dig site, and it was nice to have someone from back home. He was funny and enthusiastic, and I enjoyed talking to him. Discovering what he did was a huge shock. I never would've expected it from him. I think that's why I gave him a chance to right his wrong. If I'd caught anyone else with those coins, I would've turned them in immediately. But Ian is so young. I really thought if he had a chance to think about what he'd done, and the potential consequences, he'd realize what a huge mistake he was making and fix it."

"He didn't," Kendric said unnecessarily.

"Yeah. That's why I need to do this, Kendric," Marlowe told him. "What he did was so wrong, it's not even funny. He stole part of a country's history. He undermined the work of every archaeologist on that site. And . . . he stole the confidence I had in *myself*, and my ability to trust my instincts when it comes to people. I need to get that back."

"You don't need him to be able to do that," Kendric said.

Marlowe wished he was right, but she needed to see this through. Wanted to have a hand in making Ian pay for what he'd done. She believed in karma, but sometimes it needed a little help.

"He's arrogant," she said. "After getting away with stealing those coins, he's going to think he's invincible. And having me call him will be a huge shock. I'm sure he thought I'd be gone forever, and even if I did get out of jail, he'd have already sold the coins and there'd be no proof of what he'd done.

"I thought about it while you were talking to JJ . . . and if I demand a cut of the money from the coins, he might not suspect I'm working with the police. And if I threaten to turn him in if he doesn't agree, he'll think he's smarter than me. He'll think since he got rid of me once, he can do it again."

"I don't want him within ten feet of you," Kendric said in a low, harsh tone.

"I don't want to *be* within ten feet of him," Marlowe agreed. "He scares me. I mean, I thought I knew him, and look what he did. I'm hoping that with one phone call, this nightmare will end. I mean, I'm not naive enough to think it'll be easy. But I still think that if I piss him off enough, he might mess up and give something away. That it'll be *my* turn to send *him* to prison. Please, Kendric. I need to try."

Her man sighed and stared up at the ceiling.

Marlowe waited, giving him time to mull over her argument.

Eventually, he said, "If we do this, it's on my terms."

"Okay," Marlowe agreed immediately.

"You won't take any chances. Won't tell him where you are. Will say only what we discuss ahead of time, from a script. You'll tell him our terms, then be done."

"All right."

"I mean it, Punky. No changing the plan once it's in motion. No thinking you can get more info if you drag things out. Your idea is a good one. You'll tell him you want a cut of the money he'll get from the sale, and in return, you'll forget about him and he'll forget about you. Understand?"

"Yes, Kendric." Marlowe couldn't believe he was agreeing. She loved him even more at this moment than she did before. Which was kind of hard to believe, because she already loved him a hell of a lot.

"I can't lose you," he said in a tortured tone. "Not after I just found you."

"You aren't going to lose me. I'm right here. This is going to be over before you know it," she said, crossing her fingers that she wasn't lying.

Now that it looked like she really *would* be talking to Ian, Marlowe was a little nervous. But knowing Kendric and his friends had her back made the entire thing a little easier.

He rolled then, and Marlowe squeaked in surprise as she stared up at him. "Be careful!" she scolded. "Your back—"

"Is fine. I'm fine. And I want to make love to my wife in our bed. In our home."

Marlowe practically melted under him. "Yes. Please."

"So polite," Kendric said with a mischievous grin. "There's something else I want, that I didn't get a chance to do before."

"What's that?"

Instead of answering her verbally, Kendric's smile widened before he leaned down and kissed her. But he didn't linger. He kissed her neck. Then her collarbone. Then he suckled one of her nipples as he lightly pinched the other.

Marlowe inhaled sharply and arched her back.

He kept moving down her body, kissing her belly before ultimately settling himself between her legs. Marlowe looked down and saw him staring up at her as his hands caressed her thighs. "You liked my fingers on you. Let's see how you like my tongue."

She didn't get a chance to say anything before he'd lowered his head and proceeded to drive her absolutely out of her mind. She writhed under him as he licked and sucked and sent her flying over the edge embarrassingly quickly.

Marlowe had only had one other man go down on her, and it hadn't felt anything like that.

But Kendric didn't stop. He continued to tease her clit with his lips and tongue, even when she whined that it was too sensitive.

When she was sweaty and boneless after two enormous orgasms, he finally made his way back up her body, kissing every inch of skin along the way.

He was smiling as he hovered over her. "Love seeing you like that," he told her, before kissing her once more. Marlowe could taste herself on his lips, and with any other man she would've been embarrassed or weirded out. But with the man she loved, nothing seemed awkward.

"Like what?" she asked, when they paused to take a breath.

"Mussed," he said with a grin. Then he reached between them and lined his cock up to her pussy. "You ready for me?"

"I'm always ready for you," she said without hesitation, widening her legs, inviting him inside.

Before she could blink, he was settled deep. She sighed. He felt so good, filling her in a way no one ever had.

He closed his eyes and took a breath through his nose. When he opened them again, he said, "You've gained some weight since you've been here."

Marlowe froze. She didn't think he was complaining, but it was a little weird to talk about her weight in that moment. "Um . . . yeah?"

"You started your period again yet?"

Licking her lips and trying to control the blush she could feel blooming across her cheeks, she shook her head.

"If you want, I can start wearing condoms . . . to protect you."

Oh! That's why he was commenting on her weight.

Marlowe couldn't imagine not having him bare inside her. She liked how he felt. Loved when he came deep within her body. But was he changing his mind? They'd talked about kids, but maybe now that they weren't on the run, he'd decided that was crazy?

"I can see your mind working a mile a minute. I still want to get you pregnant," he said bluntly. "There's nothing I want more than to see you round and glowing with our baby. But things moved really fast with us. If you want to wait, I'm okay with that too."

"No," she said quickly. "I don't want to wait."

"Excellent," he said.

"Although there's no guarantee," she warned.

"I know. But we'll have fun trying," he said with a grin as he began to move, slow and steady, in and out, making Marlowe gasp and moan with pleasure.

At one point, she voiced her concern about his back again. In response, he moved faster, took her harder, and any concerns she might've had flew from her mind.

Marlowe had thought making love with him the first time was the best she'd ever had, but she'd been wrong. Being with him now, safe and comfortable, was much more exciting and fulfilling and erotic.

He made love to her, teasing her body until she was begging him to let her come. Without making her wait another second, he held himself inside her as she flew over the edge. Just like before, he seemed to crave the feeling of her rippling around his cock.

As soon as she relaxed, he began to fuck her hard, murmuring words of love and how beautiful she was, until his orgasm overcame him and he spurted ropes of come deep inside her body.

He lowered himself on top of her for a few seconds, catching his breath, then rolled and clutched her to his chest.

Marlowe wanted to protest, tell him that he shouldn't be bearing her weight because of the wounds on his back. But she loved this position. Lying bonelessly on top of him, with Kendric still inside her. It reminded her of the first time they'd made love in that barn. Only now she didn't have to worry about dirty hay or being interrupted, and there were no animals eating noisily all around them.

"I love you," she mumbled into his chest.

His arms tightened, and she felt his cock twitch inside her. "I love you too," he returned.

Marlowe kissed his neck and sighed contentedly.

"I will do whatever it takes to keep you safe," he said softly.

She lifted her head. "What?"

"When you talk with Ian. I'll do whatever it takes to make sure things don't go sideways. And that goes for life in general too. I'm going to be a pain in your butt. You're going to think I'm overprotective, because I am. I won't be controlling, you can be friends with whoever you want, go wherever you want. You can get whatever job you want, or no job at all. I don't care. But I'm probably going to be texting you constantly, making sure you're okay, asking if you need anything. And when we have kids . . . ?"

He shuddered slightly, then kept speaking. "I'm going to go completely overboard. We're talking background checks on their babysitters, coaches, teachers. Nothing and no one will hurt what's mine if I can prevent it."

Tears ran down Marlowe's cheeks.

Kendric looked alarmed. "Shit! Don't cry, Punky. I'll try to keep a lid on it, but I've never loved anyone the way I love you, and the thought of anything happening to you makes me crazy. And kids are so vulnerable. I don't want them ever questioning their dad's love for them. I'm going to screw up, I know I will, and I'm terrified that I might do or say something to turn them into psychos, but I'll still do my best to be the kind of father and husband you've always wanted."

"Kendric," Marlowe said, bringing a hand up to rest on his cheek. "You already *are* the husband I've always dreamed about."

He turned his head and kissed her palm.

"And I'm okay with you being protective, as long as it goes both ways. When you're on a job, I'll probably text incessantly to make sure you haven't been crushed under a huge tree. When you go on your hikes, your clients will think *I'm* the psycho for always checking up on you."

She smiled. "Lord, we're sappy," she finished with a shake of her head. "The Army's gonna take away your Special Forces patch."

He chuckled, and Marlowe felt it from the inside out since they were still connected in the most intimate way a man and woman could be. "They can have it. I don't care."

"Did you . . . are things okay with you and JJ?"

"Yeah. Did you think they wouldn't be?"

"Neither of you were happy when he went out to talk to you. Was he really mad that you were doing the rescue missions?"

"He wasn't thrilled," Kendric admitted. "But we talked, and I told him about how I'd been feeling . . . and about my nightmares."

"And?"

"He admitted he has them sometimes too. Said the four of us probably should talk more about what we went through on that last mission, and the stuff we're going through now. And he's not wrong."

Marlowe loved that for him. "Good."

"Although I haven't had any nightmares since I've been home."

"I know," Marlowe said calmly. They'd had that discussion earlier, and she was thrilled and relieved that he'd been sleeping so well. She'd expected his bad dreams to continue, at least occasionally.

"You can't ever leave me," Kendric said seriously. "I think you're a blocker or something. Having you in my arms keeps the demons at bay."

Marlowe wasn't sure about that, but if he wanted to think so, she wouldn't argue again. "Okay."

He smiled. "That was easy."

She shrugged. "I'm right where I want to be. Why would I protest?"

"I love you," he said.

"And I love you back," she returned immediately.

Kendric palmed the back of her head and gently pushed her down, so her cheek was resting on his chest once more. "Sleep, Punky."

"What if I'm not tired?"

"You'll need your strength."

"For what?"

"For later when I want you again."

"Is this normal? I mean, I didn't think most guys could go more than once a night."

He laughed. "It's not nighttime. And I don't know about most men, but for me, with *you*? It's completely normal. I would live inside you if I could."

Marlowe snorted. "Not sure that's practical."

One of Kendric's hands moved down her back and squeezed her ass. "Don't care."

She giggled with a small shake of her head, then snuggled deeper into him.

"For the record?" he said after a moment.

"Ummmm?" she murmured, feeling sleepy after all.

"You taste delicious, and I'm gonna be eating you out a lot."

Marlowe's face heated once more. But since she loved every second of his mouth on her, she wasn't about to complain. "Can I try that sometime? Going down on you, I mean?"

"Anytime you want, Punky. Although I don't need that from you."

"But I want to give you as much pleasure as you give me," she protested.

"You already do. Go to sleep, Marlowe."

"'Kay." It didn't take long for her to fall into a deep sleep. She'd been stressed while he was talking to JJ, then exhausted by his lovemaking.

She'd somehow found herself married to the man of her dreams. She had new friends, her brother was safe, and soon she'd make Ian West pay for what he'd done. Life was good.

Better than good.

Chapter Fourteen

"Are you really going to confront him?" Carlise asked Marlowe.

She, June, April, and Marlowe were sitting in the break room of Jack's Lumber while the guys were all out on jobs. There had been a huge rainstorm the night before, and there were trees down all over Newton. Marlowe hadn't been sure Kendric should be working with his back still healing, but he'd insisted on helping his friends.

So the four women were hanging out, trying not to worry about the guys.

"I am," Marlowe said. "Tomorrow I'm going to the police station, and Chief Rutkey is going to let me use the phone there, since it's already got all the recording stuff set up. I'll call Ian and try to get him to admit everything he's done."

"Do you think he's going to take the bait?" June asked.

Marlowe shrugged. "It could go either way, but I'm thinking he will."

"Why?"

"Because he's going to want to know what I might tell the police about him. Because he'll want to know how I got out of Thailand."

"Are you nervous? Because I would be terrified," April said.

"Honestly? A little. But Kendric will be there." And that was the clincher. If she was on her own? There was no way she'd be brave enough to confront Ian. Just knowing that Kendric had her back was enough to give her the courage to help bring Ian to justice. "Besides, Ian needs to be stopped from doing this again. From stealing the heritage out from under another country."

"That's true. What a dick," Carlise said in disgust.

"Changing the subject, how did you come to call Bob *Kendric*?" April asked with a grin. "I mean, the rest of us"—she gestured to the other women—"had a conversation once about how with a name like Bob, some women might dismiss him as a serious love interest from the get-go. I was gonna set him up with one of the women looking for a guide on the AT, and introduce him by his real name, but you beat me to it."

Marlowe laughed. "There's nothing wrong with the name Bob. But the first time I met Kendric, that's how he introduced himself. And now I can't think of him as anything else. And seriously, the way he got the nickname Bob is just ridiculous."

"Right? I don't understand guys and their stupid nicknames. At least the others' nicknames are all based on their *actual* names. Like Chapman and Chappy, Cal and Callum, and of course, JJ for Jack's first and last initials. Although I could go for some Bob Evans right about now," June said with a smile.

"That's because you're eating for two," Carlise told her.

"Wait—*what*?" April asked.

At the same time, Marlowe exclaimed, "You're pregnant?!"

June blushed, gave them a small smile, and put a hand on her belly. "Only about four weeks, but . . . yeah. Seems that Cal has *very* determined sperm. He knocked me up pretty much the second we decided to start trying."

"Congrats!"

"That's awesome!"

"I didn't mean to spill the beans," Carlise told June sheepishly.

"It's okay. Honestly. And . . . speaking of Bob Evans . . . I could eat breakfast food all the time, since I always seem to be hungry lately."

"I'm so happy for you guys," April said.

"Chappy and I are still trying," Carlise admitted with a worried look. "And while I love the attempts at baby making, I'm worried that it hasn't happened yet."

"It's been what, two point three seconds since you guys got together?" April said dryly.

"I know," Carlise said. "I'm just impatient. If we're going to have the four kids we talked about, we need to get started on that. Although I'm not opposed to adopting. Or in vitro. Or fostering. I just want a family with Chappy so bad. He'll be the best dad, and I can't wait to make that happen for him."

"It will," June told her.

"What about you?" April asked, looking at Marlowe.

"What about me *what*?"

"Are you and Bob thinking about kids?"

Marlowe blushed and nodded. "Although my body is still out of whack after everything that happened."

"I'm still shaking my head at the fact that all three of us found our men because we were forced to share a bed with them," Carlise said with a chuckle.

"Right? You with the snowstorm at the cabin, me with the bed at the hotel, and Marlowe with a pit under the floor, of all things. Although none of us were forced to get married like she was," June said.

"I'm not sure *forced* is the right word," Marlowe protested.

"What would you have done if you didn't do what that lady wanted?" Carlise asked.

Marlowe shrugged. "Kendric would've figured something out."

"I'm thinking none of the guys do anything they don't want to do," April said. "If Bob agreed to marry you, it was because he *wanted* to marry you."

"That's what Chappy said," Marlowe admitted with a small smile.

"I know the circumstances weren't romantic in the least," Carlise said. "But I can't help but feel all mushy inside thinking about how it all came about."

"The ceremony was actually really . . . nice," Marlowe said a little lamely. "The guy who married us spoke in Thai, so I didn't have a clue what he was saying, but when it came to our vows, he spoke English. I was shocked."

"Really? That's cool. So he did the whole 'have and hold, love and cherish' thing?" June asked, leaning forward on the couch, totally enthralled.

Marlowe nodded. "Yeah. Except it was a little different. More . . . I don't know . . . meaningful?"

"Do you remember them? The vows, I mean?" Carlise asked.

"Yes."

"Do you feel comfortable sharing? It's okay if you don't," Carlise said.

Marlowe spoke without effort. The words burned into her brain as if she was standing in that woman's living room all over again. "To have and hold from now to forever, for better and worse, for rich and poor, when sick and healthy, to love and protect, cherish and honor, respect and nurture, in this life and the next."

All three women sighed.

"They're Buddhist in Thailand, right?" April asked.

"A lot of people, yes. I'm not sure what religion the woman was whose house we were staying in, but she was definitely old fashioned, since she didn't want us sleeping in that hole together."

"I think she definitely was because of that last line. Most would say until death do us part, but I'm thinking Buddhists believe in reincarnation, so saying in this life and the next makes sense," April mused.

Marlowe had no clue about the Buddhist religion, but she liked the thought of being with Kendric not only in this life, but whatever happened after as well.

"What about you?" Carlise asked April.

"Huh?"

"We all did the one-bed, forced-proximity thing. What about you and JJ? How are we gonna get you two into one bed, make him stop farting around and pull his head out of his butt and admit that he's madly in love with you?"

Marlowe watched in fascination as her new friend's cheeks reddened.

"He's not in love with me," she protested.

"Oh please, he so is," Carlise said with a shake of her head.

"Well, I'm happy being his admin and friend. So no forced proximity for us." Then she gave each of them a stern look. "I mean it. If you lock us into a room with a sleeping bag or something, I'm not going to be happy."

Everyone chuckled.

"Besides, I'm too old for him," April muttered.

"What? You are not!" Carlise exclaimed. "We've already been over this. You're only seven years older, that's like nothing!"

"I've already been in a serious relationship, and it sucked," April said, ignoring Carlise's comment. "I'm happy being single. And soon, I'll get to be Aunt April to all your kids. I'll get to spoil them rotten."

"You don't want children of your own?" June asked.

April gave her a small smile. "No. Don't get me wrong, I love kids, and I know I could always adopt or something, but I'm enjoying not having that responsibility."

"It's okay if you don't want to be a mom," Marlowe felt compelled to say. "Society puts too much emphasis on women having babies. As if there's something wrong with us if we don't want to experience childbirth. But that doesn't mean you can't have your happily ever after with JJ."

"We're friends. That's it," April insisted.

But Marlowe could read the longing in her voice. She hadn't been around the woman very long, but it was obvious she couldn't take her gaze from JJ when they were in the same room together. They might snipe at each other, but Marlowe hadn't met two people with more chemistry.

"Besides, Chappy, Cal, and Bob fell in love in like two seconds. You two"—she pointed to Carlise, then June—"were married within weeks. And Marlowe, it was like five days for you!"

"The circumstances were a bit different for us," she protested. "We got married, but we didn't love each other."

"Bullcrap," April said. "Again, Bob wouldn't have married you if he didn't want to. He was already in love with you, I have no doubt about that. My point is, Jack and I have known each other for *years*. Nothing has ever happened between us. Eventually, he'll meet a woman and fall as hard and fast as the rest of his friends did. He's not going to wake up one day and suddenly realize that he loves the woman he sees at work all the time. Besides, he's my boss. That never ends well."

Marlowe wanted to argue, but wasn't sure what to say. She didn't know JJ or April well enough. Something was clearly keeping both of them from admitting their feelings for each other, and whatever it was, it might be something they couldn't overcome.

"Anyway, I can't wait for there to be babies running wild in here. I'm always available to babysit, I just want to make that clear right here and now. Okay?"

Everyone laughed.

"Good. Because with four kids, we're gonna need some alone time," Carlise joked.

"With the *two* we want, we're gonna need some alone time," June said with a laugh.

"How many do you want?" April asked Marlowe.

"I don't know. More than one, less than six," she blurted.

"Six? Good Lord," Carlise exclaimed. "I thought four was a lot."

"I just . . . I've always wanted to be a stay-at-home mom. I kind of got sucked into the archaeology thing, and while I liked it, I want to settle down. Raise a family. It's not cool these days to say I want to greet my husband at the door when he comes home from work, but . . . I do. I'm not sure how the dinner thing will go, since I suck at cooking, but I'll figure it out."

"I think that's awesome," June said.

"Me too," Carlise agreed.

"Me three. Screw what others think. You do what's right for you and Bob."

Marlowe grinned. She liked these women. A lot. "I will," she said firmly.

"So . . . is it time to check on everyone again yet?" Carlise asked with a small grin. "I mean, it's been what, twenty minutes since we last heard from them?"

"Thirty, and yes, it's time to check," April agreed eagerly.

The woman might deny liking her boss in a romantic way, but it was more than obvious that she was just as anxious as the rest of them to know their men were all right.

Once they'd reassured themselves that the guys were fine, and making great progress on cleaning up the mess from the storm, the women decided to order Granny's Burgers for lunch. Carlise went to pick them up, and they were in the middle of stuffing their faces when the guys returned.

Chappy went right to Carlise and kissed the mustard off her cheek.

Cal approached June, his hand resting on her belly as he kissed her hello.

JJ's gaze was locked on April, and he had a small, tender smile on his face as he watched her frantically try to swallow the huge bite she'd just taken when they walked in.

And Kendric headed straight for Marlowe. He didn't lean down to kiss her, though. Instead, he plucked her up and out of the chair she was sitting in and headed for the door.

"Kendric!" she scolded. "You shouldn't be carrying me around! Your back!"

"Is fine. And I just spent the day chopping and hauling huge trees around. You weigh less than they did."

Not knowing what else to do, and secretly loving being in his arms, Marlowe turned and waved to her friends. "Later!" she called out.

Everyone laughed and waved goodbye.

"What's the hurry?" she asked as Kendric walked toward his pickup truck.

"It's been fourteen hours, eight minutes, and twenty-eight seconds since I last made love to my wife," he replied.

Marlowe shook her head in exasperation, but since she wanted her husband as much as he apparently wanted her—all the talk about babies had made her horny—she wasn't going to complain.

He placed her in the passenger seat, then framed her face with his hands and kissed her long, hard, and deep. When he pulled back, they were both panting. He stared at her for a long moment, as if memorizing her features, then took a breath and stepped back, shutting the door.

They talked about their days on the way to his apartment, as if the sexual tension between them wasn't there at all. Kendric told Marlowe how good it felt to be working again. How he'd felt as if he'd let down his friends by not being able to help recently. She told him about the fun visit she'd had with the other women and how much she liked them.

After pulling into a parking spot, Marlowe was already out of the truck and waiting for Kendric by the time he reached the passenger side. He took her hand in his and led her up the stairs to his apartment. Neither spoke, but Marlowe could already feel her nipples tightening and her body readying itself for her man.

∼

Bob had never felt like this before. As if his skin was too tight for his body. He'd lusted after a woman or two in the past, but not in the desperate way he wanted his wife.

His *wife*.

It was such an odd feeling, knowing she was as tied to him as he was to her. He'd accepted he might never find the one woman who made him want to settle down, but life had a way of turning things on their head and proving him wrong.

He pulled the door to his apartment shut behind them and locked it; then he was on Marlowe. He backed her up against the nearest wall and groaned as she slipped out of his grasp and went to her knees in front of him.

When she fumbled with the fastening of his pants, he groaned again. He wanted her hands and mouth on him more than he wanted to breathe. But he'd been working all day.

"Marlowe, stop," he said, but she ignored him, pulling his boxers down so his rock-hard cock popped out of the confines of his underwear.

She looked up at him, licked her lips, and leaned in, still holding his gaze.

"I need a shower," he managed to croak out before her mouth closed over him. "Holy shit!" he exclaimed as she took as much of him into her mouth as she could and sucked. Hard.

A burst of precome left the tip before he reached down and grabbed the base of his dick to keep himself from coming right then and there. He was primed and ready, and having the woman he loved sucking him off was almost more than he could take at the moment.

She was more enthusiastic than skilled at what she was doing, and Bob had never had better head. He kept one hand around his cock, holding himself still, and the other thrust into her hair, tightening as she bobbed up and down on his dick.

She slurped and licked as she enthusiastically pleasured him. He felt her mouth touch his hand every time she bottomed out on his cock, and it was the most intimate thing Bob had ever experienced.

But he was done. He needed to be inside her when he came. As much as he loved the feel of her mouth, he wanted to feel her hot, wet body spasming around his dick as he lost it.

He reached down and pulled her roughly off his cock, then walked her backward as he locked his lips onto hers. He could taste himself, and it only turned him on more. There was no way he was going to make it to their bed.

She hit the couch. He jerked her leggings and underwear down before he picked her up and sat her on the back of the sofa, placing her at the perfect height.

Then he took hold of his cock and sank into her soaking-wet folds with one firm thrust.

"Can't wait!" he apologized.

In return, Marlowe moaned deep and low, kicking one foot out of her leggings and underwear so she could wrap her limbs around him, holding on and digging her fingernails into his shoulders.

Tingles were already shooting down his spine, and his balls had already drawn up. It was only a matter of seconds before Bob knew he was going to come. He wanted to wait. To draw this out. To make it good for her, but his body had other ideas.

Way before he was ready, Bob was shooting deep inside Marlowe's body. His vision went dark for a moment, and his knees went weak. He managed to keep hold of her, and when he felt as if he could walk, picked her up and moved around to the front of the couch. He fell onto the cushions, keeping her clasped tightly against him.

She hadn't come yet, and that was unacceptable.

"Ride me," he panted as he leaned back, balancing Marlowe on his lap and reaching between them.

They were both still mostly clothed, Marlowe's leggings and panties still trailing off one leg as she straddled him. Her hair was mussed where his hand had gripped it, and her cheeks were flushed.

"Take me, Punky. Like you did on our honeymoon." Remembering how she'd been in that barn was enough for Bob's cock to harden to half mast inside her.

She began to ride him, taking him in and out of her body as she rocked up and down. He tweaked her clit, helping her toward her orgasm even faster.

The feel of her muscles clutching him was something he'd never get tired of. The sounds their bodies made as they came together were so erotic, and Bob was relieved she was as turned on as she'd been so he hadn't caused her pain when he plowed into her earlier.

"That's it, Punky. Take your man. You're so beautiful. And all mine. God, you have no idea how amazing that feels! Do it, Mar. I've got you."

She let out a small screech as she arched, threw her head back, and came on him.

It was just as amazing as it had been the first time. Nothing could compare to her rhythmic pulses on his dick. He could feel a rush of wetness against his balls as she came.

He was smiling when she finally came back to herself. She looked at him, sweat dotting her temples, and she had a satisfied cat-got-the-cream look on her face. And she certainly had.

"Um . . . hi," she said shyly.

"Hi," he returned with a huge grin on his face. "I didn't hurt you, did I? I didn't exactly make sure you were ready for me."

"You didn't hurt me," she said. "I liked that. A lot."

"I noticed," he replied, not able to keep the note of pride out of his voice. "I'd ask what you ladies were talking about before we got there, but I'm not sure I want to know."

"Babies," she blurted.

Bob raised a brow. "Yeah?"

She wrinkled her nose. "I guess I got a little worked up. And then you swooped in and picked me up like a caveman . . . I couldn't help but jump you as soon as we got in here."

Bob laughed. "Anytime you want to jump me, feel free," he teased. "You hungry?"

"Well, I just had half a Granny's Burger. You arrived before I could finish."

"Right, so . . . you hungry?" he repeated. One thing he'd learned about his wife was that she could eat like a pro. He would have never guessed when they were in Thailand. She had to have a hollow leg or something, but he didn't mind. And no matter what she ate, she was still a tiny thing.

"Um . . . I could eat."

"Then you should stand up so I can feed my woman," Bob said.

She nodded and eased off his lap, standing with his assistance. She grabbed her panties and started to pull them back on. Still sitting, Bob caught sight of something—and he stopped her, alarmed.

"I *did* hurt you," he exclaimed as he held her hips in his hands and leaned closer. She was naked from the waist down, and he could see his come leaking down her inner thigh, but it was tinged pink. She was bleeding.

Looking down, Marlowe tried to pull out of his grip.

He wasn't letting go. "I'll call the doctor. I'm so sorry, Marlowe. I was an idiot! I'll just—"

"You didn't hurt me," she said, interrupting him. "I was more than ready for you. I think it's my period. I had cramps earlier today, but since it's been so long since I've felt them, I actually didn't make the connection."

Bob forced his gaze away from his seed dripping down her leg to look her in the eye. "Your period?" he asked quietly.

"Yeah. You know, that thing women get every month? Let me go so I can clean up."

But Bob couldn't make his hands release her. He looked back down at the pink come leaking from between her legs. He'd never thought much about a woman's time of the month. But now he couldn't *stop* thinking about the ramifications of the blood. He looked back up at her.

"You can get pregnant now," he whispered.

Her lips twitched. "Well, not right this second. That's not how it works, but yes, now that I'm getting proper meals and stuff, I'm clearly healthier, so . . . it's possible."

"I hope you aren't one of those women who don't like to make love when they're bleeding," he blurted. "Because this isn't a turnoff. At all."

"It's really messy. And blood stains," she informed him.

Bob grinned. "We'll use towels. And make love in the shower." He looked up at her again. "You didn't hesitate for even one second to go down on me, even though I've been working up a sweat all day."

She looked uncomfortable for the first time. "You being sweaty reminds me of when we were on the run. We didn't shower much, and your natural scent reminds me of when you held me tight when we hid out. Of being safe. It doesn't bother me in the least."

Bob's heart melted. He loved this woman so much. She was perfect for him in every way. "You need me to go out and get you some tampons or pads?" he asked.

Her eyes widened. "No. I can do it."

"Nope. You stay here. I'll run out and grab them. What size? Never mind, I'll get a few different things. I'll make us some spaghetti when I get back. I love you, Marlowe."

She smiled at him. "I love you too. Will you . . . will you grab me a paper towel or something?"

Bob sprang up from the couch and was back in seconds. "Let me," he insisted when she reached for the paper towel.

She blushed but nodded.

Bob wiped away the evidence of their lovemaking, a feeling of satisfaction overwhelming him.

He was a total goner. This should probably be gross, something he'd normally shy away from. Something he was embarrassed about. But how could he be, when it was partly of his own making? He'd promised to respect and nurture this woman, and this was just a part of that.

"I'll be back soon. Take some painkillers if you still have cramps."

"I'm fine, Kendric. I've been dealing with my periods for decades now."

"Right, sorry. I just . . . this is amazing."

She rolled her eyes. "It's just a period."

But Bob stepped closer and took her face in his hands. He'd pulled up his pants already, but still felt as if he was naked with this woman. She made him want to be a better person. Be the kind of man she could rely on.

"It's not *just* anything. You were starving. A function had shut down because your body was using every calorie just to keep you alive and moving. And now you're healing. Getting your period back is the first step to us becoming a family. Your body is a miracle, and I'm overwhelmed by how grateful I am that I took that job. That you were smart enough to escape when the opportunity presented itself. That you were strong enough, physically and mentally, to get us out of the country. This relationship is going to work. Nothing's going to stop us from living our best lives possible. Okay?"

He was being sappy again, but Bob didn't care.

"Okay," she agreed.

"Good." He kissed her. "I'll be back in a jiffy."

"Don't go overboard," she warned him. "I mean, I just need one box."

"Right. Got it. Love you."

"Love you too."

Bob left the apartment, feeling happier than he'd felt in ages. He didn't need adrenaline rushes or danger to make him feel fulfilled. He'd simply needed Marlowe.

Chapter Fifteen

He'd totally gone overboard.

Marlowe shook her head, still thinking about the six boxes of tampons he'd brought home, in every size and brand the small general store in Newton had in stock. He'd also bought three boxes of pads. But it was . . . adorable. It was obvious Kendric had no idea what a woman needed during her time of the month, but that made him going all out even sweeter.

When he'd gotten back from the store the night before, he'd quickly whipped up their dinner as they'd talked more about their days. She supposed most people wouldn't find it very interesting to hear what was involved in a tree-cutting or guide business, but she wanted to know every little thing about her husband.

That night, he'd held her tightly, cuddling and not pressing for sex. He flinched a few times during his sleep, but didn't wake from a nightmare. Marlowe kept her arms around him, letting him know he was safe and loved, praying it was enough to keep his demons at bay.

And it was.

Now they'd just finished lunch, and she was almost done getting ready to head over to the police station to call Ian.

Did she *want* to confront him? Yes and no.

A part of her wanted to just move on. Forget about what happened. But it would be impossible to truly move on unless she cleared her name and confronted the man who'd put her in prison. Who'd made her suffer so much.

She was both scared to death and pissed way the hell off. It was a weird dichotomy, and she wasn't exactly sure which feeling dominated from moment to moment.

Kendric was on edge. She could tell from the moment they woke up. He hadn't spoken much, although he was still as loving as ever. She supposed he was just as stressed as she was. The sooner she got this done, the happier they'd both be.

The fact that he was standing by her side while she did what she needed to do meant a lot to Marlowe. She was very aware that he didn't want her calling Ian. That he was overprotective and wanted to keep her from experiencing any kind of angst. But he was still supporting her decision.

On their way to the police station, she reached over and put her hand on his arm. "It'll be fine," she said, not sure who she was trying to convince, Kendric or herself. "I mean, all I'm doing is talking to him."

"I know."

His words were clipped. He was obviously very stressed, and Marlowe hated that she was the cause. She sighed and put her hand back in her lap.

Kendric immediately reached over and twined his fingers with hers. "I'm trying," he said softly. "But I really hate this. West will probably say something to upset you, and it sucks."

"It does suck," Marlowe agreed. "But he's not going to get to me. I survived being thrown in prison and thinking I was going to spend the rest of my life there. Comparatively, this is a piece of cake."

"Saying it like that, I can't exactly disagree," Kendric said.

Marlowe chuckled. "Nope."

He brought their hands up to his mouth and kissed her fingers. "I love you, and I'm so proud of you."

"Thanks. I just want this done, Kendric. I don't want to look over my shoulder the rest of my life, and I don't want Ian to be able to hurt anyone else the way he did me."

"I know. He won't. You'll make sure of it."

His belief in her instantly made some of the butterflies dissipate.

They arrived at the police station, and Marlowe met the police chief, Alfred Rutkey. He welcomed her and led her to a small interrogation room. The room was packed with too many chairs around a small table, and a phone was sitting smack dab in the middle.

Suddenly everything was very real, and Marlowe wasn't sure she could do this after all. The last time she'd talked to Ian, he was promising to do the right thing and reassuring her that he'd return the coins. Then the second he had the chance, he'd turned on her.

What did Marlowe know about blackmail? Or getting people to admit to their wrongdoing? Obviously not very much, considering she'd been the one who'd ended up behind bars and not Ian. But it was okay. As promised, she, Kendric, and his friends had devised a loose script with talking points designed to coerce a confession. She could do this.

"You've got this, Punky," Kendric said into her ear, reading her thoughts. He was behind her, with a hand on the small of her back.

She took a deep breath and felt more centered, walking into the room and taking a seat at the table. Chappy, Cal, and JJ followed them in and sat as well. The police chief took the seat across from her, and Kendric pulled a chair up so close, his thigh was plastered to hers when he sat down. His hand rested on her leg, grounding her.

"Right, so this call is to let West know you're back in the States," the chief coached. "Follow his lead, but also try to chat with him about nothing for a while, see if you can get him to lower his guard. If he asks how you got out of jail, be vague, say that you had a really good lawyer who convinced the judge to release you on a technicality or something. Don't accuse him right off the bat. Feel him out.

"When you think he's relaxed a little, use your talking points. Turn the conversation to the dig. The coins. Remind him that you know he took them—then reveal that you *also* know he's got a buyer. Threaten him with the authorities if he won't cut you in on the deal. He might not care. He'll know he can turn you in just as easily. But hopefully the threat alone will be enough to make him agree to your terms."

The chief gave her a look. "If he won't agree, then remember—at the very least, we need him to admit that he planted the drugs. Above all else, we need to get those charges against you dropped. Do you have any questions?"

Marlowe took a deep breath and let it out slowly. She'd been over all the details with Kendric several times already. She'd been told what the computer guy, Tex, had found out about the seller, and how Ian was auctioning the coins on the dark web. She had all the info she needed to scare the crap out of him and hopefully get him to slip and admit he had the coins. She just had to be strong and get through this call.

There was a lot riding on the next few minutes, and Marlowe hoped she didn't screw it up.

"No questions. I'm ready," she said more confidently than she felt.

Kendric squeezed her leg, letting her know without words that he was there. That he believed in her.

Chief Rutkey nodded and pulled the phone over to him and hit the speaker button. The dial tone sounded especially loud in the small room. He dialed a number, then turned the phone around so the speaker was in front of her. This was it. There was no going back.

∾

Bob didn't like this. Not at all. But Marlowe needed the closure this call with West could provide. She was as stiff as a board next to him, and it was killing him that the only thing he could do to try to make this easier was remain close.

The phone sitting on the table rang three times, then West finally picked up.

"Hello?"

"Hello, Ian. It's Marlowe Kennedy."

Bob flinched. No. She was Marlowe *Evans*. His wife. But he obviously couldn't correct her.

There was silence on the other end of the phone for a moment before West replied.

"Holy crap, Marlowe? Are you okay? Are you home?"

"Yes, and yes . . . no thanks to you."

So much for the chief's suggestion about being polite and working her way into the conversation. Bob tightened his hold on her leg. She was angry, it was easy to see.

"What do you mean?" Ian asked, trying to sound innocent.

"Cut the crap, Ian, you know *exactly* what I mean," Marlowe said, leaning forward. "You planted those pills in my stuff and called the cops on me."

"What? No, I didn't!"

"Yes, you did. There was no one else who had any reason to get me out of the way except for you. We had that conversation about you stealing those coins, and you promised to return them. And the next thing I know, I'm being interrogated and thrown in jail, scared out of my head. That was your plan, wasn't it? Get me out of the way so I couldn't tell anyone what you did. And now you're back here in the States, looking for a buyer for those coins."

"Look, I know I screwed up on the dig, but I did just as you asked," he blurted, talking fast. "I returned the coins. They're back in Thailand where they belong."

"You're such a liar. Do you think I'm an idiot?" Marlowe asked, bitterness lacing her question. "Don't answer that, I know you do. I've been a good person, Ian. Nice. Easygoing. But I'm *done* taking shit from people. And lucky you, you get to experience my newfound backbone firsthand."

"I don't think you're an idiot. And you *are* nice, Marlowe," Ian said.

Bob was impressed. It was obvious West hadn't expected Marlowe to be so forceful. She was playing this exactly right, putting West on the offensive right from the start. He'd been proud of her before, but now he was even more so.

"How'd you get out?" West asked.

"My brother," Marlowe said shortly. "He has some amazing connections, and he got me a lawyer who knew exactly how to get me out of that hellhole. And now that I'm back, your little plan to get rich off those coins is shot to hell."

Ian was quiet for a moment. "What do you want?"

"I *want* to go back to being naive. I *want* to think that the people I work with are trustworthy. That they wouldn't throw one of their coworkers under the bus for money. But I can't have that, can I? No," she said, answering her own question. "So now, I want to discuss the deal you're making for the coins."

"What deal?"

"Honestly, you playing the innocent dumbass is getting old," Marlowe barked. "You think I'd call you if I didn't know what you were up to? I know you've been trying to sell those coins on the dark web. I know that you've had some interest. And I know that you're on the verge of making a deal. I want in."

"In . . . ?"

"Yes. *In.* You owe me, Ian. Big time. I was going to demand that you give me a percentage of the money you stand to make on those coins, but now that I'm talking to you, I don't trust you not to screw me. *Again.* So instead, I want one of the three coins. I'll make my own deal."

"I . . . I don't have any coins."

"Yes, you do," Marlowe said calmly. "And I want one of them. I'll find my own buyer. And if you don't give me what I want, I'll go to US Customs *and* Homeland Security, and tell them everything. How you pocketed the coins when you were on that site. How you smuggled them into the US. How you framed me. They might not believe that I was framed for those pills, but when I show them the screenshots I have of your little advertisement on the dark web—and how the IP address leads straight to your parents' house—*you'll* be the one behind bars."

She let her words sink in for a moment. Then added, "Oh, and your mom and dad just might end up there with you. You know . . . since they're aiding and abetting and all."

"You *bitch!*" Ian hissed.

Bob stiffened. And there he was. The real Ian West.

Marlowe was doing amazing. She was tense, but there was no way West would know that from the sound of her voice.

Now she laughed, a short, bitter sound. "Yup. Guess I learned to toughen up after my little stint in that prison in Thailand. I know how much those coins are worth—a million each. You'll still get two million after you hand one of them over to me, and be grateful I'm not asking for half of everything. After this transaction, you and I are done. I'll disappear from your life, and you'll be free to do whatever the hell you want. Go on more digs, steal more shit . . . I don't care."

"I don't believe you," Ian said. "I can't trust you."

"I don't trust you either," Marlowe retorted. "You've already proven that you don't care who you step on in order to get your way. Give me one of the coins and we're done. Forever. I don't ever want to see you again. And besides, look at it this way—when I have one of those coins, I'm just as guilty as you are. Why would I turn you in when it would put me right back in prison as well? I just want what you owe me."

There was silence on the other end of the line, before Ian West said in a hard voice, "Fine. But not in Boston. There are too many cameras in the city. I'll come to you."

"No."

"Then we have nothing else to talk about. It's my way or no way."

Bob felt Marlowe tense next to him. Her gaze came up to his, her brows furrowed. It was obvious she wasn't sure what to do now. He gave her a little headshake.

"Marlowe? You have three seconds to agree before I'm hanging up. And don't think I just believe your little story about being let out of prison. All it'll take is one call to confirm if that's true—and if it isn't, one *more* call to get you on every most-wanted list in the US."

"Fine. Where?" Marlowe blurted.

Bob's heart rate increased, and he could see the tension stealing over every man in the room. No! He didn't want her coming face to face with the asshole who'd already double-crossed her.

"Wherever you are. An out-of-the-way spot. And if you even think about setting me up, you'll regret it."

Marlowe paused for a few seconds. Then said, "I'm in Newton, Maine."

Ian chuckled, but it wasn't a humorous sound. "Maine isn't too far. Where can we meet?"

His friends were shooting looks at each other and Bob. Marlowe had given up her location! And there wasn't a damn thing he could do about it now.

"Newton is a small town. There aren't any traffic cams, and the police department's a joke. It won't be an issue to meet here. There's a park off of Highway 2, right before you get to town. I'll meet you there. Two days from now. One o'clock. Be there and bring me my coin, or I swear to God, I'll make you regret ever meeting me."

"I already do," Ian growled.

"The feeling's mutual," Marlowe fired back. "Don't screw me over again, Ian. Trust me, prison sucks. See you in two days."

Marlowe reached out and clicked off the connection, then immediately lowered her head, resting it on top of her hands on the table.

The room was silent.

Bob wrapped an arm around her back and leaned into her. "Punky?"

"Give me a second," she mumbled into her hands.

"Holy crap. That was *awesome*," Chappy exclaimed. "Not the part about the meet, but the way you smoked him."

"If I wasn't already happily married with my first child on the way, and if you weren't already hitched to one of my mates, I'd ask you to marry me," Cal said.

Bob ignored his friends. His full attention was on Marlowe. "Are you all right?"

She nodded but didn't raise her head.

"Okay, well, *that* wasn't how I suggested things go, but . . . I honestly think it might work out," Chief Rutkey said.

He felt Marlowe take a deep breath, then she sat up and looked around the room. "I'm so sorry. I hope it was okay that I told him to meet me at that park. He blindsided me by insisting we meet in person."

"We'll make it work," Rutkey assured her.

"He'll be planning something," Bob warned. "He wouldn't insist on meeting in person if he just planned to give up a coin."

"I agree. I'll get with Tex about some high-grade video and audio equipment so we can monitor the meeting," JJ said.

"I'll go scope out the park and find places for us to position ourselves, so we're nearby at all times," Cal added.

"We can use my Jeep for the meet," Chappy offered. "We obviously can't use Cal's expensive monstrosity, and Bob's truck has more power than my vehicle. We'll want to have that as backup."

Bob didn't like the sound of that, but he knew it was a smart decision.

"Thank you. I appreciate you all being here and willing to help. But I . . . I need to go."

Marlowe's voice cracked on the last word, and Bob could tell she was on the verge of losing it. He stood when she did and grabbed her hand, leading her toward the door. "Keep me in the loop," he told his friends, before getting Marlowe out of the room and the building, into the fresh air. He went straight to his truck and hoisted her inside, then jogged around to the driver's side.

He immediately started the engine and said, "Hang on, Punky. Five minutes and I'll have you home."

He glanced over and saw she was sitting as stiff as a board. Her gaze was fixed forward, and her hands were clasped together in her lap. He drove quickly but safely, and within minutes he was parking the truck in the lot at his apartment complex. Marlowe met him at the front of the truck, and they headed up the stairs hand in hand.

The second the door shut behind them, the tears Marlowe had so valiantly kept at bay let loose. Bob scooped her up, carried her to the couch, and sat down with her on his lap. She was crying so hard, he was somewhat alarmed, but he didn't try to convince her to stop. Simply let her get all the emotion out.

She clung to him, her body shaking with her sobs, and Bob felt completely helpless. It took another ten minutes or so, but finally her crying lessened. He leaned over and grabbed a tissue from a box next to the sofa and gave it to her. She gave him a watery smile and blew her nose. Then she snuggled back into him.

"Feel better?"

She shrugged. "I guess. I don't know why I was even crying."

"Because that was very stressful," Bob said. "Because you had to act like someone you weren't. Because you're scared. Because talking to the man who caused you so much pain and terror wasn't fun. Because you're a kind person who doesn't like hurting others."

Marlowe snorted. "You make me sound like a paragon of virtue. I can be a bitch."

Bob rolled his eyes. "Uh-huh."

She lifted her head so she could see him. "I can," she insisted.

"Name one time you were bitchy to someone else," Bob challenged.

Marlowe frowned in concentration, then looked at him and said, "I refused to let one of the women in prison take my spot on the floor next to the window."

Bob shook his head. "Doesn't count. Anything you did while incarcerated was fully justified. Try again."

Marlowe huffed out an adorable breath. "Fine. The last time I drove on the interstate around DC, before I went to Thailand, there was construction and the right lane was closing. But I didn't get in the left lane right away. I drove all the way to the front of the long line of cars and forced my way in."

Bob burst out laughing.

"What? That's bitchy!" Marlowe insisted. "I should've gotten into the left lane along with everyone else, instead of passing them all and sneaking in."

"Yup, you're a coldhearted bitch, all right," Bob told her.

Marlowe sighed, then rested her head against his chest again. "Fine. It's not in my nature to be mean. I don't like it. Even if Ian deserved everything I said, I still feel . . . weird about it."

"You were amazing. And while I initially agreed with the chief's plan for how he thought that call should go, you actually played it much better. In hindsight, West would've been suspicious if you had a bunch of small talk, then suddenly did a one-eighty and tried to blackmail him."

"I don't know what happened," Marlowe said. "I was planning on asking how he was, how long he'd been back in the States, how his family was doing . . . but the second I heard his voice, I kind of saw red and just blurted out what I was thinking."

"Again, you did good."

"Do you think he'll actually show up?"

"Yes."

"You can't know that," she protested.

"Marlowe, you threatened to turn him in. You gave him enough detail about the sale of those coins and how you knew he was on the dark web . . . he's gonna show. He's not going to risk being arrested before he can make that sale," Bob said firmly.

"I don't want to see him again," Marlowe whispered.

Bob tensed, and he opened his mouth to tell her that she didn't have to, that they'd figure something out, but she continued before he could speak.

"But I have to. I need to look into his eyes and see if he has even a speck of remorse for what he did to me. And I know that today's call might not be enough to put him in jail. He didn't actually admit to anything. It's an okay start, but he'll be *really* screwed if he shows up with those coins."

She was right . . . damn it. "We'll get Chappy's Jeep completely wired up, in a way that West won't be able to tell. And you won't get out. You can talk to him through your car windows. He won't get near you. And Tex is really amazing at tracking devices. We'll get you some earrings or a necklace that will record both video and audio, just in case. We're gonna get him, Punky. Thanks to you."

"I should feel guilty about what's going to happen to him. But I don't. Does that make me a bad person?"

"No. It makes you human," Bob reassured her.

"I'm scared," Marlowe said, barely audibly.

Bob's arms tightened around her. "I won't let anything happen to you."

She nodded, which made Bob feel better, but she didn't relax in his arms.

"I just . . . I want this over. I want to be able to live my life. I want to explore Newton, hang out with Carlise, June, and April. I want to eat more Granny's Burgers. I want to have my brother and his family come up and visit."

"And you'll get to do all of that," Bob said, fairly alarmed now. "Why would you think you wouldn't?"

"I don't know."

But he knew she was lying. She clearly had a bad feeling about this, and he couldn't blame her. Bob was frustrated and stressed out himself, and even though he had faith in his ability to protect her, and the abilities of his friends, he still worried that something might happen that none of them could prevent.

"You can always stop this," he told her. "At any point, you can call it off."

"And let him get away with what he's done?" Marlowe said. "No. I want to do this. I want to make him pay for stealing those coins. We can't allow him to sell them. They should be returned to Thailand. And I don't want to be watching my back for the rest of my life, wondering if I'm gonna be thrown back in jail." She shifted in Bob's arms until she was straddling him. "Can I go with you on your next tree call?"

"What?" he asked, confused by the abrupt change in topic.

"I don't want to think about Ian West, or prison, or coins, or anything else until I'm forced to. I'd love to go with you the next time you have a call. See a bit more of Newton. See what it is you do. I can help too."

Bob smiled at her. "You ever use a chain saw?"

She wrinkled her nose. "No, but I can carry stuff for you, or put on a yellow vest and direct traffic away from the tree, or simply talk to you while you work. Please?"

"Of course you can come. But it's not that exciting."

"I'm sure you'd say that about an archaeological dig too, but you'd be surprised at how fun it can be."

"All right."

"Yay," she said with a smile.

Bob was relieved to see the spark back in Marlowe's eyes, but he was still worried about the upcoming meeting with West. Desperate men did desperate things. He knew that better than most. And while he was supportive of Marlowe wanting to do what she could to take the asshole down, he didn't want her getting hurt in the process. The only reason he wasn't trying to talk her out of this entire thing was because West had no history of any kind of violence in his past.

"So, now that I'm over my freak-out, what do you want to do for the rest of the day?" she asked with a grin.

The first thing that sprang to Bob's mind was taking her back to bed, but he had a feeling that wasn't what she needed.

"How do you feel?" he asked.

"Fine, why?" she said without hesitation.

"No cramps?"

She blushed a little and shook her head. "No."

"How about a little hike? This part of the country is beautiful, and there's an overlook called Table Rock that I think you'd love. There are a lot of places with that name around the country, but this one is the most impressive."

Marlowe tilted her head. "How do you know? Have you been to them all?" she teased.

He chuckled. "No. But I've been to one out in New Mexico. I have a friend who owns kind of a resort with his buddies out there. It's a place where people who suffer from PTSD can go to completely relax. It's pretty, but our Table Rock has theirs beat."

"With that kind of buildup, I definitely want to see this place now," Marlowe teased.

Bob leaned forward and kissed her. It wasn't short, but it wasn't a precursor to taking her to bed either. "I love you," he said when he'd lifted his head. "You're the kind of woman a man looks for all his life. I know I've hit the jackpot, and I'm going to try like hell not to screw this up."

She shook her head. "I'm nothing special, Kendric. I'm just a hardworking woman who does her best to be kind to those around her, and who's muddling along the best she can."

"You go right on thinking that, Punky. I know the truth," he told her.

"Whatever. What should I wear? How long are we going to be gone? Do we need snacks?"

Her excitement couldn't be contained, and Bob was thrilled. He was looking forward to showing Marlowe everything about this little corner of Maine. It might not have been his first choice in where to live out the rest of his life, but he was learning to love it more and more.

"Layers. Just in case you get too hot or cold. And your hiking boots. It'll be four or five hours probably. I'll make us a lunch and include snacks as well."

"Sounds perfect." Then she leaned down and kissed him briefly, before hopping off his lap and heading for the bedroom. She turned around at the last minute before she disappeared down the hall. "Kendric?"

"Yeah?"

"I love you too. Thanks for letting me cry on you. I promise not to make a habit of it."

"Doesn't matter if you do, it won't make me love you any less," he reassured her.

She gifted him with a huge smile, then spun and disappeared down the hall.

Bob sat there for a moment and took a deep breath as his smile slowly faded. He was more worried than he'd let on about this meeting with West. But if the man showed up, he and his former Deltas would make sure nothing happened to his wife.

He stood and headed for the kitchen. He had lunches to make and snacks to pack, and he made a mental note to let April know he would be unavailable for the rest of the afternoon.

He was looking forward to the hike. To getting both their minds off Ian West. Tomorrow, he'd figure out the tracker, and the audio and visual equipment. Today . . . he was going to enjoy spending time with the woman he loved.

Chapter Sixteen

Marlowe fidgeted in the chair as Kendric and his friends went over the plan for what seemed like the hundredth time. She was nervous, and listening to them talk about what to do if something went wrong wasn't helping.

She was wearing a pair of onyx earrings, each of which held a tiny camera that recorded visual and audio. Chappy's Jeep had a camera in the rearview mirror, as well as one on the central high-mount brake light, both filming the interior of the vehicle. She wasn't wearing any kind of police mic, because no one wanted Ian to accidentally spot it or insist she prove she wasn't wired.

No one was planning on Ian West getting anywhere near her, but everyone wanted to cover all the bases and make sure they captured the evidence they needed not only to get the charges against Marlowe dropped, but to bring West down at the same time.

The chief of police and his deputies were ready to pounce the second Ian produced the coins—if he actually brought them. There was also a representative from the FBI in town, two from US Customs and Border Protection, and a woman from Homeland Security, who would all be watching the feed from the chief's office. Rutkey had secured written promises that Marlowe wouldn't be extradited, since she was cooperating with the authorities to get the priceless artifacts returned.

Of course, if Ian didn't produce the coins, or he didn't admit to his role in Marlowe's arrest, things could get messy for all three agencies, since she was still technically an escaped fugitive. They were all banking on Ian not being able to keep his mouth shut.

Everyone wanted to take him down, but they had to have irrefutable proof that he'd broken the law. Any good lawyer would be able to rip apart a circumstantial case. So it was up to Marlowe to not only get Ian to admit he'd pilfered from the dig site—and framed her for the pills—but convince him to actually give up one of the coins.

It was a lot of pressure, and honestly, Marlowe was second-guessing her insistence on being the one to meet with her former coworker. What did she know about being undercover? Nothing. That's what.

She much preferred to be hanging out with Kendric when he was on a job.

Their hike to Table Rock two days ago was awesome. It was much nicer being in the woods of Maine than the jungles of Thailand. They'd laughed as they'd hiked and talked about nothing and everything. And he'd been right, the view from the huge boulder that seemed to be hanging off a precipice as if by magic was spectacular. Even the turkey-and-ham sandwiches Kendric had made them for lunch seemed to taste better when enjoyed with an amazing view.

She couldn't wait to see the same view in the fall when the trees were changing colors. Kendric had promised to bring her back.

Then yesterday, she'd gotten her wish to accompany Kendric when he'd been called out to cut down a tree that looked as if it was one storm away from crushing a house. She'd been fascinated by the precision and planning it took to ensure the tree didn't fall in the wrong direction and cause property damage or hurt someone.

And seeing her husband in a tight T-shirt, his muscles bulging as he operated the chain saw and cut the tree into manageable pieces, wasn't exactly a hardship. She'd helped him pick up the smaller pieces and load them into a trailer, and throughout it all, she couldn't stop smiling.

Now she was back in the small interrogation room at the police station, getting ready to meet with the last person she'd ever wanted to see again.

"Are you listening, Marlowe?" the chief of police asked.

Mentally scolding herself, she nodded.

"Good. Because once you get in that Jeep, you're on your own. We'll be listening, and people here at the station will be watching, but we won't be there to give you advice or tell you what to say."

Marlowe nodded again, chastised. She knew this was high stakes for everyone involved, but she simply wanted to go back home and climb into bed with Kendric. He'd woken her up early and had made slow, sweet love to her. She was nearing the end of her period, and he made it seem like not a big deal at all . . . which was a refreshing change from some other men she'd been with, who'd acted as if she had the plague when it was that time of the month.

Everything to do with Kendric was going amazingly well. He'd even brought up last night how he was looking into the details involved to make sure their marriage was legal here in the States. She loved him so much, it was almost scary.

"I'm thinking the faster you get to the point, the better," Chief Rutkey said. "Just like you did on the phone. Get him to give you one of the coins if he brought them, try to get him talking about the drugs found in your tent, but don't push too hard. And get out of there as quick as you can. Understand?"

"Yes."

"Okay, we've got thirty minutes until go time. We all need to be in place and ready, if and when our mark shows up. Marlowe, we'll do some audio and visual checks before you head out. Two of my deputies will be playing Frisbee at the park and can get to you in seconds if you need them. Bob and JJ will be in the woods around the parking lot. Cal and Chappy will be in their cars down the street. As soon as West arrives, I'll be blocking traffic along Highway 2 to make sure he can't get away, and the reps from the various agencies will be here, watching and listening to everything. We've got this."

Marlowe was reassured by all the planning the chief had done. It was highly unlikely anything would go wrong, but if it did, there were a lot of people who would be nearby, ready to help.

April, Carlise, and June had insisted that as soon as the meeting was over, she come to Jack's Lumber, where they'd be waiting to hear all about how it went . . . with champagne. They wanted to celebrate Marlowe successfully taking down Ian. She was humbled by their confidence.

Knowing she had such good friends, and so many people at her back, made her feel a little more confident about what she was about to do. But she was still uneasy. She'd been a little rash in suggesting she take center stage at his takedown, but she'd so desperately wanted to help. To ensure Ian suffered the consequences for what he'd done.

Everyone began to stand up, and sudden panic made it hard for Marlowe to breathe. But then Kendric was there. He took her elbow and helped her stand, leading her out of the small room and toward the front door of the station.

The soup she'd had for lunch before they'd left the apartment churned in her stomach.

Kendric led her toward Chappy's Jeep and turned her so her back was to the door. Then he took her in his arms and held her so tightly, it was almost painful. But she welcomed the slight hurt. She held him just as securely.

"I'm going to be just out of sight," he murmured into her hair as he held her. "I'll be patched into the audio feed, so I'll be able to hear everything that's going on. You've got this, Punky. I've got your back, and all my friends do too."

She nodded and closed her eyes. It wasn't until then that she realized how badly she was shaking. The hair on the back of her neck was standing up. She wanted to call this whole thing off, but it was too late. The chief had already set everything up. His deputies had been taken off other jobs to assist. The other agency representatives were in town, leaving the physical surveillance to Chief Rutkey and his officers. Kendric's friend Tex had overnighted the earrings.

So many people had done their part in what was about to happen. She had to suck it up and do hers.

Not to mention, Ian was almost there. The mysterious Tex had been tracking traffic cameras, letting everyone know his progress as he headed north.

"Bob? It's time!" JJ called out.

Marlowe took a deep breath and let her arms loosen around Kendric. He held on for a beat longer before moving his hands up to cradle her face. "Whatever happens, know that I'm here," he said earnestly. "If shit goes sideways, you just hang on, stay in your role. I'll get you out."

"It's going to be fine," Marlowe reassured him, only half believing what she was saying. "Ian will pull up, we'll talk through our windows, he'll give me a coin. Easy peasy."

Kendric's expression didn't lighten in the least. "Tonight," he said, "we move on with the rest of our lives."

"Okay," she agreed.

"We'll start looking around here for a house with several bedrooms for our kids. I've got a ring that I was going to surprise you with, but you know I suck at secrets. It's waiting for you back at the apartment. I'm going to put it on your finger, and it's never coming off."

She smiled at that. "All right."

"You're mine," he said fiercely. "My friend, my inspiration, my love."

"I love you," she whispered.

"Not more than I love you. Now . . . go kick some butt."

"I will."

Marlowe wanted to cry again, but she held back her tears. She needed to look tough, not greet Ian with a blotchy face and red eyes. She'd see Kendric again in less than an hour. They'd celebrate with the girls back at Jack's Lumber and go home, she'd get her ring, and then she'd show him exactly how much she loved and appreciated him.

It was eerie how alone she felt as she drove Chappy's Jeep toward the park. Even knowing people were listening and watching her, she still felt as if she was the only person in the world at that moment.

Her heart beat way too fast in her chest and her hands shook as she parked the Jeep in the spot that had already been staked out ahead of time. She saw two men about fifty yards away, Newton officers, playing Frisbee in the grass. Their car was the only other one in the lot.

Looking into the trees, she couldn't see any glimpse of JJ or Kendric, but they were there. She knew that down to her toes. She could do this.

Taking a deep breath, Marlowe removed her seat belt. Kendric had told her to do so, wanting to be sure she could bolt out of the car if necessary. Minutes seemed to go by like hours. Ian was apparently mostly on time, but there weren't traffic cameras on the outskirts of Newton, so they were flying blind as far as his exact arrival time was concerned.

Just when Marlowe didn't think he was going to show, that he'd changed his mind and turned around and headed back to Boston, a black older-model Honda Civic pulled into the parking area.

Her heart immediately started pounding once again as adrenaline shot through her. Marlowe took a couple of deep breaths, trying to calm herself. Ian parked to her right, backing into the spot. He rolled down his window, motioning for her to do the same.

Marlowe did as he asked, glad that things were going according to plan.

But that feeling disappeared with his next words.

"Get in," he ordered, gesturing to his car.

That wasn't part of the plan. She'd specifically been told several times not to get out of the Jeep. Not to go *anywhere*. To stay right where she was.

She shook her head. "No."

"Do you think I'm stupid? You've probably got your car wired. I don't trust you. Get in and we'll go somewhere else to talk."

"I don't trust *you* either," Marlowe said, feeling the same irritation and bravado that she'd had while talking to him on the phone.

"Then you aren't getting the coin," Ian said flatly. "Your choice."

"And you'll go straight to jail. No collecting two hundred bucks," she countered.

Ian studied her, and Marlowe had a split second of relief, thinking she'd be able to stay put in the Jeep . . .

Before he lifted his hand—and she was staring down the barrel of a gun.

"Now. Or you're dead," Ian threatened.

Her stomach dropped violently. Just a few feet separated their cars. Too close for Ian to miss. Yes, he'd definitely be arrested if he shot her— but it would be too late for Marlowe. If she complied, at least she'd have a slim chance of surviving.

Reluctantly, she reached for the handle of the Jeep.

She could practically hear everyone watching and listening, screaming at her to stay put, but she couldn't let this deal fall through now. If she died, it couldn't be for nothing.

She climbed out of the Jeep and slammed the door, standing there for a moment with her hands on her hips. "You want to strip-search me as well?" she asked sarcastically, doing everything in her power to stall, to give someone time to get to her.

But no one came. Either something was wrong with the audio and video, or the officers playing Frisbee weren't aware of what was happening. Which seemed unlikely. The whole reason they were there was for her safety.

"Get in," Ian ordered. "Hurry up."

Marlowe held her breath as she reached for the door handle. She couldn't imagine why the officers weren't intervening, why Kendric and JJ weren't rushing in from the forest the second they saw the gun.

Like a bolt of lightning, it struck her that if anyone moved in, Ian would shoot her before they could get near her. It was the logical conclusion—and Kendric and the others would know that.

It totally sucked, but she understood it.

She had no choice but to finish what she'd started . . . and trust that Kendric would get her out of this, just like he'd gotten her out of that prison.

The second she was inside the car, Ian pulled out of the parking space and took off. There was no sign of Chief Rutkey, and Marlowe couldn't decide if she was pleased or upset about that. She imagined there was a lot of scrambling going on to figure out how to follow them while not being spotted.

She also didn't see the roadblocks that were supposed to be put up after Ian pulled into the park. She wasn't sure what happened to them. Maybe they just hadn't had time to put them up yet? Ian had acted very quickly, after all. She was in his car seconds after his arrival.

"Where are we going?" she asked as Ian turned east, both for her own knowledge and for those listening.

"There's a cemetery not too far from here. I figure that'll be private. I'll be able to see if anyone follows us."

Marlowe rolled her eyes and crossed her arms over her chest as she spoke with more bravado than she was actually feeling. "No one's following us. Haven't you figured that out yet? I'll be in just as much trouble as you if anyone sees you giving me a coin. I'm not an idiot."

Ian didn't respond, simply kept driving. It took longer than Marlowe would've liked to reach the cemetery. And he was right. There was absolutely no one around, and to her dismay, there weren't a ton of trees either. So it would be harder for anyone to hide and come to her rescue if needed.

If she thought she was alone before, she felt even more so now.

Ian parked the car in the parking lot and unclipped his seat belt. Marlowe hadn't even put hers on; it had simply slipped her mind with everything else happening.

"So?" she asked. "You have the coins?"

"I don't get it," Ian said conversationally, not moving to reach into his pocket, or the glove compartment, or the console between them. Anywhere he might have stashed the coins.

Marlowe sighed. "Don't get what?"

"How the hell you're here. No matter how good your lawyer is, Thailand is known for locking people up for life for drug offenses."

"Yeah, well, too bad for you, I also have a powerful brother. Now stop stalling. Give me my coin and take me back to the park."

"I thought you were a pushover," he went on, staring at her with dead blue eyes.

Marlowe resisted the urge to shiver. She had to stay strong. Make him believe she wasn't bluffing. She looked straight at him, wanting to get everything he said on video and audio.

"I had you pegged for a Goody Two-shoes. Weak," he said. Then he smiled slightly, the look so sinister, her gut clenched. "I mean, look how easy it was to plant those drugs in your tent that night. It was bad luck that you caught me with the coins, especially since that dig was one of the easiest ones to steal from yet. You were a complication that I thought I'd already dealt with."

"And yet, here I am," Marlowe said darkly, her heart beating so fast she felt almost light headed. He'd admitted to planting the drugs and stealing the coins! Actually *admitted* it!

"Here you are," he agreed.

"So you've done this before? Stolen artifacts from other digs?" she asked, knowing this was also important info.

"Of course. It's not hard. People pay top dollar for arrowheads and shards of pottery and other stupid shit they think means something."

Marlowe frowned. "Then why are you living with your parents?"

Ian chuckled mirthlessly. "Subterfuge. It wouldn't be smart for someone as young as I am to flaunt my wealth. And believe me, I *am* rich. I've got money socked away in several foreign banks, and when the time is right, I'm going to move somewhere with lots of sun and easy women, and live happily ever after."

Marlowe's blood ran cold. She'd had no idea this baby-faced moron was a hardened criminal. She suddenly felt way out of her league and wanted to go back to the park, now. "Great. Woo-hoo, you're rich. But you still owe me, Ian. You had me thrown in a damn foreign prison. I want my share. Give me the coin and you can go on your way. I'll go mine, and we'll call it even."

Ian laughed again, and Marlowe's skin crawled at the sinister sound. He'd kept the gun in his hand throughout the drive, and now he placed it on the dashboard, then leaned to his left and reached into his pants pocket. He fumbled a bit, then drew his hand out.

"You mean these coins?" he asked.

And there, sitting on his palm, were three innocent-looking coins. They each had a hole in the middle and seemed completely ordinary. But Marlowe knew she was looking at something worth millions.

Irrationally, she had the urge to scold him like a child, tell him he shouldn't be handling ancient coins with his bare hands, that the oils from his skin could literally disintegrate the metal of the precious artifacts. But she managed to swallow the words.

She reached for his hand, wanting to get this over with, but he fisted the coins and said, "Ah ah ah, not so fast."

"What now?" Marlowe seethed, trying to sound annoyed instead of completely freaked out.

"How do I really know you aren't going to turn me in the second you have one of these coins in your hand?"

She huffed impatiently. "How many damn times do I have to spell it out for you? If you go down, *I* go down. I can't explain it any simpler! I'm done going on digs. I'm sick of it. Sick of not speaking the languages, sick of the dirt, sick of not getting the money I deserve for the work I do. I want to settle down right here in Nowhere, Maine. Live off the money from the sale of that coin. I deserve it. After everything you put me through, after all the work I've done for other countries to save their heritage, I'm *owed* this!"

He stared at her for a long moment before nodding. "Yeah, you probably are," he agreed.

Just when Marlowe felt as if this was going to be over soon, he lunged.

"What are you—!"

That was all she got out before her words were cut off by the hand closing around her throat.

Immediately, her own hands flew to his fingers, trying to pry them off her neck. But it was no use. Ian was taller, meaner, and stronger than she was.

Before she could blink, he'd hauled her up and over the front seat to the back.

He slammed her onto the back seat and brought his other hand up to join the first, wrapping it around her throat.

"Fucking whore! *No one* blackmails me!" he gritted out as he tightened his hold. "I'm not giving you a damn penny. You should've stayed where you were, locked away in that shithole prison. You're a pain in my ass, and there's no way you're getting a fucking cent! I was gonna shoot you in the head, but that would be too easy. I want you to look me in the goddamn eye while I watch the light go out in yours!"

Marlowe wasn't thinking about anything other than getting oxygen. She raked her fingernails down his face, but he growled and simply held on tighter. She kicked, tried to use her knees to throw him off her, dug her nails into the skin of his hands.

And he still didn't loosen his hold even a fraction.

"Die, already! Just fucking *die*!" he shouted as he leaned forward, putting more weight on her neck.

Blackness began to creep in behind Marlowe's eyelids—and she had a moment of such sorrow, it felt as if she was having a heart attack. Everything she wanted to do, she'd no longer get the chance. Her life with Kendric. Watching her nephew and niece grow up. Celebrating the births of her new friends' babies, having her own . . .

Everything was being taken away from her because she thought she was some sort of badass undercover spy.

Her last thought before blackness overwhelmed her was of Kendric. How he'd probably blame himself for not protecting her. Even though it was Marlowe who'd been stupid enough to get into Ian's car.

Kendric would start having nightmares again, would never forgive himself for what he'd perceive as his own mistakes . . . and it was all Marlowe's fault.

～

Panic threatened to overwhelm Bob as he watched West drive out of the park with Marlowe in the passenger seat. He was utterly livid that she'd gotten into the man's car, but even more pissed at the officers in the park for not preventing it from happening. Something had briefly interrupted their audio, so he didn't know what West had said or done to get her in the car, but now her life was in serious danger. He knew it down to his bones.

Their departure from the park left everyone scrambling to follow. Rutkey hadn't had a chance to put the roadblocks in place, and he was still trying to troubleshoot the faulty audio feed for the officers at the park when West pulled out. They could all hear the conversation in the car and knew exactly where they were headed. Bob hadn't been to the cemetery Ian was allegedly driving toward, but he'd been in the area on a job in the past.

Cal's SUV careened to a stop in the parking lot, and he and JJ hopped in. Before the door was even shut, Cal was moving. Bob heard Chief Rutkey talking to his deputies on the radio, but it was as if the man was speaking down a long tunnel. All Bob's concentration and thoughts were of Marlowe.

There was only one road leading to the cemetery, and thankfully there was a large curve right before the entrance, which allowed Cal's vehicle—and those of the other officers and Chappy—to stay out of sight. Bob didn't even wait for Cal to stop before he opened the door and ran toward the scant grouping of trees way too far from the parking lot.

He and JJ went to their bellies and crept as close as they dared while watching the Civic. They could hear the conversation between Marlowe and West as if they were standing right by the car, but they couldn't see what was happening. They didn't have access to the video portion of the recording. Only the agents back at the station in Newton were watching.

Bob stiffened when he heard West brag about how rich he was, how he was going to move somewhere warm with his ill-gotten gains.

"This guy's unhinged," JJ whispered.

Bob nodded. He was, and they'd all missed it. They'd assumed he was a harmless kid, taking advantage of an opportunity for crime. While he might be young, he was anything but harmless.

"We need to get her out of there," he told his former team leader. In situations like this, they all fell back into the familiar roles they'd played while on missions for the Army.

"I know," JJ said. "But there's no cover. The second we stand up, he'll see us, and Marlowe is a sitting duck in there with him."

Bob scowled with frustration.

He heard West ask, "*You mean these coins?*"

Bob assumed he'd finally revealed them. Satisfaction swam through his blood. West had screwed himself. No matter what happened, Marlowe would get those coins on video. Ian had proved to everyone that he really did have the artifacts, that he'd stolen from a dig site, just like he'd apparently done many other times before.

West replied, "*Yeah, you probably are,*" in response to Marlowe's statement about being owed—then a loud scuffling sounded over the audio.

Bob frowned, trying to see what was happening in the car. He could only see shadows, and . . .

And the car rocking slightly, from the movements of the people inside.

The hair on the back of his neck stood straight up, and Bob felt sick. Something was wrong.

"Fucking whore! No one *blackmails me! I'm not giving you a damn penny. You should've stayed where you were, locked away in that shithole prison. You're a pain in my ass, and there's no way you're getting a fucking cent! I was gonna shoot you in the head, but that would be too easy. I want you to look me in the goddamn eye while I watch the light go out in yours!"*

Bob was on the move before West had barely begun speaking. He had no idea what was happening, but it was bad. He knew that without a doubt. He saw Cal and Chappy running toward the car from the other side of the parking area. They'd obviously managed to work their way around and hide out in the scant trees, or maybe even behind the tombstones.

Bob felt as if he was running through molasses. He couldn't get to the car fast enough. The woman he loved was in danger, and he couldn't get there! It was as if he was living one of his many nightmares. Not being able to get to his teammates when they were being tortured.

He ran and ran, but didn't seem to get any closer.

Then he heard West shout, *"Die, already! Just fucking* die!"—and Bob nearly had a heart attack right then and there.

Suddenly, he wasn't running anymore. He was slamming into the car.

He wrenched the door open and grabbed West by the back of the shirt and hauled him off Marlowe's eerily still body, onto the gravel lot. He punched the man in the face once. Twice.

He had his fist cocked back to punch him again, but JJ caught his arm.

"Bob! *Marlowe.* See to Marlowe!"

Without hesitation, Bob let go of West's shirt and turned back to the car. He vaguely heard JJ dragging West's unconscious body away, but all his attention was on Marlowe.

He was afraid to touch her for a second. Then his brain kicked in. He'd seen West's hands around her throat, but he prayed it hadn't been long enough to kill her. It took no time at all to make someone pass out, but several minutes to kill someone by strangulation, and she'd been talking not that long ago . . .

He crouched in the open car door and leaned over the woman he loved, putting two fingers to her carotid artery—and the relief that swept through him at the feel of her steady pulse would've brought him to his knees if he wasn't there already.

"Marlowe!" he yelled.

To his surprise and relief, her eyes popped open, and she gasped. Then she began to thrash and fight. Her arm flew up, and her fist popped him right in the eye. It hurt like a mother, but Bob didn't back away.

"It's me!" he shouted. "Kendric!"

She was lost in her terror, and either didn't hear him or didn't understand. She tried to sit up, but Bob grabbed her shoulders.

"No! Nonononono!" she yelled as she fought and kicked.

Even as he struggled to subdue her as gently as possible, Bob couldn't help but be proud of her for fighting with everything she had. "You're safe! It's me, Kendric. He can't hurt you anymore, you're good," he reassured her.

It took several more seconds of his calm words to break through her panic. Before she finally stilled and looked up at him.

"Kendric?" she croaked.

"Yeah, Punky, it's me. You're safe. I've got you."

Bob expected her to burst into tears. Instead, she took a deep breath, closed her eyes, and simply nodded.

"Marlowe?" he asked gently, concerned about her unexpected reaction.

"Did you get him? Did they get all that on tape?"

"Yes, and I'm assuming *also* yes."

"Good. Can we please go now?"

Worried that she was suffering from shock, from the idea that she'd almost *died*, Bob lifted his head to look at Chappy, who was crouched in the back door opposite him, the same concern reflected in his gaze.

"In a second," Bob reassured her. "Can you sit up?"

She nodded and slowly sat up. Bob moved to sit on the seat next to her, his arm around her back. "Do you feel dizzy? Light headed?"

"No," she said. "Although I could use some water or something. My throat hurts."

Of course it did. West had his damn hands around her neck. Bob could see dark bruises already forming on the skin of her throat, and it made him want to finish what he'd started when he'd hauled the asshole out of the back seat.

He forced himself to stay next to Marlowe as he said, "Yeah, Punky, we'll get you a water real soon."

She looked down at her hands then, and frowned. She held them up. "I scratched him," she said.

Bob saw blood under her fingernails. She'd done more than scratch West. She'd gouged the hell out of his skin. He took hold of one of her hands, and to his surprise, found his own eyes filling with tears. His lip began to quiver.

He'd never been as scared as he'd been in the seconds between realizing something was wrong, and when he'd reached the car.

He'd almost been too late. He'd promised to have her back, that he'd keep her safe, and yet, West had almost killed her with his bare hands.

A sob escaped, and Bob frantically tried to stop the others that wanted to follow. Marlowe was alive, but she wasn't all right. She was acting as if she was in a fog. She was clearly in shock, and it was the most distressing thing he'd ever witnessed.

But when he made another choked sound, Marlowe turned to look at him. She stared for a beat, then blinked.

And that seemed to be all it took for his Marlowe to return. One blink.

"No," she said firmly, shaking her head.

"No what?" Bob managed.

"You don't get to feel guilty. I knew you would. As I lay there under him, and he was choking me, I *knew* you'd blame yourself. It was my last thought. Stop, Kendric," she begged. "You got him. You saved me. We're going to have a ton of babies and live happily ever after. Got it?"

Bob couldn't help but laugh at that. "Yes, ma'am," he said.

"Good. Can you please get me out of this stinky car now? I have a celebration to get to."

Bob looked behind him at the still-unconscious Ian West. JJ had trussed him up so tightly, he wasn't going anywhere anytime soon. Bob could hear sirens coming in hard as well. His hand flexed as he thought about hitting West one more time, but a touch of Marlowe's hand to his arm had him forgetting about the man in an instant.

"Kendric?"

"We're going," he told her, gesturing to the other door, where Chappy was still hovering. He didn't want her even looking at West. "But we're going to make a stop at the clinic before we do anything else."

"I'm fine," Marlowe insisted as she scooted across the seat.

"Humor me," Bob pleaded.

Chappy grasped her hand and carefully helped her out of the car. Bob was immediately at her side. Marlowe turned to him and leaned her forehead against his chest. They stood like that for a long moment, soaking in the fact that they were both alive and well.

He caught a glimpse of Chief Rutkey running toward them as other officers screamed into the lot, sirens blasting, driving way too fast.

Marlowe looked up at Bob and smiled. "Men and their toys," she joked quietly.

Bob closed his eyes for a fraction. He'd almost lost this. Her. He needed her so badly, had no idea what he'd have done without her. By the grace of God, today wasn't the day he'd find out.

He opened his eyes and touched a gentle finger to her neck.

Marlowe reached up and took his finger in her grasp. "I'm okay. Honestly."

Bob nodded.

They both turned as Alfred Rutkey reached them. "Are you okay?" he barked gruffly.

"Yes," Marlowe said. "Did you get it? Was it enough?"

Alfred smiled. It was a satisfied and almost bloodthirsty grin. "It was more than enough," he told her.

"Good. Oh! He had a gun," she blurted.

Bob thought his knees might give out yet again at hearing that. He clutched her to him even tighter as she continued.

"That's why I got in his car. The *only* reason. It was either get in and hope I survived, or let him shoot me in Chappy's car." She turned to Bob. "I had to do it. If there was even the slightest chance I'd get back to you . . ."

Bob couldn't possibly love this woman any more than he did right that moment.

Before he could speak, Rutkey nodded and said, "We know. Got a call from one of the agents watching the feed. You were in the car before I could even notify my officers on the scene, but I wouldn't have let them intervene regardless. The chance of Ian shooting you if he realized he was being watched was too high."

Marlowe seemed to take that information in stride. She nodded, then said, "I don't know where the coins went. He was holding them when he grabbed me. They might be on the floorboards or something. But . . . if it's okay, Kendric and I are going to leave. We'll be at Jack's Lumber if you need a statement. Although I'm probably going to have too many drinks, so it might be better if you waited until tomorrow to talk to me."

The police chief smiled. "All right. I think we're good. I mean, we have the recordings, so there's no pressing need to interview you immediately."

"Right."

"Although, if I can make a suggestion?" Alfred said, still smirking.

"Yeah?"

"Don't forget to take off those earrings. Wouldn't want you broadcasting anything you'll be embarrassed about later."

Marlowe looked up at Bob, and he almost melted at the look of love on her face. "Right, I'll do that," she agreed.

Bob could practically read her mind. He wanted to take her straight home, strip her, and check every inch of her body to make sure she really was all right. Then he wanted to bury himself inside her and not leave for the rest of the night.

"Party," she said, as if she could read his mind.

"Doctor, then party," he countered.

Marlowe pouted but took a deep breath and nodded.

She turned to Chappy then, and surprised him by hugging him hard. "Thank you for having my back."

"You're family," he said simply.

Marlowe grinned.

Bob wasn't surprised when they stopped near JJ on the way to Cal's SUV, and she hugged and thanked him too. She also thanked the deputies and the chief, and when she got to Cal, wrapped her arms around him as well. "Thanks for getting here so fast . . . although I'd expect nothing less from a car that costs more than most houses."

Cal grinned. "Knew there was a reason I bought this car."

Bob helped Marlowe into the back seat, then turned to Cal. He was suddenly at a loss for words. His teammates had been there for him without question once again. He'd lied and gone behind their backs, and yet they still hadn't hesitated to support him and Marlowe when they needed them most.

Cal shook his head. "No, mate. I get it. I've been where you are. When June was lying on that floor, bleeding out . . ." His voice trailed off before he cleared his throat. "I was going to get you here before it was too late, no matter what."

"Thank you."

"You're welcome. Now come on, let's get Marlowe looked at, then we'll go meet everyone at the office."

Bob had a feeling Cal needed to see June, to make sure she was all right. Everything that just happened had reminded him of almost losing his wife, and yet he was still going to stick with him and Marlowe until she was cleared by the doctor.

Surprising himself, and Cal, Bob grabbed his friend and gave him a hard hug, thumping him on the back before letting him go. "Right. Let's get this hunk of junk moving," Bob quipped.

Cal chuckled. "Hunk of junk, my arse," he mumbled before climbing behind the wheel of the ridiculously expensive SUV.

Bob carefully buckled Marlowe's seat belt before doing the same for himself. Then he took Marlowe into his arms once again. It would be a long time before he'd be able to stop touching her, but he didn't even care. That had been way too close of a call.

Chapter Seventeen

"I'm fine, Kendric," Marlowe said for what felt like the thousandth time that night.

What happened with Ian was horrific, but surprisingly, Marlowe really *did* feel as if she was doing okay. She'd gone to the medical clinic without protest. She had pretty nasty bruises on her neck that would only continue to darken, looking worse than they felt. Her throat was scratchy, as if she had a bad cold or something. But overall, she'd been tremendously lucky.

Kendric had hovered all afternoon, as had his friends . . . *their* friends. After everything that had already happened to Carlise and June, no one was happy with how things had played out with Ian.

Jack's Lumber had been packed, and even though Marlowe was tired, she hadn't wanted to leave. It felt as if half the residents of Newton had stopped by, wanting to make sure she was all right. She had no clue how anyone knew about what had gone down, but . . . small towns. She didn't question it too hard.

Despite the office being closed for the party, April had been slammed with people inquiring about getting trees on their property pruned or removed. Everyone wanted to support them somehow, and it seemed one of the ways they felt they could do so was by hiring Jack's Lumber.

Carlise, June, and April had been understandably shocked by Ian's actions, even though Marlowe had tried to downplay them. Everything had happened so quickly, Marlowe wasn't sure there should be this much fuss over an attempt on her life that was thwarted in less than sixty seconds.

JJ went out and got Granny's Burgers, which he wasn't charged for, and between bites, Marlowe found herself consoling her friends. She hated that everyone felt so awful. She was the one who'd put herself in a position for Ian to do what he did. She was the one who couldn't let him get away with making money on Thailand's heritage, who hadn't been able to forgive him for putting her in prison. She'd knowingly put herself into a potentially dangerous situation.

Marlowe had even spoken with the mysterious Tex, who was a man of few words. He'd called to talk to Kendric, and had asked to speak with her as well. The conversation was short. She'd said hello, Tex had asked if she was all right, she said yes and thanked him for the earrings that had caught every second of what happened, ensuring Ian wouldn't get away with any of his crimes. Tex had said he was glad she was safe, told her no thanks were necessary, then asked her to put Kendric back on. She'd done so with an amused chuckle.

The day had been long, and after just a few hours at Jack's Lumber, Marlowe was exhausted. Kendric finally put his foot down and told everyone he was taking her home. Then he simply picked her up and carried her out of the office and to his truck, which seemed to be his new favorite thing.

Now they were home, and Kendric had already asked if he could get her anything three times and had practically buried her beneath a mound of blankets on the couch. He'd made sure she took some painkillers, and at the moment, he was currently in the kitchen doing God knows what.

"Kendric, come here," she ordered gently.

He immediately put down whatever he was fiddling with and sat down next to her. But he didn't pull her into his arms, which was where she desperately needed to be.

For a moment, a flash of uncertainty went through her. Had something changed between them? Was he reconsidering being with her? Had she been too reckless in insisting on meeting with Ian, then getting into his car?

"Why are you all the way over there?" she asked with a small frown. It wasn't as if he'd sat down on the extreme opposite end of the couch, but he wasn't touching her, and that freaked her out.

Kendric studied her for a long moment, then he sighed. "I don't want to hurt you."

Marlowe shook her head. "Touching me won't hurt me." He still didn't move, and her heart fell. "I mean, if you're mad at me or something, please just tell me. If you've changed your mind about us because I screwed up today, I want to know."

"Changed my mind?" he asked incredulously.

Before she could blink, she was sitting on his lap, blankets and all, and his arms were around her, holding her close.

Sighing in relief, Marlowe snuggled into him, wrapping an arm around his neck and holding on tight.

"You didn't screw up today. I did."

Marlowe shook her head, but he didn't give her a chance to protest verbally.

"I did. I told you that I'd have your back, and yet I hesitated just long enough for that asshole to get his hands on you. I'm so sorry."

"Don't apologize," she begged. "You saved me, Kendric. He was going to kill me. He'd somehow hidden who he *really* was from everyone, until the moment he tried to squeeze the life out of me. I saw it in his eyes. The greed, the hate, the disregard for anyone other than himself. If you weren't there . . ." Her words faded.

"I know," he said, his voice breaking. "I know. I can't go through that again. Seriously. I know you needed to do all this to fix what happened to you in Thailand, but nothing about that situation felt right. I didn't want you to think I was being a controlling husband, refusing to allow you to make your own decisions. But I think deep down, I suspected West was unstable. That he'd do anything to get his hands on the money he felt he was entitled to.

"I want you to be independent. I want you to be the strong, competent, and amazing woman you are. But I won't let you put yourself in danger again. I just can't."

"Okay," Marlowe said without hesitation. She wasn't upset that Kendric wanted to protect her. Wasn't that what she'd wanted all her life? Someone to lean on when the going got tough? To protect her and their children from anyone and anything that might hurt them?

Kendric nodded against her, and she felt him take a deep breath. He was just as affected by what had happened today as she was. Maybe even more so. He'd been the one to see Ian with his hands around her throat. She'd been unconscious when Kendric had opened the car door, but she'd heard from the others how he'd wrenched Ian off her with one hand. How he'd beaten the crap out of him before turning his attention to her. He'd had to see her in that back seat, lying motionless, and probably thought he was too late.

Yeah, his perspective on what happened today was probably worse than what she'd actually experienced.

"Take me to bed?" she asked. She needed to hold her husband. Reassure him that she was all right. He'd probably have nightmares tonight, which she hated because it had been quite a while since he'd had any. It killed her that she would be the reason for his relapse.

Kendric moved immediately, scooting to the edge of the couch before standing. He carried her to their bedroom and placed her on the mattress.

"Do you need anything? Use the restroom? Wash your face?"

"I'm good," Marlowe told him. She'd changed into her pajamas earlier and had brushed her teeth when they'd gotten home.

He nodded and went to the dresser and pulled out a T-shirt. He stripped out of the clothes he'd been wearing all day and put on the clean shirt. He went into the bathroom, and Marlowe heard the water running as he brushed his teeth. The toilet flushed a moment later, then finally he was climbing under the covers with her.

He lay on his back and pulled her against his side. Marlowe rested her head on his chest and sighed with contentment. Kendric's fingers brushed against the nape of her neck and tickled the hairs there.

"Kendric?"

She felt more than heard his chuckle. He'd admitted once that he loved how she always said his name, as if asking permission, before she asked a question or told him something. She hadn't realized she was doing it, but now she couldn't stop.

"Yeah?" he asked.

"I love you."

"I love you too," he said with no hesitation whatsoever.

"I feel as if I owe you an apology."

"You don't," he told her.

"I do," she insisted. "I shouldn't have met with Ian by myself. We both knew that he'd do anything in order to steal those coins. I mean, he had no problem getting me thrown in jail. There was no reason to think that he'd ever agree to give me one of them. I should've let you and your friends think of something else. Or let Customs and Border Control handle it. I got caught up in proving that he was a thief, in proving that he'd set me up. And proving that he hadn't broken me. I ignored the very real threat he could pose."

"Your bravery is what I love most about you. You don't let anything get in your way. You just forge forward no matter what. You don't owe me an apology. We both made mistakes, and thank goodness we're both still here to learn from those mistakes and improve going forward."

"Yes," Marlowe breathed.

"I've made my own share of other mistakes. In fact, we're so much alike it's not even funny. I didn't trust my best friends to understand why I needed to work with Willis. I lied to them, and didn't even give them a chance to have my back. You, my love, acted in much the same way. Wanting to do all the work yourself to bring West down, despite having me and my friends here to help. I'm thinking we both learned that trusting others isn't a bad thing."

Marlowe shook her head against him. "It's not. And you're right."

Kendric turned his head and kissed her temple. "Sleep, Punky. Tomorrow's a new day."

"Yeah." She lifted her head and met his gaze. "I don't want you to have any nightmares tonight," she said firmly.

He chuckled. "I don't either. But I'm not sure saying it makes it so."

"I know," she sighed, putting her head back on his chest. "But I feel guilty knowing that they might come back because of me."

"If they do, they do," he said nonchalantly. "You'll be here to talk me down if I have one."

"Damn straight," Marlowe muttered.

"I used to dread going to sleep," Kendric admitted. "Because I knew I'd dream and relive the worst moments of my captivity. But now? I'm not scared. You'll be here when I wake up, and somehow the power of those dreams has lessened, knowing what I have now."

That was . . . sweet.

"And learning that Chappy, Cal, and JJ have also struggled with nightmares makes me feel not as weak. I never really asked them if they were having trouble reacclimating to civilian life after we got out of the Army. I just figured it was only me, because they all seemed to be coping so well. Even Cal, who definitely had it worse than the rest of us. But they were hiding their pain, and the fact they were having issues adjusting too. Not that I like that they were suffering, but it makes everything seem not quite so . . . lonely."

"I'm glad you have them," Marlowe said. "This goes without saying, but I'm going to anyway. Anytime you need to talk, I'm here. I wasn't with you on that mission, so I get that there are things you can only talk about with the others, but if you ever need an ear, I'm all yours."

"I know you are, Marlowe, and I appreciate it more than I can say. And the same goes for you. You haven't talked much about your experiences in that prison in Thailand, but I can imagine they weren't great. I probably have a larger capacity than others to understand some of what you felt being locked away."

"Thanks," she whispered. He was right. She'd pushed her time in prison to the back of her mind because she'd had other things to worry about, like getting out of the country without being recaptured. Now that she was safe and happy, she knew memories might overwhelm her at times, and it would be nice to have someone to talk to about them.

"Sleep, Punky. If you wake up in the middle of the night in pain, I put some pills and water on your side of the bed."

"I'll be okay," she said. All of a sudden, the events of the day caught up to her, and she couldn't keep her eyes open anymore. "Love you," she murmured.

"Love you too."

～

Bob didn't know what time it was. It was pitch dark outside, and he wasn't sure what had woken him.

Then Marlowe jerked against him and muttered, "No!"

He was immediately awake. He hadn't had a nightmare tonight, but it looked like his brave, stoic, and seemingly unflappable wife was.

"Kendric!" she suddenly screamed, scaring the shit out of Bob.

"Shhhhh," he murmured, tightening his arms around her.

That seemed to make whatever she was seeing in her mind worse.

Bob rolled onto his back, taking her with him so she was on top. The last thing he wanted to do was remind her in any way of being helpless underneath someone bigger and stronger, as she'd experienced with West.

"No! Let go! *Keeeeeendriiiiic!*"

"I'm here," he told her sternly. "I'm here, Punky. Open your eyes. Look at me."

One second she was thrashing in his arms, and the next, her eyes popped open and she stared down at him.

Bob was more grateful than he could put into words that she seemed to recognize him immediately. Her pajama top was askew, and he could see the horrible marks on her neck against her pale skin, even though there weren't any lights on in the room. The light from the moon shining through the window was enough for him to be able to see the awful results of the previous day.

"You're okay," he said gently. "I've got you. I'm here."

She sighed, then lowered herself back onto his chest. Well . . . lowered wasn't exactly the right word. Plopped was better. She simply went boneless and collapsed against him.

"Shoot," she mumbled.

Bob couldn't help but smile at that. It was such a Marlowe thing to say. He speared his hand in her hair and wrapped his other arm around her waist, anchoring her to him.

"I wasn't the one who was supposed to have a nightmare," she complained.

Bob's smile grew. He couldn't believe he found any humor in this situation, but she wasn't wrong. It was a miracle he hadn't had a nightmare. The sight of her in that car, unconscious, with that asshole's hands around her throat was burned into his brain. He'd thought he'd lost her. He had no doubt at some point he'd dream about that moment, but apparently not tonight.

"Want to talk about it?" he asked.

She sighed, and Bob felt the warm exhale even through his shirt. "It was his eyes," she said softly after a moment. "They were dead. I mean, I worked with Ian. Shared meals. We laughed together. I was the one who gave him a tour around the dig site when he first arrived.

"But when he was strangling me . . . I saw nothing but deadness in his eyes. He could've been peeling a carrot for all the emotion he had. I mean, I would've expected to see anger, hatred, something. His words *sounded* furious. But he was completely blank. I knew then that it didn't matter what I said or how hard I fought, he was going to kill me. And that sucked because all I could think about was all the things I'd miss out on with you. Laughing, loving, our kids . . . all of it."

"Punky," Bob said in a strangled tone.

Marlowe lifted her head. "But I'm okay now. You're here."

"I am," he agreed.

"And if I have any other dreams, you'll wake me up and reassure me that he didn't win."

"Damn straight."

She nodded, then lowered her head back to the crook of his neck. "You know, this is weird," she said after a moment.

"What is?" Bob asked, running a soothing hand up and down her back.

"Lying on top of you without being naked and you inside me," she said.

Bob snorted. "We slept like this a few times as we made our way across Thailand," he reminded her.

"Yeah," Marlowe agreed. "Kendric?"

"Yeah, Punky?"

"I'm thinking three."

"Three what?"

"Kids. So we need at least a four-bedroom house. The kids can share when they're young, but they'll want their own space when they get older. And I want to find a house with a huge porch, and a big backyard. And not too far from Carlise and June, because I want our kids to play with theirs."

The images her words put in Bob's head were so visceral, so real, it almost hurt. "Okay, Punky."

"I don't know how we'll pay for it, but we'll figure something out."

"We will," Bob agreed. He'd do whatever it took to give his Punky everything she ever dreamed about.

"My brother's going to come up soon with his family," she went on.

It seemed as if his woman was wide awake now, and wanting to talk. Bob had no problem with that. "Good. I'm looking forward to getting to know them."

"What did Tex tell you today?" she asked. "I mean, after he said like two words to me." She chuckled.

Bob's smile died. He didn't really want to talk about this right now, but he knew Marlowe would need to know what was happening with Ian in order to move on with her life, and hopefully banish the nightmares for good. "He was updating me about West," he said after a moment.

"And?"

"Are you sure you want to hear this now?"

"I'm wide awake," she said with a shrug.

He nodded. "West is being charged with a whole slew of things. Kidnapping, attempted murder, money laundering, smuggling, and a bunch of other charges I forget right now. The maximum charge for the smuggling alone is twenty years in federal prison."

Marlowe lifted her head. "Yeah, but he'll only have to serve a portion of that before he's eligible for parole, right?"

"True, but customs wants to charge him separately for each coin."

"Oh, that's good," Marlowe said.

"They're also going to dig into his past, check into the other sites he worked on, continue to scour the dark web, and see if they can find evidence of other artifacts he stole and sold . . . and charge him for those too. And since they believe his attempt to kill you was premeditated, they're going to go for life in prison. It's all on audio and video. His intent was to get you to an out-of-the-way place, kill you, collect on the money from the buyer of those coins, and go on with his life. He's not going to get away with any of his crimes."

"And the coins will go back to Thailand?" Marlowe asked.

Bob closed his eyes and pressed his lips together. He shouldn't have been surprised that she was so concerned about the coins going back to the country that had imprisoned her, but he still was. "Eventually, yes."

"Good."

"And Tex is working with a lawyer over in Thailand to get the charges on you overthrown. They're using the evidence that you got today as proof that you had no knowledge of the yaba pills found in your stuff, and that it was all West."

Marlowe nodded against him, but didn't comment for at least a minute. Then she lifted her head and stared at him in a way that Bob couldn't read.

"What is it, Punky?" he asked.

"I love you."

He smiled. "I love you too."

"Since we're both awake and all . . . I'm thinking we should find a way to pass the time. It's way too early to get out of bed." One of her hands trailed down his side and pushed under the waistband of his boxers.

He quickly caught her hand in his. "You were hurt yesterday," he said.

"I was," she agreed, holding his gaze. "But I'm okay now."

"Are you in any pain?" he asked.

She shrugged. "I'm a little stiff and my throat is sore, but otherwise, I'm good."

"I'm thinking we should give it another few days," he started, but Marlowe shook her head and shifted until she was straddling his stomach. She stared down at him.

"I'm *fine*," she insisted. "And I need you, Kendric. For a moment, I thought I'd never feel you inside me again. Would never watch you fly over the edge. Would never see the adorable little grimace you make when you come." She grinned. "Please?"

Well, hell . . . how could he resist such a pretty plea? The truth was, he couldn't. Bob had a feeling that didn't bode well for him. Anything his wife wanted, he'd cave in a heartbeat when she looked at him like she was right now.

"I don't grimace when I come," he protested.

She giggled. "Uh-huh, sure you don't. Prove it."

"A challenge. I like it," he said with a grin. "But then again, I'm tired. I think you should do all the work."

Bob was surprised at how quickly his wife moved. She stripped off her pajamas and was sitting astride him naked as the day she was born before he could blink.

The next twenty minutes were the most erotic of his life. He made love to his wife, just as she made love to him. They reaffirmed their feelings with every touch, with every thrust of their hips. Being able to be with her like this again was a true gift, and Bob vowed never to take her for granted. Ever.

When he'd made her come twice, and had emptied what seemed like gallons of come deep within her, she was once more lying boneless on his chest, his half-hard cock still inside her, their juices dripping out of her body onto his balls. Bob had never felt so content.

"This is more like it," Marlowe said sleepily.

"Yeah," he agreed.

"And you totally grimaced," she said. Bob could feel her lips curl up in a grin against his chest.

He wasn't surprised. Every orgasm with her felt as if he was being turned inside out. It hurt in the best way. "Whatever," he fake grumbled.

Marlowe giggled, and the sound went straight to Bob's heart. He'd do anything, give anything, to hear that small giggle every day for the rest of his life.

She yawned and sighed sleepily.

"I've got you, Punky. Sleep."

"I don't want to dream."

"I know." And he did. "But if you do, I'm here."

"Yeah, you are."

He felt her breaths get slower and deeper against him, and by the time his cock softened enough to slip out of her body, she was asleep once more. Bob shifted her so she was lying against his side, and he pulled up the covers that they'd kicked off in their lovemaking.

Usually when he lay in bed, his mind wouldn't shut down. Visions of his past flickered through his brain like a movie. But tonight, it wasn't his past that kept him awake . . . it was his future. The house Marlowe described. Their kids running around, shrieking like little hellions, laughing with Chappy and Cal's children.

He fell asleep with a smile on his face. He had no idea what their future would actually hold, but whatever it was, he'd be with Marlowe. He had no doubt whatsoever about that.

Epilogue

Five Months Later

Marlowe smiled as she watched Chappy, Cal, JJ, and Kendric unloading the moving truck. It had taken a while to find the perfect place, but as soon as she'd laid eyes on this house, she knew it was the one. It needed some work, but Kendric promised to make it shine, and she had no doubt he'd do just that.

He seemed content. Sometimes she worried that he'd get bored and want to go work for Willis again, but he'd assured her over and over that he was done with that. That he was satisfied being here in Newton with her and his friends.

He worked a lot, but Marlowe didn't mind. He needed to stay busy, and if chopping trees and leading people on hikes on the Appalachian Trail kept him occupied and satisfied, she would never tell him to stop.

Ian's trial was still pending, and while that was frustrating, Marlowe knew it was for the best. He was being held without bail, at least, and the lawyers were doing their due diligence, covering all their bases so he wouldn't ever get out of jail. All the money he'd hidden in offshore accounts had been confiscated, and customs, Homeland Security, and the FBI were still tracking down some of the artifacts he'd stolen before he'd gone to Thailand.

So with Ian in jail and Kendric settled . . . things were going great in Marlowe's life, and she couldn't be happier.

She rubbed her growing belly and smiled as Carlise and June came over to stand next to her.

"Look at us, the three fat little pigs," June joked.

Marlowe laughed. She'd gotten pregnant surprisingly quickly. Less than a month after she'd started getting her period again. It was as if her body had just been waiting for Kendric's sperm or something. Chappy had also finally knocked up Carlise, and Marlowe was thrilled that all their children would be born around the same time, only a few months apart.

Cal's house wasn't too far from the one that Marlowe and Kendric had bought, and while Chappy and Carlise were still living in their apartment in town, they were building onto their cabin in the mountains.

"I'm so happy for you," Carlise said, resting her head on Marlowe's shoulder—and bending awkwardly to do so. The other woman was so much taller than her and June, she frequently joked about using their heads to rest her elbows.

"This house really is perfect," June added.

"Yeah," Marlowe agreed.

"Should we feel guilty that we're just standing here watching our men do all the heavy lifting?" Carlise asked after a moment.

Marlowe laughed. "Ha. I tried to help, but Kendric yelled at me. Told me to 'go eat some pickles or something.'"

The other women chuckled.

"Right?" Carlise said. "It's as if they think we're completely helpless, simply because we're pregnant."

"Now that I'm nearing the end of my second trimester, Cal's become super paranoid," June agreed. "I swear if we stand here for too much longer, he'll be running over with a chair and insisting I sit."

"The other day, when I tried to tell Riggs that I wasn't done with the translation I was working on, he came over, picked me up out of my chair, and carried me into our room, saying that I'd spent enough time working and needed to rest."

Marlowe smiled. Kendric wasn't that bad . . . yet. But she had no doubt his overprotectiveness would be emerging more and more as their child continued to grow. "Do we hate it, though?" she asked.

Carlise and June grinned.

"Nope."

"Not in the least."

Marlowe nodded happily.

"You know what's missing here?" Carlise asked after a moment.

"What?" Marlowe and June asked at the same time.

"April."

Marlowe frowned. Carlise was right. It seemed as if their friend was hanging out with them less and less . . . and it was as confusing as it was hurtful. "Where is she, anyway?"

"At the office, where else?" June replied.

Marlowe sighed. "She works too hard. She's always there. Do you think she's upset that we're all pregnant?" she asked.

"No," Carlise said without hesitation. "I really don't think she wants kids, so it's not that. Something else is bothering her."

"I wish she'd talk to us," June said.

"Me too," Carlise agreed. "But she's always been pretty close lipped about her personal life. She hangs out with us and everything, but it still feels as if I don't know that much about her."

"I thought it was just me!" Marlowe exclaimed.

"Well, I know she was married before, and things just kind of fizzled out, but that's all she's told me," June said.

Carlise straightened as JJ came out of the house, waved at them, and disappeared back into the truck Kendric had rented to move their stuff. "I'm thinking enough is enough, and we need to get JJ and April to pull their heads out of their butts and admit that they like each other. It's almost painful to watch them stare at each other when they don't think anyone notices. The puppy dog looks and sad eyes are killing me. They both seem so unhappy."

"What can we do? I mean, they're adults," June said.

"Force them to share a bed one night?" Carlise suggested.

Everyone laughed.

"Well, it worked for the three of us," she argued.

"True, but I'm thinking that's not going to work for them."

The three women sighed as they racked their brains in silence.

"I got nothin'," Marlowe admitted after a minute or two.

"Me either," June agreed.

Carlise sighed. "Yeah, I have no idea what to do."

"We're just going to have to let the two of them figure it out," Marlowe reasoned.

"I guess. I just want them to be happy. They both work so hard, and they're so awesome. I know they'd be perfect together if they just gave it a chance," Carlise said.

"Yeah," Marlowe agreed. She was still racking her brain, trying to figure out a way to help JJ and April's relationship along, when Kendric exited the house with a huge smile on his face.

"All done," he said as he got close. He wrapped an arm around her shoulders and pulled her into him. "Well, I mean, everything's in, not unpacked. I'll start on that later. You want to see?"

"Duh," Marlowe told him with a small laugh.

"I'm gonna take June home, she's been on her feet long enough today," Cal said as he claimed his wife by wrapping an arm around her waist.

June gave the other women a look as if to say, "See?"

"Yeah, Car and I were going to head up to the cabin for the weekend. If anything comes up and you need me, let me know," Chappy said, taking Carlise's hand in his.

Marlowe waved to her friends and promised to text them pictures later when the house was more settled.

"And I guess I'll just get out of your hair," JJ said with a grin. "Head to the office. I know when I'm a third wheel." He slapped Kendric on the back and headed for his Bronco.

"You look happy," Kendric told her as his friends walked toward their various cars, all parked on the road.

"That's because I am," she said with a smile.

"Good. Me too."

Gazing at her new home, Marlowe had the thought that everything she'd been through, all the terror, the uncertainty, the flight through Thailand, almost being killed . . . every single thing had been worth it. She was married to the man of her dreams, would be having their child, and now was moving into her dream house. She'd go through it all again if it meant she'd end up right here.

"Let's go see our house," she said. "Maybe even christen some of the rooms."

Kendric grinned huge. "Sounds like a good plan to me."

He swept her up bride-style and strode toward the front porch. He carried her over the threshold and stopped, leaning down to kiss her. "Are you sure you aren't upset that you never had a real wedding ceremony?"

They'd decided to go to the justice of the peace and get married here in the States, just to make sure their marriage was legit. It had just been the two of them, and the two witnesses, employees who worked in the building. Neither had wanted to make a big deal out of it, because as far as they were both concerned, they were already married. That was just a formality.

"I *did* have a real wedding ceremony," Marlowe insisted. "I wore a cream dress, we said our vows, and we have the certificate to prove it."

The piece of paper was a little worse for wear, wrinkled and torn at the corners, and the ink was smudged from his fall into the canal, but it would always hold a special place in Marlowe's heart. Kendric had gotten it framed, and she had no doubt he'd already hung it in their bedroom, where it had been in their apartment for the last five and a half months.

"I love you," Kendric said.

"I love you more."

"Not possible." Kendric kissed her again.

He was about to close the door when he heard a sharp whistle coming from behind them. He turned and looked around—and immediately put Marlowe on her feet when he saw his friends gathering. Something was up, and it didn't look good.

Kendric and Marlowe turned their backs on their new house, putting their christening plans on hold to go see what was happening.

~

April sighed as she hung up the phone. She was at the office instead of hanging out with her friends. She wanted to be there, but lately, being around Jack was excruciating. Despite her protests to the other women . . . she loved the man. And being nothing but his friend for years was slowly killing her.

She wasn't even sure when it happened, precisely. She supposed it was a gradual thing, seeing how dedicated Jack was to the business, how much he loved his friends. He'd drop everything to help the ones he loved if they needed it. She'd seen it firsthand over and over. He was everything she'd ever wanted in a partner.

She hadn't come first in her own marriage. Her ex-husband wasn't a bad person, he was simply . . . self-absorbed. He'd felt as if his work was more important than hers. If she had a doctor's appointment, and wanted him to go with her, he'd always insisted he couldn't because of a meeting at work or something. She couldn't rely on him for *anything*.

They'd loved each other at the beginning of their marriage, but as the years passed, they grew apart. By the time she'd finally asked for a divorce, they'd been nothing more than roommates.

April had a feeling Jack would be an amazing husband. Attentive, protective, and he'd never blow her off if she asked him to come with her to an appointment, or a party, or simply to sit with her at home and have a meal together.

Sighing, she shook her head. She and Jack weren't meant to be, that much was clear. They'd worked together for years. If he had any feelings toward her other than those of a boss toward his employee, he'd had plenty of time to act on them.

Since he was currently with everyone else, helping Marlowe and Bob move into their new house, she'd gone to Jack's Lumber. It was the weekend, and she didn't need to be there. The phone service would alert her to any emergency calls. But she couldn't be near him any more than she was already, even if she wanted to be, so coming into the quiet office was her best option.

While she attempted to keep her mind off her friends, the phone rang. It was one of the ski resorts nearby. A massive tree had fallen near one of the popular ski runs, and they wanted Jack's Lumber to haul it away. April told the man that everyone was out of the office, but she'd come out and take a look.

Pushing the chair back from her desk, she stood. She'd just assess the job quickly, so she'd know how many of the guys to send out tomorrow. It wasn't something she usually did, but she needed to get away from her thoughts. She was being a coward when it came to Jack, and she knew it. She wanted to admit her feelings to her boss, but was scared that if she did, and those feelings weren't reciprocated, things would get weird and she'd have to leave a job she loved.

April grabbed her purse and jacket and headed out the door of Jack's Lumber, climbing into her red Subaru Forester and taking off toward the mountains. She vaguely noticed a black pickup truck behind her, the only other vehicle on the long stretch of road, but her mind remained on her destination.

She was mentally putting together a proposal for the ski resort, just in case they wanted Jack's Lumber to check the trees along all the slopes, removing any others that seemed in danger of falling, when something alongside the road in her peripheral vision caught her attention.

Instinctively, she slammed on the brakes.

A large moose stepped out onto the road, and April jerked the wheel to the right. As she began to slide, she immediately attempted to correct the sharp movement, but it was too late.

She spun, the scraping sound of rocks against the metal undercarriage of her car loud as she ran off the side of the road.

April was jostled in her seat, her head smashed into the window to her left as she let out a small scream—then she was airborne.

The moose had picked the worst possible place to wander in front of her car, because there was a shallow ditch . . . then a twenty-foot drop off the side of the rural road to the forest floor below.

The car hit the ground at the bottom of the hill with enough force to take April's breath away. That might've also been the seat belt tightening around her chest and lap, or the airbag going off with a loud *poof* and scaring the shit out of her.

Spots swam in front of her eyes. Her head throbbed, and she could feel blood dripping down the side of her face. Everything had happened so quickly!

Seconds went by as April realized she'd never been in this much pain before. Her head pounded so badly, she couldn't keep herself from puking. Luckily, the airbag had slightly deflated, so the vomit didn't spray back in her face, but it was almost just as bad when it landed on the roof of her car.

Wait . . . the roof?

Turning her head, she blinked in confusion at how the world seemed to be topsy turvy.

Then she realized it wasn't the world that was upside down—it was *her*. The car was lying on its roof, and she could see the road she'd driven off, far above her.

The moose was long gone, but the black pickup truck that had been behind her was up on the road. She couldn't make out who was behind the wheel, but just as she had the relieved thought that whoever it was would surely help her . . . the truck began to move.

To her utter shock and confusion, it drove away, leaving nothing but silence in its wake.

The longer April lay in her wrecked car, the more her head throbbed. She tried to convince herself that whoever was in the truck probably hadn't had cell service, they'd just gone down the road to get help. But for some reason, she knew that wasn't the case.

Whoever it was, they had left her there. Hurt, bleeding, and trapped.

She wanted to cry. Wanted to scream. But her body was shutting down. The pain was too intense. Her head felt as if it was going to explode.

The last thing she thought about before she went unconscious was how quiet the area seemed. The silence was absolute, and it was the scariest thing she'd ever heard in her life.

JJ was frustrated and grouchy. He'd been looking forward to helping Bob and Marlowe move into their new home because it meant he'd get to see April outside the office—except she never showed up. In fact, she seemed to have an excuse every time she was invited to hang out with him and his friends lately.

The woman drove him crazy. He wanted her, *badly*, but he had no idea how to change the status quo between them.

She was always so professional. And he hated it. Didn't like the distance she kept between them.

April Hoffman was everything he'd ever wanted in a woman. Tall, smart, down to earth, and hardworking, and more than anything else, she was a wonderful friend. She was *his* friend. But he wanted more. Was desperate for more. But he didn't know how to make that happen.

He should've made his interest known years ago, but the more time that went by, the harder it was to figure out how to make a first move. And he was afraid he'd lost his chance. Aside from hanging out less and less with Carlise, June, and Marlowe, she seemed to be making an effort to put space between herself and JJ, in particular. Even trying to avoid being in the office at the same time as him. It sucked, and JJ wasn't sure how to fix it.

After all the furniture and boxes had been moved off the truck and into Bob and Marlowe's house, JJ finally excused himself when his other friends headed for their vehicles. He was walking toward his Bronco when his phone rang. When he saw the unknown number on the screen, he frowned and brought the cell up to his ear.

"JJ here."

"Is this Jackson Justice?" an unfamiliar voice asked.

"Yes. Who is this?"

"My name is Patrick Stewart. We found your number under April Hoffman's emergency contacts. I'm calling to let you know that she's in our ambulance and we've called in air flight to take her to Bangor."

JJ's heart stopped beating. "What? April's hurt?"

"Yes, sir. Her car ran off Mountain Road, and a bystander called it in."

"JJ? What's wrong?" Chappy asked, materializing at his side.

But he couldn't concentrate on anything other than the voice on the other end of the phone. "Is she . . . is she going to live?" he whispered.

"Yes, but she's unconscious and has a serious head injury. As I said, she's being life flighted to Bangor, and you were listed under her emergency contacts in her phone. Is there anyone else we should call?"

"What hospital?" JJ barked, ignoring the question. Every molecule in his body was urging him to jump into his car and get to her side.

The paramedic told him, and JJ nodded. "I'll be there. Tell her . . . I'm coming," he begged.

"She's unconscious, sir, but I'll tell her if she wakes," the paramedic assured him.

"Thank you." JJ hung up and started for his car again, but Chappy's hand on his arm stopped him.

"What the hell's going on?" he asked.

"April's hurt! She was in a car accident. They're taking her to Bangor. I need to get to her."

"We'll go with you. Hang on," Chappy ordered.

JJ shook his head. "I can't . . . I need . . . I need to go!"

"And we're going," Chappy said calmly. He turned and whistled loudly.

For the first time ever, JJ had no idea what to do. He was always in control. He'd been the leader of their Special Forces team. The one everyone looked to when shit went south. But the second he heard April was hurt, it was as if he was suddenly incapable of making even the smallest decision.

Every molecule within him was urging him to get to her side. To make sure she was all right.

He heard his friends talking as if from a long distance away, and the next thing he knew, Cal was steering him toward his SUV. "I'm driving," he said firmly.

JJ didn't protest. Cal's Rolls-Royce had some serious power under the hood, and he could get to Bangor faster than JJ in his Bronco.

He heard his friends talking all around him as they climbed into the vehicle, but all he could think about was April. Why was she on that road? Would she be all right? Was she terrified when it happened? Had she even been aware, or was she instantly knocked out?

And underneath all his fear and worry . . . determination. Stronger than any other emotion.

No more waiting. When she recovered—and she *would* recover, she had to—he'd make sure the woman knew how much he loved her. He'd wasted enough time. No more dicking around.

April Hoffman was his—and he'd do whatever it took to get her to love him as much as he loved her. No matter what obstacles might stand in his way.

Turn the page to see a preview of Susan Stoker's book *The Lumberjack*!

THE LUMBERJACK

GAME OF CHANCE SERIES, BOOK FOUR

Chapter One

It took a few seconds after she woke up for April to realize where she was. What had happened. Well . . . what she'd been *told* had happened. She was in the hospital because her car had run off the road. She didn't remember any of it.

In fact, she didn't remember much of the last five years of her life.

The doctors claimed to have high hopes that her loss of memory was just a result of the bruising on her brain from the accident, and her memory would return in time.

But high hopes weren't super comforting. She would've preferred they told her in no uncertain terms that her amnesia was temporary. The thought of never remembering anything about her life from the last five years was terrifying.

She remembered who she was—April Hoffman. That she was forty-six and her mom was her only family left. She recalled everything about her childhood and most of her adult life. But the hole in her memories about what she'd been doing for the last five years was, quite frankly, freaking her out.

Not because she thought she'd done anything horrible, or had been a person she might not like. But because she'd had a steady stream of visitors who seemed to be worried about her . . . and she couldn't remember any of them.

She didn't like to see them upset, and it was clear they were just as stressed as she was about what had happened . . . and she couldn't ease their minds by recalling who they were, what they'd meant to her.

Her head throbbed, and April kept her eyes closed. The light in the room exacerbated the headache she'd had since waking up in the emergency room days ago.

She heard shuffling footsteps from the direction of the door, and she vaguely wondered who was visiting her this time.

From the moment she'd been assigned a room at the hospital—a hospital in Bangor, Maine, she was told—she hadn't spent any time alone, even at night. It was disconcerting that the people constantly sitting vigil next to her bed, these men and women who were so loyal, were now strangers.

She'd never had that many friends, not that she could remember. And certainly none who would put their entire lives on hold just to remain by her side, even while she mostly slept.

The truth of the matter was, the April she *remembered* being was a loner. She'd always wanted to have close friends she could hang out, shop, and laugh with. It seemed that whatever she'd been doing the last five years had finally resulted in just that. She just couldn't remember any of it.

Her eyes opened when she heard a whispered argument nearby. Turning her head, she saw the back of a man standing just outside the door. His legs were shoulder-width apart, like he was blocking access to her room. She could tell he had his arms crossed over his chest as he had a very heated conversation with someone.

She stared at the man's back and desperately tried to remember something, anything, about him. She knew his name was Jackson Justice, but only because he'd told her. And he'd been a steady presence in her life from the moment she'd woken up, scared and hurting.

She didn't remember him . . . but something deep down inside her immediately trusted the man.

When the doctors realized she had amnesia, Jack was the one she'd instinctively looked to for reassurance and comfort. When she'd woken up in the middle of the night with her head throbbing so badly she thought for sure she was dying, he'd been there, holding her hand, calling for a nurse and promising her that she was going to be all right. He'd helped her to slow her breathing, staying right by her side until she'd fallen asleep again.

Even when the other men and women visited her room, Jackson was the one she looked to when she got overwhelmed. He was the one who shooed them away when she needed a little break from everyone's concern.

All the others called him JJ, but for some reason, that name didn't feel right to April. When she admitted as much to him, he told her that she always called him Jack. *That* felt familiar. It was probably the first thing that had felt right in the last week.

Jack had said they were friends, that she worked for the business he owned with the three other men who'd been regular visitors over the last several days, along with their wives—who, apparently, she was also close to—but he hadn't gone into any more detail than that.

It felt as if she and Jack had more of a connection than simply boss and employee, but anytime she brought it up, he quickly changed the subject. She was beginning to think that maybe they'd dated at one time and things hadn't ended well. Or maybe they'd had a one-night stand.

The not knowing was driving her crazy.

April watched as Jack's muscles tensed before he consciously relaxed. He leaned toward the other person standing just out of sight, said something too softly for April to hear, then stepped aside. As he did, he looked into the room and saw she was awake.

She saw him tense up again, but he still allowed a man to enter the room. As soon as April saw who it was, she understood the animosity in the air.

It was James Neal . . . her ex-husband.

Jack had also been with her the first time her ex had visited. James had run into her room, gasped when he saw her, rushed to her side, grabbed her hand, and proceeded to fake cry all over it.

April had been annoyed, but not terribly surprised. Jack, however, had responded as if James was a serial killer. He'd grabbed him, wrenched him away from April, and slammed James into the wall on the other side of the room, as far away from her as he could get the man, asking who the hell he was.

James had sputtered a bit and said that he was her husband.

That had caused Jack to nearly lose his mind.

Of course, April had been shocked herself, as she hadn't remembered remarrying James after their divorce. But it wasn't long before he admitted that he was her *ex*-husband. It hadn't been an auspicious beginning for the men, and in the two days since, both of them had been on edge and, it seemed to April, on the verge of coming to blows every time they crossed paths.

"I'll be down in the cafeteria if you need me," Jack told April from the doorway.

"She's not going to need you," James sneered.

Jack ignored her ex and held eye contact with her. "Okay?" he asked.

"Okay," April told him softly.

She wasn't sure how long they stared at each other—the connection she felt with this man was captivating—before he finally nodded and stepped out of her sight.

"I can get him barred from your room if he's bothering you," James insisted as he pulled a chair closer to the bed. The sound it made as it scraped along the tile floor made April wince and her head throb.

"He's not bothering me," she replied.

Her ex huffed out an annoyed breath, then leaned back in the chair and put his feet up on the mattress next to her hips. "I hate hospitals. They smell funny, and everything is so depressing," he complained.

Apr

The Lumberjack

April pressed her lips together and wondered why he was here. Only her memories from the last few years had been affected by the accident. But despite remembering her divorce clearly, she was still having difficulty remembering much about her marriage to the man. Probably because it was so unremarkable.

She *did* recall that they'd simply been coexisting at the end. They didn't talk or even interact much at all in the last year or so before the divorce.

Honestly, she wasn't sure why she fell for him in the first place, all those years ago. Sure, James was fairly good looking. He was around her height, five-nine or ten, and had dark-brown hair and hazel eyes. He wasn't fat, but he wasn't skinny. He was just . . . perfectly average.

Upon arriving at the hospital, he'd told her that her mom had called him, letting him know she'd been in an accident and asking him to go to Maine to check on her, since her mom couldn't travel. And after seeing for himself that she wasn't at death's door, he'd done nothing but complain about nearly everything.

Bangor, the weather, the flight here, how expensive the rental car was, the size of the hospital, the lack of his favorite restaurants . . . the list went on and on.

He continued to do so now, bitching about the uncomfortable bed at his hotel.

"You don't have to stay," she interrupted. "You've seen for yourself that I'm okay. You can go home."

At that, James dropped his feet from her bed and leaned forward.

April braced herself for whatever he was going to say next. He didn't make her wait.

"It was a mistake. Us getting divorced. We should give things another go. We were good together, Ape."

April wanted to roll her eyes at the nickname. She'd always hated it. Had told him more than once, but he'd ignored her and kept using it, thinking it was a cute way to shorten her name. It wasn't. It was annoying.

267

"We were once," she agreed. "But can you honestly say you were happy toward the end of our marriage?"

"Yes," he said without hesitation.

"I wasn't," she countered.

That seemed to shock James.

"We never did anything together anymore. I could've put on a dinosaur suit and danced around the house and I don't think you would've noticed."

"That's not true."

"I appreciate you coming to check on me, James, but we're over. We've *been* over for years," April said firmly, not wanting him to get any ideas in his head that maybe they could work things out and get back together.

James sighed. "I miss you," he whined.

"No, you miss not having to worry about anything having to do with normal responsibilities. Paying bills, being at the house when the exterminator showed up, cooking and cleaning. You took me for granted, James. We weren't husband and wife, I was your live-in help. That's not a marriage."

"That's not true," he protested.

"It is. We grew apart. It happens," she explained. "I appreciate you coming all this way to see me, but you hate it here. It's time you went home."

James studied her for a long moment. "I never understood why you chose Maine. Why you'd come all the way up here. The winters are awful, and it's so isolated."

April shrugged. She wanted to tell him that it was as far away from him as she could get at the time—and that she knew he'd never follow her. But she kept her mouth shut.

He sighed. "That JJ guy . . . he's not good for you."

April stiffened. There was no way she was going to discuss Jack with her ex. She had no idea where she stood with her boss, but James didn't get a say in what she did now. "James, no——" she started, but he interrupted.

"Seriously, Ape, he'll run roughshod over you! The man's bossy as hell, and he's probably the reason you're in the hospital in the first place. You shouldn't have been on that road. If he'd been doing his job, not having his secretary do it for him, you wouldn't have been hurt."

"It's time for you to go," April said sternly. "You don't know what you're talking about, and I won't have you bad-mouthing Jack."

"That's the problem—*you* don't know what you're talking about either," James fired back. "Because you can't remember. That guy can literally tell you anything right now and you won't know if he's lying or not. You aren't safe until you get your memory back, *if* you get it back, and you're completely vulnerable in the meantime. He could say that you're lovers and have you flat on your back with your legs spread, and you'd have no idea if he was lying or not!"

April saw red. She pushed herself into a more upright position. "You're right, I don't know where my relationship with Jack stands, but he's been nothing but respectful. He's been a rock at my side ever since my accident. I trust him, James, more than I trust *you*, and I remember most of our marriage . . . so that's saying something, don't you think?"

She took a deep breath, trying to calm herself. Her head was throbbing even more now. "Go home, James. You've done your duty."

"You're making a mistake," he warned as he stood up, the chair making that horrible noise once more.

"Maybe so. I've made a lot of mistakes in my life—including staying in a loveless marriage for way longer than I should have—but I know without a shred of doubt that the people who've rallied around me since I've been here aren't among them. Chappy, Carlise, Cal, June, Bob, and Marlowe have been better friends than I've ever known, and that's just in the last few days, since I don't remember our history. As for Jack? I don't know what our relationship involved, but at least he doesn't come in here bitching about how much he hates hospitals and trying to make me feel guilty for being here in the first place."

April was breathing hard when she was done. It felt good to stand up to James. She hadn't done it much when they were married. It had been easier to just go with the flow and not upset him. But she was done with that. She and James were divorced. She'd apparently taken her maiden name back, and she wasn't going to let anything he said influence her ever again. She'd already done that once, for way too long.

"Don't come running back to me when you realize how much of a mistake you made moving to Maine," he growled.

April chuckled, even though it jostled her aching head. "It's been five years, James, I don't think I'll be running back to you anytime soon."

"Your mom is going to be disappointed," he told her.

April shrugged. "She's always disappointed in me," she returned. "She'll get over it."

With one last shake of his head, James turned and headed for the door.

April held her breath until he left the room, then scooted back down on the bed. The relief she felt when he was gone was almost overwhelming.

At that moment, it occurred to her that when Jack left her room, she felt anything *but* relief. It was almost as if sadness coursed through her veins anytime he was out of her sight.

It was that realization that made her sure she'd made the right decision. James was her ex for a reason. And while she could be grateful he'd taken the time to come up to Maine to check on her, she was never, ever getting back together with him.

"April?" a woman's voice asked tentatively from the doorway. "Are you okay? I saw James leaving, and he didn't look happy."

Turning her head, April saw a very pregnant June peeking into the room.

"Come in," she said, gesturing for the petite woman to enter.

June entered and pulled the chair James had been sitting in closer to the bed, being careful not to let the legs screech against the floor. She eased herself onto it and leaned forward, putting her hand on April's forearm. "Are you okay?" she asked again.

"I'm fine. James won't be back . . . at least I hope not."

June smiled. "Really?"

"Really."

"Good. Oh! I mean . . . that was rude. Sorry. But he wasn't ever very considerate of you."

"Or of you and the others," April said with a small smile. She hadn't missed the way James had dismissed June, Carlise, and Marlowe.

All three women were in various stages of pregnancy. June was about six months along and definitely waddled when she walked. Marlowe wasn't too far behind her at five months, but her baby didn't seem as big as June's, and Carlise was just shy of four months along. Their men were constantly making sure they had enough to eat or drink and were comfortable when they visited April.

It didn't even seem to cross James's mind that maybe the pregnant ladies might need or want to sit. The man had never bothered to give up his chair when any of the women visited.

June nodded. "Yeah. JJ will be glad he's gone too."

April's doctor had warned her not to push too hard to try to remember the last five years. He'd told her that he had every expectation her memories would return after her brain healed from the trauma it had experienced.

But at that moment, April wanted to know about the time she'd spent with June and the other women. Wanted to know the stories of how they'd met their men.

And she very much wanted to know why she felt so comfortable with Jack, and why she trusted him so readily.

"Why?" she blurted.

"Why what?" June asked with a tilt of her head.

"Why would Jack care?"

For the first time since she'd been visiting, June looked uncomfortable. "I'm not sure I'm supposed to talk about that with you."

"Please," April whispered. "I'm so confused. Were we lovers? Did we date? I don't understand why I'm so drawn to him, and yet he treats me as if I'm his sister or something. He's clearly very protective and concerned about me, but he's keeping his distance. Did I do something to upset him? Was I a bitch to him or something?"

"No!" June exclaimed so vehemently, it made April feel better instantly. "You haven't dated, and he *definitely* doesn't think of you as a sister," she said. "Things between you two have been . . . complicated. And that's all I'm going to say. I don't want to do or say anything that will hinder your healing. Besides," her voice lowered a little, "I don't actually *know* much about you and JJ. You guys are both super close-mouthed about what's going on.

"But I'll tell you this . . . when JJ heard you were hurt, he couldn't get to you fast enough."

April's heart swelled at hearing that. She was still confused about where things stood between her and Jack, and in the absence of her memory, she couldn't help comparing him to James yet again.

At one point in their marriage, she'd been rear-ended while driving. It hadn't been that big of a deal, but her neck was stiff, so she'd gone to the hospital just to be safe. She'd called James while in the ambulance on the way to the hospital, to let him know what was going on . . . and the first question he asked was how badly their car had been damaged.

Then he told her that he'd be working late that night, asking if it would be okay for her to take a taxi home.

The difference between the two men's reactions to the respective accidents was night and day. Maybe the two situations couldn't be compared because they were so different in how badly she'd been hurt . . . but she had a feeling Jack would've reacted the same way in either scenario.

June squeezed her arm, then drew in a surprised breath.

"What? What's wrong?" April asked in concern.

"Nothing, it's the baby. He's kicking hard today. Wanna feel?" Without waiting for her response, June stood up and brought April's hand to her belly.

"It's a boy?"

"Oh . . . I forgot that you don't remember. We weren't going to find out, but the second Cal saw his little wiener on the ultrasound, he got so excited that there was no way to keep him quiet." June chuckled. "You scolded him for like fifteen minutes, telling him that he shouldn't be so proud of a penis on a baby that hasn't even been born yet."

April smiled, a little sad that she couldn't remember. She was happy, however, that June didn't feel weird about sharing the memory. She felt movement under her palm and smiled up at the woman. "He's strong."

"Yeah," the other woman said with pride.

It was obvious how happy June was to be pregnant, and April had no doubt she was going to make an amazing mother.

The doctor chose that moment to enter the room, along with the two interns who'd been glued to his heels every time he'd arrived to check on her.

"I'll leave you guys to chat," June said. "And I'll find JJ and let him know that James is gone," she told April with a wink before waddling toward the open door.

The doctor was all business as he checked her vital signs and asked the same questions he asked every time he came to see her.

"Any memory returning?"

"Not really," April told him. "I mean, the stuff that happened in my past is becoming clearer, but I still can't remember the accident or anything about my life in Newton."

"The results of the MRI you had last night are promising. The swelling in your brain has stopped, and it's even shrunk a bit. I'm confident that with time, you'll regain most of your memory of your life here in Maine."

"How much time?" April asked with a frown. She was impatient to get her life back, and that couldn't happen without her memories.

"There's no telling," the doctor said.

April sighed.

"I know it's frustrating, but you've made a very fast recovery so far, and I have no reason to think you've lost those memories forever. Just be patient. Take things slow. Your memories could return gradually, one at a time, in pieces, or they could snap back all at once. How's the pain today?"

"Around a five," April told him. If Jack had been there, she probably would've downplayed the throbbing in her head and said around a three, because she didn't like to see the worry on his face, but since she was alone with the doctor, she was more honest.

He nodded as if he'd expected that. "As your brain heals, you'll continue to experience some pain. Don't try to force your memories, that'll just make the pain worse. Wear sunglasses when you go outside and in bright light, and continue to get plenty of sleep and eat well-balanced, nutritious meals. I'm going to discharge you this afternoon . . . as long as you have someone who can stay with you for the next few days at least, to keep an eye on you."

April smiled. Oh, she so wanted to get out of this hospital room. But then reality crashed in on her. She had no idea what her living situation was. Did she have her own house? An apartment? She didn't know if any of her female friends could stay with her as the doctor wanted. Hell, she had no idea if she even had a guest room, or a place for someone to sleep—

"She'll be staying with me," a deep voice interrupted from the doorway.

Get *The Lumberjack* now!

ABOUT THE AUTHOR

Susan Stoker is a *New York Times*, *USA Today*, and *Wall Street Journal* bestselling author whose series include Badge of Honor: Texas Heroes, SEAL of Protection, and Delta Force Heroes. Married to a retired US Army noncommissioned officer, Stoker has lived all over the country—from Missouri and California to Colorado and Texas—and currently lives under the big skies of Tennessee. A true believer in happily ever after, Stoker enjoys writing novels in which romance turns to love. To learn more about the author and her work, visit her website, www.stokeraces.com, or find her on Facebook at www.facebook.com/authorsusanstoker.

Connect with Susan Online

Susan's Facebook Profile and Page

www.facebook.com/authorsstoker

www.facebook.com/authorsusanstoker

Follow Susan on Twitter

www.twitter.com/susan_stoker

Find Susan's Books on Goodreads

www.goodreads.com/susanstoker

Email

susan@stokeraces.com

Website

www.stokeraces.com